THE MINUTE MEN

Retrostep 1

SIMON WINSTANLEY

Other books by Simon Winstanley:

Field One

Blackbox: Barcode

Field Two

Boundary

EVA

Inside the Field: The visual guidebook

The Bridge

Rez Point

The Olympus Key

The Reality Forge

www.futurewords.uk

ISBN-13: 978-1-914989-21-6

THE MINUTE MEN

THE BRIXTON JOB

The Brixton job was supposed to be [illegible]htforward. Non-specialist equipment. Fast tu[illegible]nd. Good money.

But looking at the blueprints, he cou[illegible] that they weren't entirely up to date.

He stood still and assessed the room.

At some point, somebody had decide[illegible]eir home would be more fashionable if they bl[illegible]f the old fireplace and chimney breast. Where th[illegible] had once stood, a bulky floor-to-ceiling rectangular [illegible]protruded into the room.

His job was to remove the fireplace a[illegible] the living room an open, decluttered space, fre[illegible] distracting indents. The poorly constructed boxy m[illegible]vould slow everything down. From his experience o[illegible]onstruction jobs, he knew that removing someone [illegible]ork always added days, or sometimes weeks, to the [illegible]chedule.

There was no point whining about i[illegible] In fact, the ugly protrusion would only make his fin[illegible] look even better.

When people visited the website an[illegible] the before

and after photos of the detached house, it would make the property development company look good. And if *they* looked good, he thought, then they'd keep giving him work.

His 2009 flip phone was now two years old but, despite being bashed about and flecked with paint, it was as sturdy as a brick. He flipped open the lid and used the arrow buttons above the keypad. Moving the on-screen cursor, he navigated to the icon of the camera and pushed the keypad's enter button.

Holding his phone sideways like a normal camera, he looked at the digital image on the screen and pressed the special shutter button that was built into the side of the phone.

The first few images came out blurry, so he found the option to turn on the flash and tried again. After a minute or so, he had a fairly respectable set of photos that showed what things looked like before the intended improvements.

Snapping the phone shut, he returned it to his overalls and walked to the middle of the room.

The previous owner of the house had apparently sold it 'as is'. The sofa and armchair had been left behind, as had an ageing side table and floral-looking vase. They'd all need removing or covering with plastic dust sheets before he could begin work in earnest. It was getting late, but he knew he could start some of the inspection work right now.

He walked to the protruding chimney block and tapped at the wallpapered surface. Plasterboard, he thought. Taking his claw hammer from his tool belt, he drove a blunt hole into the wall, then worked it larger with his fingers. Pulling away at the layers and layers of once-fashionable wallpaper, he found old plaster with wooden slats in it.

This stuff would take ages to remove.

Groaning to himself, he left the living room and began making a mental list of the tools he'd need to fetch from the van. He'd just reached the hallway when an ear-splitting burst of noise erupted from somewhere behind him; pushing at the air and vibrating the ground under his feet. As suddenly as it had started, it was all over.

The house was quiet.

Faint whirls of dust were drifting towards him along the hallway.

Half crouched, unable to speak, it took him several seconds to persuade his feet to move again. Creeping slowly and cautiously, he retraced his steps and entered the living room.

His first impression was that someone had just put a wrecking ball through the wall, except that he couldn't see the street. He swore in utter disbelief at the swirling mass of dust that hung in the air. It looked like the entire chimney breast had just collapsed.

The sofa, armchair, and side table lay tipped over and coated with chunks of debris. The vase was now an unmade jigsaw of china pieces that were strewn all over the floor.

Staring at the hammer that was still in his hand, he whispered a selection of expletives into the swirling dust.

He was in trouble.

There was no way that the company would believe that this level of damage had happened spontaneously. They'd assume that he'd botched the job.

He carefully put the hammer back in his tool belt.

As he wondered what to do next, he remembered what somebody had once told him.

Unlike proper cameras, so-called camera phones had a way of recording the time that photos were taken. He didn't have the first clue where that information might be stored, but if push came to shove, and lawyers got involved, he could find out. He'd be able to prove that the damage had happened mere seconds after the original photos.

Flipping open his phone, he quickly found the camera icon on the screen and pushed the enter button. Trying to hold his hand steady, he began taking photos of the destruction. With any luck, he thought, the images would show that dust was still in the air.

After capturing several wide shots of the toppled furniture and tragic fragments of vase, he moved forward to the ruined chimney breast itself and framed up the dark hole that was surrounded by torn wallpaper, plaster, and bricks.

He pushed the shutter button and saw the flash go off.

On the phone's small screen, he saw that the hole had an oddly shaped lighter patch at the centre.

Frowning at the shape, he stepped closer and pressed the shutter again. The flash went off, clearly exposing what was within.

Yelling out in sheer shock, he backed away.

NEW CLASS

Diane Sellick held her thick folder and walked on through the busy corridor. As though caught in the wake of a passing ship, students efficiently flowed around her without a second glance; their attention focused on their own endeavours.

Noticeboards on either side of her bristled with timetables and invitations to join clubs and societies. Where the display space had been insufficient, posters had migrated onto the surrounding walls, reminding people to buy their tickets for the 2015 Christmas Ball.

Leaving the corridor, Diane took hold of the door handle and made her way into the rear of the lecture room. Immediately, the familiar hubbub of youthful conversation surrounded her. Despite the number of years that she'd lectured here at the university, the sound of new students always remained the same: a barely contained enthusiasm to begin life as an independent adult.

In previous years, she'd greeted the new intakes and outlined the general rules and regulations, then directed people to their different faculties. Today, however, would be different. Tucking her thick reference folder under her arm, she descended the steps between the raked lines of benches.

As she progressed further into the room, people began to spot that an older authority figure had arrived. With each row that she passed, conversations became quieter. By the time she'd reached the floor level, only a handful of voices persisted. They would be the most confident ones, she thought, but they wouldn't necessarily be the candidates she wanted.

Standing behind the lectern, she placed her folder down and opened it to a double-page spread of stamp-sized student photos, some of which had an asterisk next to them. When the room was quiet, she looked up and studied their faces. Although they couldn't know it, the reduction procedure had already begun.

She stood up straight and took an audible breath.

"Why did you all become quiet when I stood behind this lectern?" she looked out and studied them.

As expected, there was no response, just a vague sense of uncomfortable shuffling in seats. She knew this was simply a symptom of posing a question to a group; each person in it assumes that someone else will reply. Even though she didn't know any of them yet, she knew that a pattern breaker would shortly emerge. As expected, the most confident person raised his hand.

"Yes," she pointed at him.

"Respecting our elders?"

His smirking glance at the others next to him instantly told her that he was more concerned with gaining their approval than with thinking carefully.

"No," she dismissed him, "Anyone else?"

As the young man recovered from his embarrassment by whispering to his neighbour, she quickly scanned the rows. Most of them were glancing between themselves, eager to see who would speak next, but a small scattering of individuals were taking notes during the silence.

Another hand went up, so Diane gave an assenting nod.

The young woman cleared her throat, "Learnt response?"

The room was small enough for her voice to be easily heard, so clearing her throat was either an indicator that she was nervous, or that she wanted people to pay her attention.

"Better," Diane acknowledged the answer.

The young woman gave a fleeting glance in the direction of the man who'd answered incorrectly. It seemed that the cough had been little more than the preening of social feathers.

"What I was looking for…" Diane raised a finger, "was *conditioned* response. From an early age, each of you were conditioned to respond to a mentor figure in a particular way."

She straightened her folder and watched as some students drew lines across their notes to make a new section. Those people were the ones who would have manipulable personalities, so she took mental note of those who differed.

"Mentors come from all walks of life," she continued, "but your parents are the main ones. All I can say is that they did a damn good job of preparing you to learn here!"

She smiled and looked around at them all.

As expected, the timing, cadence and mild curse word gave them all the chance to express relief. Many of them interpreted this as permission to smile or to let out a polite laugh. Again, she took note of the small subset who hadn't made this assumption.

"From this point on," she said, "as you young adults enter your various faculties, you will become mentors to each other, so remember to show each other the same respect that you showed me."

There was a minor ripple of note taking, head nods, discreet fist bumps, and a few eye rolls.

Her mental list narrowed further. Perhaps a dozen candidates remained.

"Now," she refocused them, "I'm afraid the staff class allocation list isn't complete yet, so today's session is little more than me welcoming you."

After a glance back at the photos in her folder, she checked that the potential candidates were present in the room. Some of them were absent and had thereby eliminated themselves from the process.

"The good news," she smiled, "is that most of you get to leave here early."

Her smile was almost immediately reflected back at her by the students, some of whom were already beginning to adjust their bags.

She filtered several more people away.

Three asterisked photos and four unmarked ones remained in the process.

"Unfortunately, because the finance office has managed to misplace a ream of paperwork, a few of you will need to stay behind."

Referencing her chosen subset of pupils, she called out their names and directed them to sit in the front row.

After the unsuccessful students had finished leaving the lecture room, she turned to face the three candidates who were now occupying the seats directly in front of her.

"Like everyone who just left, each of you has first class potential, and high-paid careers await you upon completion of your various courses. But you knew this already. Your motivation to succeed, at least in part, is driven by the crippling level of debt that each of you will accrue over the next few years."

She saw that, without exception, each of them had shifted slightly or had taken a deep breath.

"I don't believe in the notion that debt should *ever* be used to motivate a worthy mind. But I do believe that people should remain invested in their own future. With this in mind, I'm giving you an opportunity to join me in a different class."

She looked at the three of them.

"Let me be clear. By joining me, you will leave here without debt, but any idea you might have had about your future earnings must be left behind. The only thing I'm offering you is the chance to engage in a new field of research."

She closed her folder, "Any questions?"

Each of them raised their hands.

"Excellent," she said, "Follow me. I'm about to make your day more interesting."

She led the way up the lecture room steps and back through the bustling space outside. After several turns down quieter side corridors, the colourful posters and notices abandoned the unfashionably old walls, and she arrived at her office. Unlocking the door, she moved inside and her three guests followed her in.

None of them had hesitated. A good sign.

She locked the door again, sending the click echoing off the largely empty walls. She then weaved her way through stacks of boxes that now contained the contents of her room. Tomorrow, her time here would be over, and a new phase of her life would hopefully begin.

"Please," she gestured to a line of bulky packing cases, "take a seat."

It was interesting to watch the dynamics of who assessed the cases, who moved a small box in order to do what they were asked, and who tried to avoid disturbing the layout of her temporary environment.

"No doubt you're wondering why I haven't just offered this opportunity to people who have already *completed* their degrees."

As anticipated, there were nods.

"To reach this point in your education," she said, "you've all ably demonstrated that you can quickly absorb information, and be examined on it. The truth is that I don't need graduates with minds that are full of neat methodology and conditioned responses. I need *open* minds that are at the peak of their ability to explore new concepts. In short, information can be taught, aptitude can not."

Diane moved to her tripod-mounted video camera and turned it on. Looking at the fold-out screen on the side of the camera, she adjusted things until all three students were in frame, but didn't hit record.

"In a moment, I'm going to ask you to jointly sign a non-disclosure agreement, witnessed by this camera. Before that, I'll allow each of you to ask me one question."

As expected, there was a short pause while they navigated the non-verbal cues of deciding who would speak first.

"Hi," the ginger-haired student half raised his hand then pointed at the boxes, "You mentioned we'd be joining a new class, but it looks like you're packing to leave."

"What's your question?"

"The class," he frowned, "It isn't connected with the university, is it?"

"No," Diane admitted, "In fact, the term *class*, is something of a misnomer. In reality, it will be more like a well-funded collaboration."

"Collaborating on what?" he tried to get her to react.

"Nice try," she told him, then gestured at the video camera, "but until you sign the forms, I can't answer that question."

He smiled and gave a shrug, "It was worth a shot."

The second student drew breath, but then she seemed to consider her choice of question more carefully. After looking at the other two students, she tucked a strand of hair behind one ear and glanced at Diane's thick folder.

"I think you had a page for everyone in that lecture room," she said, "Why did you pick just us three?"

Diane couldn't help smiling. It was true that she'd researched all the potential candidates thoroughly before selecting three, but it was impressive that one of them had picked up on the detail.

"No university course in the world can teach the area we'll be exploring," she replied, "Your various backgrounds, your interests, even your reactions in the lecture room told me that you'd all be a good fit for the project."

The third student, who had quietly waited until the others had exhausted their questions, now spoke.

"OK," his eyes darted about the room, "You're leaving here because theoretical research must have taken you as far as you could go. If the venture is well funded, then my guess is that we'll be dealing with some sort of *practical* application."

Correct on both counts, she thought.

"Good," she said, "but did you have a question?"

He looked at the others before turning back to her.

"What will be our *general* area of development?"

Hoping to keep them intrigued enough to join her, she tried to think of the broadest possible way to describe the phenomena.

"The mapping of complex information."

2023

Ryan waved the remote control at the TV to bring it out of standby. While the progress indicator chased itself in circles, he rubbed at his eyes and turned to face his kitchen.

The open pizza boxes and empty snack packets were still there; fallen casualties of last night's workload and poor diet choices. He'd made the deadline and had managed about four hours of sleep, but the new day wouldn't wait for him, or care if he was tired.

If he was to stand any chance of functioning properly today, he knew he'd have to use the machine.

The psychoactive toxin would adjust his neurochemistry and alter his thought processes, but he needed the edge. The black elixir of life would return him to his senses.

He topped up the water, pushed an espresso cartridge into place, and set the coffee machine running.

While waiting for the coffee, he improvised a breakfast from stale pizza crusts, then cleared away the grease-stained boxes and tidied up the piles of printouts and notes that were on his kitchen worktop.

The Fortean Eye was of course a digital publication these

days, but he still preferred to make his research notes on paper before typing up his work. Even after uploading his articles about unexplainable events, he preferred to hold onto his paper copies and photos. For him, it almost felt like a safeguard; some unquantifiable essence always seemed to evaporate when experiences were reduced to a purely digital form.

Over a fading percolation sound, the coffeemaker gave a discreet bleep and Ryan gratefully removed the cup. Taking a moment to savour the sweet punch to the tastebuds, he faced the TV.

Although the sound was still muted, he could see the morning news show presenters were in the middle of discussing something that warranted the use of serious expressions and furrowed brows. The edited segment that followed confirmed it: a grim-looking report seemed to be focusing on capital punishment.

A video of guards patrolling elevated walkways now dissolved into a grid of barred cells. One by one, each cell was covered by an arrest mugshot and an execution date.

Ryan became aware that the caffeine must be working.

He found himself staring at the last of the dead-eyed mugshots, and having an odd thought. Did you become a hardened criminal first, and *then* get awarded your aggressive facial tattoo? Or was it something you did to yourself *beforehand,* so that you felt you were really committing to a career path?

Stock footage of an execution chamber and high prison walls transitioned back to the news studio, where the presenters were now seated on a sofa and petting a cute-looking puppy. He almost laughed at the editorial decision: people are horrible, but here's something sweet to take your mind off it.

Distraction for the masses.

In a way, the Fortean Eye did the same sort of thing. In a

digital world that bombarded you with facts and figures, sometimes people wanted the distraction of a little mystery.

Taking another sip of coffee, Ryan opened his laptop screen and looked at his newly finished article on the website.

The face-like rock formation on Mars had been the subject of debate for decades. Some people swore it was evidence of an ancient Martian civilisation, others dismissed it as human psychology needing to see faces where none existed.

It wasn't his job to resolve such debates, but it *was* his job to write sceptically toned pieces while simultaneously highlighting the theories that couldn't be disproved. In that respect, the long night had been worth it.

On the worktop next to him, his phone rang. Picking up the round-cornered rectangular device, he saw that his co-editor was calling. Tapping a phone icon that now bore no resemblance to the actual device itself, he answered the call.

"Morning Omar," he said, "You all set?"

"Yeah," he sighed, *"just in the departure lounge now."*

From the early hour, Ryan guessed that this wasn't a social call.

"What did you forget?"

"Call forwarding," he said, *"Would you mind redirecting the office landline number to your cell while I'm away?"*

"No problem," he scribbled a quick note on a scrap of paper, "So, the big vacation, huh? Do you know which areas you'll be hitting?"

"Temple of Seti the First, obviously," he said,

"Obviously," Ryan smirked, "Can't go all that way and not check out the Abydos helicopter hieroglyph."

"It's stupid," he laughed, *"but I know I'll regret it if I don't tick it off the list."*

Still smiling, Ryan pictured old Omar standing in the ancient temple.

"Get some good photos, and you could claim the whole thing was a business trip."

Again he heard Omar laughing.

"I'll bear that in mind."

"So, where next?"

"Leisurely trek north, probably."

"Giza Plateau?"

"Yeah… the pyramids have been around for ages, but I won't be," he gave a sigh, *"I've always wanted to see the massive blocks up close. The way they were constructed is -"*

"Omar," he smiled, "We both know that aliens assembled them using their tractor beams."

"Don't get me started on that old gem," he said, *"Listen, I have to go, but could I ask you a favour?"*

"You can certainly ask."

"I was going to tackle this when I got back, but subscriptions are levelling off."

Ryan couldn't help sighing, "I know."

"I hate to do this, but is there any chance you could write something that would pep up the front page?"

Ryan glanced at his laptop.

"What about the stuff I wrote last night?"

"The pareidolia piece is brilliant…" Omar sounded like he was walking at speed, *"But I think we might need something more current. Something that'll appeal to old and new faces."*

"Old and -"

"Really sorry," Omar was out of breath, *"They're boarding. Maybe we should look at this when I -"*

"It's OK," Ryan told him, "I'll think of something, just have a good break."

There was a muffled thanks, then the call ended.

He set the phone down and stared for a moment, unsure how to go about turning Omar's vague idea into a new headline item.

"Old and new faces," he spoke to the empty room.

The news show presenters concluded their cute puppy segment with a smile at the camera, then the shot changed to show a bulldozer pushing down the wall of an old building.

Drinking the remainder of his coffee, he watched the shot transition into an artist's rendering of a new housing complex.

Old and new faces, he thought.

He found himself staring at his laptop.

Looking at the grey face-like image he'd used in the Mars article, he couldn't shake the idea that he was missing something. He'd had this feeling hundreds of times before. Arguably it was what made him suited to his job.

He drummed his fingers on the worktop.

Something he'd seen in the last few minutes was trying to connect to a memory. He just had to be patient and retrace his steps.

"Old and new faces," he pointed at the phone, then began moving mentally backwards, "Demolition… Grey face… Puppy… Death Row… Facial Tattoo."

There was a link here somewhere. A link to something he'd seen before. The only thing that didn't seem to fit was the puppy. He mentally removed it and slowly ran through the highlights again.

As though appearing through a mist, he caught glimpses of the key elements. A memory sprang into focus.

An old Fortean Eye article.

"Got you," he smiled.

In all likelihood, the mugshot he'd seen a few minutes ago had started triggering some low-level recognition, but the image alone hadn't been enough to give him the historical context.

The old article wasn't on the website, but he knew where to start looking for it. He felt a slight thrill at the thought of consulting a reference system that was off the digital grid.

He left the kitchen, headed up the narrow stairs to the top floor, and looked up at the hatch in the ceiling.

Most people in this area of North London had converted their attics into additional bedrooms to appeal to the property markets, but he'd made no such effort. Apart from the installation of some much-needed insulation, the mid-terrace attic was still a relic of the late 19th century.

Reaching up with a hook pole, he pulled open the hatch and grabbed hold of the sliding ladder.

The ladder wasn't one of the wooden types that would have been better suited to the aesthetic of a haunted attic; it was a lightweight metallic affair that seemed possessed in a different way. It insisted on retracting itself if there was no weight on it: a useful feature when it wasn't being used, but an annoyance at every other time.

Again reminding himself that he should probably just take five minutes to adjust the tensioning springs, he negotiated passage into the attic and switched on the bare lightbulb. With an almost self-satisfied twang, the ladder finished retracting and pulled the hatch closed behind him, leaving him in the oddly still space.

Stacks of cardboard boxes cast angular shadows onto the sloping sides of the roof, and the unused air felt as if sound had been subtracted from it.

He'd never fully boarded over the floor, so in some places the exposed wooden beams were still visible. Treading carefully between islands of supportive planks, he made his way over to the dimmer recesses where the older boxes were covered with a light dusting of cobwebs.

Meticulously labelled by year, each box contained his father's old copies of the Fortean Eye: saved for posterity but now read by no-one.

Even when his father had been running the magazine, print had been in decline. After his father's death, Ryan had taken up the heavy reins of ownership and had reluctantly decided to move things online. Bit by bit, the old analogue world was fading away. Even old Omar had begun taking what he called 'final trips' to places. It would be a while before quantum computers filtered down from the large tech corporations to the consumer level but, qubit by qubit, the day would arrive: the analogue world would be left behind and his father's boxes would become an abandoned relic.

Turning on his phone's light, he began searching.

He could picture the front cover that he wanted to find, but he only had a vague notion of the date that it had been published. Eventually, after a search through half a dozen boxes, he found the article he was after: a twelve-year-old case from 2011.

In the glare of his phone's light, the headline read 'The Brixton Live Burial'.

According to the story, an unnamed builder had been carrying out renovations on a house, when a wall had suddenly collapsed, exposing an old fireplace. Inside a space that had been sealed for many years, the builder had discovered the body of a man who had been horribly tortured. Skewered by old iron and woodwork, the man had been standing upright when he'd been walled in.

Although these gorier details weren't discernible in the photos of the semi-demolished chimney breast, one of the close-up photos showed that the man's body hadn't decomposed; something that was mysteriously at odds with the length of time it had been within the wall. In fact, this was commented on within the write up. There were mentions of divine incorruptibility, countered by theories that the space may have contained a preserving vacuum.

Ryan turned the page and found himself looking at a grey-scale photo of the man's prominent facial tattoo. This was definitely the image he'd remembered seeing. It was surprising how similar it was to the one he'd just glimpsed on the news.

Picking up his phone, it was a simple matter to search online for the criminal who'd been executed a few years ago.

It didn't take him long to find the exact mugshot that had been on the TV.

Holding the image next to the photo on the printed page, he could see that the tattoos looked startlingly similar. This was it, he thought. This was the mysterious story that would get the Fortean Eye the attention it needed.

DOTS

Diane watched the black-and-white noise fizzling on the screen. The grain was now much finer, and the curving contours were more clearly defined. Even now, eight years after recruiting her eager young collaborators, she found it hard to accept the sheer scale of the advances that were being made.

Turning away from the screen, she picked up her spoon and began stirring her cup of tea.

She remembered her cramped old university office, and telling the three of them that they'd be working on the mapping of complex information: a purposefully dry description to veil the first step in the process.

Things had moved quickly.

Barely eighteen months after freeing herself from the constrictions of an academic budget, their collaboration had started to yield results. Six months after that, experimental verification had begun to exceed, and then replace, accepted theory.

The high walls of limitation, walls that had been in place since the 1927 Solvay Congress, quietly fell. Transformations of Lorentzian complexity pushed the Planck length into abstraction, and sent old principles of uncertainty swirling into the hole in Dirac's turbulent sea.

The surface of her tea puckered and dipped at the centre.

Adding a drop of milk, she watched it follow the curving contours of the swirl and fold itself into the mix.

A knock at the office door broke her introspection, and she looked up to see that the ginger-haired Alec Wright was standing in the doorway.

"Got a sec?" he said.

"Of course," she set her cup aside and beckoned him in, "Make my day more interesting."

He exhaled a short laugh but by the time he'd walked over to her, his characteristic levity had ebbed away.

"Remember McCairn?" he said.

"How could I forget?" she said, "The whole thing cost us six months."

He nodded and held out his computer tablet.

"I found him," he said, "Or rather, somebody else did."

Not really believing him, she took the tablet and looked at the title displayed at the top of the screen.

"What is this?" she frowned, "Some sort of fringe science thing?"

"Just scroll down," he told her.

"If this is one of your practical -"

Stunned, she stopped scrolling.

Staring back at her from the screen were a pair of tattooed faces.

She scanned through the article at speed and saw what the story was hinting at. It hadn't quite joined the dots, but the dots were now visible and in the public domain.

"Alec," she said, "How did you find this?"

He gave a shrug.

"AI got an image recognition hit. Apparently it was uploaded yesterday."

"If anyone out there takes this seriously," she considered the ramifications, "they could put it all together."

She saw he was nodding.

"You wanted your day to be more interesting?" he said, "Check out who wrote the article."

Scrolling down to the name, she went cold.

"But…" she managed.

He exhaled a hollow laugh, "Exactly."

She could feel a knot forming in her stomach. There was only one possible course of action.

"We have to bring him in," she said, "Quietly. Nothing that might introduce an occlusion."

"That's what I figured," he nodded, "Theo's already looking into it. He'll have an address soon."

"And the website?" she nodded at the tablet.

"It should be four-oh-four in the next few minutes."

Sighing, she shook her head at the webpage.

The Brixton incident had been described as a gruesome impalement followed by a live burial of the victim. Having the benefit of hindsight, she could understand why people would have seen things that way, but the explanation was hopelessly wide of the mark. The modern-day update to the article had pointed out a blurry similarity of the facial tattoos, but had also failed to grasp the true facts of the situation.

When placed side by side, both parts of the web article were problematic, but they still weren't the most worrying aspects of the case.

"Alec," she said, "Let me know as soon as you find him."

With a nod, he turned and left the room.

404

Sitting in the silent attic space, amid the boxes of his father's old paperwork and back issues of the Fortean Eye, Ryan felt a curious chill.

His father had often described it as the feeling of someone walking over your grave. Since childhood, he'd always found it an odd expression: it was, after all, describing a macabre event that hadn't yet happened for you.

The more he tapped at his laptop's refresh key, the more distinct the eerie feeling became. He'd spent the last day writing a new front-page article for the website, but despite uploading it several hours ago, it was now inaccessible. In its place was an unhelpful '404' message, telling him that the page couldn't be found. Either there was a problem with his wireless connection or, worse, the disappearance was due to something he'd done during the upload.

The still location, early hour, and old magazines of unexplained phenomena were doing little to dispel his sense of unease.

A sudden vibration came from the box next to him. After almost jumping out of his skin, he realised it was just his phone.

Picking it up from the top of the box, he glanced at the screen.

The display read 'North London': obviously the cell network didn't have the faintest clue who was calling him at six in the morning.

Distracted by his recent thoughts, and the timing of the call, he cautiously tapped the answer button.

"Hello?"

"Er... hi," came a woman's voice, *"I was hoping to leave a message for Ryan Pryce."*

Still feeling unsettled, his first thought slipped out.

"How did you get this number?"

The woman's reply was hesitant, but she sounded like she was stating the obvious.

"It was on your website," she said, *"Sorry... have I got the wrong number?"*

He suddenly remembered that, of course, the office number was now being forwarded to *his* phone while Omar was away.

"No, sorry, it's the right number. I've just been having a few... technical issues this morning."

"Ah, OK. So, would I be able to leave a message for him?"

"I'm Ryan," he rubbed at his eyes and stifled a yawn, "How can I help?"

There was a long pause.

"I read your story," she said, *"The one about the guy in the wall."*

Despite the early hour, he couldn't help smiling. The headline article was obviously starting to draw attention; it was just a pity that he couldn't see it himself at the minute.

"I know the article," he said.

"Twelve years ago, no-one could ID the body, right?"

"What was left of it," he recalled, "It wasn't exactly in one piece when they cut it out of the iron and brickwork."

"And fingerprints couldn't be identified -"

"Because there was no way to separate his hands and arm from the surrounding concrete. Listen, what's this all about?"

"I've got information," she said, *"Certain… intelligence agencies are using pre-digital mugshots to falsify modern-day execution records."*

"You're saying the Death Row prisoner wasn't the man in the photo?"

There was a short pause.

"I'm not saying anything," she said, *"Not over the phone."*

Putting aside the fact that she'd already said a fair amount over an open phone line, he tried to phrase things politely.

"You realise how all this sounds?"

"Listen," she said, *"Yesterday, I got logged out of my email, and after I reset my password, I found a completely blank message had been sent from my account back to itself."*

Ryan looked at the unresponsive webpage and felt another shiver.

Perhaps his article had touched a nerve somewhere, and the webpage removal was evidence of a heavy-handed agency response. Perhaps he himself would soon be receiving a curiously blank email.

He knew there was a fine line between 'unexplained coincidence' and 'conspiracy theory', but in the isolation of the quiet attic, he genuinely couldn't decide which side of the line he was on.

"I have a photo," she said, *"One that shows the tattoo in detail."*

"There's already a photo in my article."

"Not like the one I'm holding," she said, *"You'll want to see it in person. Trust me."*

When it came to matters of trust, he usually trusted his gut. Right now, in the early hours of the morning, his gut was telling him he was hungry.

Clearly the woman was suggesting that they should meet up. But if there was even a scrap of truth to her claims, then bringing himself to the attention of an unknown intelligence agency would be the last thing he'd want.

Looking at the vague caller ID on his phone screen, he spotted a solution; one that would satisfy the woman's need for a covert-style meeting, and his need for food.

"My phone says you're calling from North London," he said, "why don't we meet up now?"

"Now?" she sounded surprised.

Thinking of the various conspiracy theory movies he'd seen over the years, he constructed a reply that might sound plausible to her.

"When you're concerned that your actions are being monitored," he said, "You have to react fast. Don't give anyone time to prepare."

"That's..." she seemed to consider the logic, *"really good thinking."*

"OK," he said, "You don't have to give me your real name, but you should at least tell me what to call you."

She told him, and in under a minute they'd agreed on a mutually accessible public place to meet. When Patricia asked about wearing a flower or some sort of disguise, he suggested a more subtle approach for recognising each other.

After hanging up, he restarted his laptop. Perhaps the old solution of turning it off and on again might clear the problem by the time he got back home.

He moved back through the stacks of boxes, but while negotiating the ladder, he succeeded in putting a rip in his trouser leg. Stepping off the lowest rung, he cursed the long flap of cloth that now trailed at his ankle. There wasn't enough time to change into something else. He'd have to go as he was.

Leaving the hatch to spring shut behind him, he headed downstairs to the kitchen. He pushed his phone into his coat pocket and grabbed his trusty paper notepad from the worktop. When devices ran out of power, it always paid to have a more analogue solution in your pocket.

Looking at the clock on the wall, he could see he had about twenty minutes to get to the meeting. He turned off the lights, left the house, and headed out into the early morning streets.

It had been raining lightly overnight, so the wet roads were still reflecting the streetlights, and the tyres of electric vehicles were adding a faint swish to the gentle tapestry of sounds.

For him, there was something comfortable about pre-dawn London. The world hadn't fully woken up yet, and there was a sense of calm potential to the air. An impression that there was room to breathe.

He took a leisurely breath from the pleasantly cool air and walked on, allowing his thoughts to wander slightly.

He'd been in the attic because he'd been struck by an idea that had come to him in his sleep. The Fortean Eye had been moved online, but the old paper issues hadn't made the transition. Although he much preferred the tactile quality of the physical publications, his father's boxes of files weren't easily searchable, and stories couldn't be cross-referenced.

Having now looked through the volume of material in the attic, he knew it would take a while to digitise the back issues. The project would be an effort but, in the long term, his father's legacy may stand a better chance of being preserved.

Turning to go down a street, he found it was closed off for roadworks. Although the actual work hadn't started, he knew he'd still have to go the slightly longer way around. Things like this were always frustrating, but diversions and delays were just part of life here. London was a city built on centuries of previous settlements and roadways. Its historic layers and strata were always being excavated to repair the thin veneer of the present day.

In the end, the diversion only added a few extra minutes

to his journey, and he was soon turning down a quiet side road.

Ahead of him, the glow of the all-day breakfast cafe spilled out onto the dark street. The perfect meeting place: public but quiet, and food to eat.

As expected, it was already open for its early morning customers. With any luck, he thought, Patricia should have found her way here on time.

Walking through the door, a wall of warmth wrapped around him, and the smell of frying food hung in the air. In one corner, mounted on the wall, an old flat-screen TV was murmuring the morning headlines to itself, while half a dozen people sat at different tables and ignored it.

He moved past them and walked up to the counter, where a tired-looking old man stood wiping his hands on a towel. After a perfunctory exchange of early morning greetings, Ryan ordered a bacon sandwich and a mug of instant coffee. The sandwich was going to take a few minutes to make, but the coffee was ready by the time he'd waved his phone at the payment pad.

Taking the steaming mug, he turned away from the counter.

Most of the people in the cafe were simply digging into their breakfasts or checking their phones, but one person caught his attention: a duffle-coated woman, who was wearing thick-framed glasses. She made eye contact with him and then attempted to look away nonchalantly. A moment later, she used her elbow to nudge a paper napkin off the edge of the table.

This was the action that he'd agreed with Patricia over the phone, but it had been carried out so heavy-handedly that all covert subtlety had been lost.

Sighing to himself, Ryan walked between the tables and sat down opposite her.

"Sorry, there were roadworks," he pointed at her

obviously full mug, "But I'm guessing you haven't been here that long either."

She gave him an appraising look, then straightened her glasses.

"You're good at this," she nodded, "Thanks for meeting."

As Ryan unzipped his coat and pulled out his notepad, he saw Patricia slide a printed photograph across the table.

As far as he could see, it was the same man that had appeared in the news and the Fortean Eye. This image was in colour though, and the background featured what looked like out-of-focus machinery; a detail not present in either of the images he'd dealt with.

He lowered his voice to blend in with the background noise.

"Where did you get this?" he looked at the crystal-clear markings.

Patricia twisted her mug from side to side. Clearly, she was one of those people who liked to cradle their drink until it had almost gone cold. Either that, or she wasn't quite ready to trust him yet.

"Query," she looked directly at him.

"Go on," Ryan nodded for her to continue.

"Does it mean anything to you?"

He found himself frowning.

"Does *what* mean anything?" he hesitated, then pointed back at the photo, "The tattoo?"

She assessed him for a moment, as though he was being deliberately unhelpful, then tilted her head.

"Sure."

Hoping to gain her trust, he began talking through the various markings that were in the photo.

"OK, there's hints *here* that a swastika may have been concealed by the addition of later floral motifs. Covering up a mistake of youth isn't uncommon, but the radial lines *here* could be read as the Sumerian symbol for longevity, so it's possible that he -" Ryan broke off, suddenly aware that she wasn't looking at the photo. She was just watching him.

Pushing his mug aside, he faced her.

"I came here because you said there was more to this story," he kept his voice low, "I'm listening, but you've got to start telling me something."

"How can I put this?" she lowered her voice to match his, "You're up to your neck in something, but you're not seeing the whole picture."

He leaned forward.

"So you *do* know how all of this is connected?"

She took a deep breath, "You really should've left this alone."

Ryan saw something shift slightly in her posture, and he felt vaguely uneasy.

The side-to-side twisting of her mug quietly stopped.

"Please," she now stared at him, "don't make a fuss. Just keep your hands where I can see them, and you won't get hurt."

It took him a second to realise that she wasn't giving him general advice, she was actually threatening him.

Unsure how seriously to take her calmly spoken words, he started considering how he might make a swift escape. He glanced at the cafe door. Nothing lay in his way.

"I really wouldn't try that," she seemed to read his mind.

Fighting a strong urge to get out of the cafe as quickly as possible, he picked up his notepad and put it back in his pocket. Doing his best to keep his voice stable, he looked at her.

"We chose somewhere nice and public on purpose," he said, "If I tip this coffee over, *everyone's* gonna look."

"I think you're misreading the situation."

"You really think so?" he said.

Without saying a word, she now quietly lifted her mug from the table.

Instantly, and in perfect synchronisation, four other people in the cafe stood and turned in his direction.

Patricia took a calm drink from the mug, then set it aside.

"Yeah. I really think so."

He saw her gaze dip slightly to one side, then she began talking. From the tone of her voice, he realised that she must be using some sort of concealed microphone.

"Do we need to query anything?" she said.

There was a short pause, then she adjusted her glasses and spoke to the people who were standing around the cafe.

"OK," she said, "we're clear."

Ryan suddenly knew he wouldn't be leaving here by himself.

"You're not Patricia," he managed.

"No," she agreed, "but I *am* the person who called you. We *do* need to talk."

He glanced around the cafe. Someone had timed things perfectly to arrange this setup. He now wondered if they'd also been responsible for the roadwork signs that had delayed his arrival.

"You want to talk," he folded his arms, "Go ahead."

She stood, "Not here."

The others were looking at him, clearly expecting him to stand.

"You guys got some sort of ID?"

When none of them responded, the woman gestured for him to get up.

There was no point fighting this, he thought. They were controlling the whole environment. He was outnumbered and couldn't call for help. In this moment of realisation, he felt curiously free to speak his mind.

"Fine, but one of you needs to grab my bacon sandwich."

BLUE BUTTON

Theo looked over his figures again. When time wasn't against you, he thought, it always paid to check and recheck your workings.

As he carefully wrote additional glyphs on the whiteboard, it reminded him of his school years. His early life had imprinted on him a strong academic work ethic: if you wanted to succeed, then you had to work well with others and apply your talents. And apply himself he had.

Since his teens, he'd always thought that there was an elegance in the mathematics of modelling the undetermined state: a world of infinite possibility, described without having to collapse probability to one singular outcome.

When he'd joined Diane Sellick and the others, the theories he'd learnt in his youth had quickly escalated into astonishing practicality. But, despite all the advances that they'd made, the humble whiteboard still had its place.

He stood back from his handiwork and took in everything he'd written. According to his calculations, a tenfold increase in particle resolution should be possible without upgrading any of their current hardware. He wanted to give the good news to Diane immediately, but he knew she was focused on other matters at the moment. It would have to wait until later.

In a move that had now become habit, Theo looped his hand back and forth, then underlined the final version of his solution.

"Long-term storage," he tapped at his temples.

Satisfied that he'd committed his calculations to memory, he picked up the board rubber and wiped the surface clean.

He was just putting the rubber away when he heard a call coming in on the computer console. Leaving the whiteboard behind, he walked over to the screen and tapped the answer icon.

A video window popped up on the display: a live camera feed from Petra Defaye's glasses. She must have been looking into a mirror, he thought, because he could see she was still wearing her duffle coat.

"Hi Duffy," he said, "Where are you?"

She tucked a strand of hair behind one ear and adjusted her glasses.

"I'm outside Diane's waiting room," she said, "You can start now."

"Thanks," he turned away and pushed the blue button on the console, "Query running."

QUERY

There was a basic chair in the corner of the featureless room, but Ryan demonstrated what little freedom he had by not sitting in it. Instead, he walked back and forth between the room's two closed doors, and mentally reviewed what had happened.

When he'd heard stories about people being abducted, the narrative usually contained themes of manhandling and physical unpleasantness, but his experience had been somewhat different.

Although they'd walked him from the cafe to the back of a dark van, they hadn't laid a finger on him. They'd asked him to sit in one of the comfortable forward-facing seats, and then three of them had joined him.

He'd expected them to put a bag over his head, but the only bag he'd encountered had been made of paper and contained the bacon sandwich he'd ordered. They hadn't answered any of his questions, which had felt awkward, but the most uncomfortable part of the journey was eating his breakfast while they silently watched him.

When the van had stopped, the duffle-coated woman had led him to this blank windowless room, opened the door, and asked him to wait inside. After pointing out the chair, she'd left by the same door, leaving him to walk around on his own.

In comparison to everything he'd been expecting, the entire abduction had been almost polite.

But this was still an abduction, he reminded himself. He'd been brought here against his will, using a quiet display of force. If he'd reacted aggressively, things may not have gone so smoothly.

The door at the opposite end of the room opened and he turned to see that an older-looking woman was standing in the doorway, holding a computer tablet.

"Mr. Pryce," she smiled and stood slightly aside, "I'm Diane Sellick. Please… come in."

Ryan glanced back at the door he'd entered by, "Do I get a choice here?"

"Let me put it this way," she said, "Only one of these doors will give you answers."

Through the open doorway, he could see an office with a single desk that faced some sort of video projection wall. The image on the wall was a fizzing blur of static noise.

Curiosity getting the better of him, he walked forward and more of the office became visible. The desk was cluttered with stacks of folders, a small picture frame, and a collection of metal components; almost as if she was in the middle of disassembling a small fridge and had run out of space.

Passing through the doorway, he could see that the wide projection wall was slightly curved, and that a modestly padded upright sofa had been positioned to face it. From the static on the screen, he guessed that something must be wrong with her elaborate home theatre setup.

"Please," she gestured to the sofa, "have a seat."

He purposefully folded his arms, "I'll stand."

"Entirely up to you," she turned away and started tapping at her tablet, "Sorry I had to keep you waiting. I had to finish up an important presentation."

"Let me guess," he forced a mirthless smile, "Interpersonal skills for henchmen?"

"No," she said, "The presentation was for you."

She tapped once more on the tablet.

The fizzing noise on the projection wall seemed to ripple and fold into discernible shapes. A black-and-white image now emerged: a grainy, static-filled video that showed him pacing up and down outside the room.

"This," she pointed, "is one minute ago."

Looking at the video's low definition and obvious lack of colour, he couldn't help voicing his first thought aloud.

"I think your CCTV needs an upgrade."

"Perhaps you'd prefer an alternative angle?"

He saw her tapping at her tablet, then the view on the wall changed.

His pacing continued, but the camera's high viewpoint smoothly shifted, orbiting around him before coming to rest a few feet above the floor.

He knew for a fact that there hadn't been any flying cameras in the room, but the fuzzy video was showing him a perspective that was completely at odds with his recollection.

"Is this some sort of... computer manipulation?" he pointed, "You tracked my motion and mapped it onto a -"

"There were no cameras in the room," she continued to watch the screen, "No depth or infrared sensors."

He pointed at the noisy image, "Then what am I looking at?"

She turned to face him.

"You're looking at a real-time view of the past."

He actually felt his thoughts stop.

Unable to process what he was hearing, he coughed a laugh.

The idea was ridiculous.

"Your reaction isn't uncommon," she stared at him, "It's a difficult thing to accept."

On the screen, his grainy counterpart walked forward and passed straight through the position that would have been occupied by a conventional camera.

"So that was me?" he glanced back at the door, "When I was waiting around out there?"

"From a certain perspective, you're *still* waiting around out there," she said, "Except *that* point in time isn't now."

The sofa now seemed like a good place to sit.

Without taking his eyes from the noisy, flickering image, he lowered himself into a more comfortable position.

"What is… this?" he gestured at the wall.

"Quantum Resonance Imaging," she said, "Q.R.I."

He now remembered a word that duffle-woman had used.

"Query," he quietly pronounced the initials as one word.

Diane appeared to assess him for a moment.

"That was fast," she said, "Clearly my team should have been more careful when speaking in public."

She sat next to him on the sofa, and tapped at her tablet.

His blurry alter ego halted mid-stride, and the viewpoint shifted smoothly again to orbit a moment that seemed frozen in time.

"Query," she said, "A three-dimensional cross section, taken from a four-dimensional topology."

He couldn't help staring at the mesmerising image on the wall. It was impossible, but the man on the screen was definitely him: he could even see the flap of ripped cloth in the leg of his trousers.

He now felt unaccountably cold, as though a surrounding crowd had suddenly fallen silent and had turned to focus on him. Somehow, he was at the epicentre of recent events and he had no clue why. The tattooed man, the Brixton Live Burial, and this fantastical technology were all connected. One thing was for sure: conspiracy theories were less entertaining when you found yourself in the middle of one.

"I'm involved in all this, aren't I?"

She actually gave a short laugh, as though the answer was obvious.

"Absolutely," she said, "But I can almost guarantee that whatever reason you're imagining will be the wrong one."

She tapped at her tablet and the grey-scale tableau unfroze. His duplicate resumed his pacing, then turned to face the door. As the door opened, the scene lost resolution and appeared to melt into a mass of static.

"What just happened?" he pointed at the screen.

"The historical segment that we were witnessing began to overlap with the moment when we first met. The resulting uncertainty created a form of temporal feedback."

Mind still reeling, he looked at the noise that continued to fizz on the wall.

"And… that's why we can't see anything?"

Her frown, and the slight tilting of her head, told him that she was weighing up the validity of his question. She pointed at the visual static.

"The closer we get to a point of quantum overlap, the more feedback noise we get," she now seemed to stare through the wall, "Ironically, it's this very interference pattern that allows us to search for temporal occlusions."

He felt lost, "Occlusions?"

"Overlaps," she said, "In some ways, they're similar to the one you've just seen… Areas in time where the present day intrudes on the past, and leaves a mark."

While the static continued to fizz, she drew a thin black line on her tablet's white screen.

"Think of this as our timeline," she then began adding dots to the line, "and these points are past events."

She zoomed in on one of the dots and began adding red hatched lines to the area on the left of the dot.

"Each time we 'query' a past event, we introduce a little interference. If the interference we make becomes sufficiently heavy," she added more hatched lines, "then it creates an occlusion. This occlusion overlaps the event itself, and then disappears just after it."

She repeated the process for the other dots until each of them had been overlaid by short diagonal scribbles. She zoomed out to show him the finished timeline that featured several red shaded areas.

"The difficult thing to grasp is that, if all these occlusions are firmly in our timeline's *past*, then they must logically have *always* been there."

"What?" he frowned at the dots on the line, "These things are there before you've even made them?"

"That question is something of a Schrödinger's Cat conundrum. It depends on whether you consider the timeline to be outside or inside the box. Indeterminable until the end result is known."

He pointed at one of the dots.

"What if you chose not to look at an occlusion?"

She gave an understanding nod.

"In reality, these things aren't as obvious as neat dots on a line. We're talking about a very long line, coupled with every explorable point in three dimensions. You don't find them by accident. You have to go looking."

Recalling his alter ego pacing in the outside room, he made an educated guess.

"You can look back even further than a minute ago, can't you?"

She gave him the sort of look that implied the task was trivial.

"History is a big place."

Only now did the enormity of what she was suggesting start to sink in.

These people could examine time itself.

"As you can imagine," she continued, "The search area is large, so we use historical records to narrow the region we want to study, and then use our system to scan for an upkick in the interaction between the covariant field and -"

"Wait, wait," he held up his hand, "What?"

She paused, and he got the uncomfortable feeling that she was trying to think down to his level.

"Think of a metal detector finding a buried coin," she said, "It doesn't detect metal, it detects eddy currents that the metal detector *itself* is inducing. It beeps because there was an interaction, not because there's metal. It's the *interaction* that we scan for, an interference pattern that tells us that we've found the right point."

Staring at the static that continued to fizz on the wall, he struggled to get his head around the concept.

"So," he rubbed at his eyes, "an interference pattern lies in the past. You later scan for it, which then *creates* the pattern that you end up scanning for. The whole thing's circular logic."

"It's a question of temporal perspective," she pointed at her tablet screen, "From our point of view, we're looking at an interaction that has already taken place in the past. It's part of our history. We're just *seeing* that there was an interaction, later. A closed-loop consistent chronology, viewed after the events are already resolved."

His head swam.

"So all this is *fate* then? You do something because you were always predestined to?"

She shook her head.

"All we're talking about is the ability to *detect* quantum overlapping," she said, "Free will remains intact."

"How exactly?"

She looked at the static-filled wall screen.

"Just because a metal detector tells you where there's buried treasure, it doesn't force you to dig it up. In theory, you're still free to walk away."

Theory, the word stuck out.

If the past hour had taught him anything, it was that Diane Sellick and her team didn't do things theoretically.

"You guys didn't walk away from buried treasure, did you?"

"No," she stood, "We built the spade."

OBSERVERS

Petra watched the video feed on her laptop. Although there were no cameras in the waiting room, one had been placed in Diane's office. For the past few minutes, she'd been observing the conversation. As Diane had requested, Alec was at her side, providing a second pair of eyes.

"What do you think?" she asked.

Alec shook his head, "He didn't even give it a second glance."

"Maybe he didn't spot it?"

"No, he looked straight at Diane's desk when he walked in. If he'd recognised it, his behaviour would've been different."

She'd known Alec since the three of them had met in Diane's old office and signed the NDA. She'd grown to trust his instincts over the years, but if he was right, then the situation was more complicated than they'd feared. She hated not knowing.

"All things considered," said Alec, "I think he took it well, but Diane didn't sound too pleased when he guessed the QRI slang."

Petra straightened her glasses and glanced over at her

duffle coat on the nearby chair. Perhaps seeking a little protection from her verbal slip-up, she found herself pushing her hands into the warm pockets of her comfortable hoodie.

"Back at the cafe," she said, "I only mentioned the word to check his reaction."

"Yeah, I know," Alec pointed to her glasses, "I was watching your video link the whole time."

"And did you see anything?"

"Not a flicker," he breathed out heavily, "He just focused on McCairn's tattoos."

She shook her head and sighed.

"Do you think he's worked it out yet?"

"I doubt it," Alec now pointed at the screen, "but I don't think it'll be long."

Petra looked at the video feed and saw that Diane was getting up from the sofa. The next movement was subtle, but she saw her turn to the camera and give a discreet nod.

"That's it," said Alec, "They're on the way."

Still picturing an exotic-looking metal detector, Ryan kept pace with Diane as she walked with purpose away from the waiting room.

"What do you mean, you built a spade?"

"We'll get to that," she said, "I promise. Along with why we brought you here. But I want you to meet some people first."

Although the statement sounded faintly ominous, he tried to hold onto what he already knew. If their intention had been to harm him, they'd already had ample opportunity. From the careful way they'd handled him so far, he knew he must be important to them somehow.

He'd spent a large portion of his life looking at unexplained phenomena and then suggesting mysterious connections between them. Today's experience was beating them all. Each answer was spawning two new questions, but he knew the pattern couldn't continue indefinitely.

"I try not to assume," said Diane, "but would I be right in thinking that you have no experience of quantum mechanics?"

"Isn't it when they tell you *two* mechanics are fixing your car, but in fact there's only one?"

Diane neither smiled nor broke her stride.

"We started all this eight years ago," she gestured loosely at the long corridor, "but things went in a direction that none of us anticipated."

"So," Ryan glanced behind him, "all that quantum resonance stuff -"

"Developed out of a different brief."

"Which was?"

"The mapping of complex information," she said, "To begin with, the task was to take the quantum state of one particle, and transfer it to another particle ten metres away."

"It worked?"

She nodded.

"The quantum teleportation effect was verified and then surpassed," she said, "Within three years, we were doing the same thing with physical matter."

"Bullshit."

"No, we never actually tried it with manure," she kept a straight face, "but by year four, we'd succeeded in transporting an ostrich egg fifty metres."

As his mind stumbled over the latest revelation, she turned a corner and walked on again at the same speed.

"Originally, Query was an analysis tool for mapping atomic momentum. The grainy three-D image is just a visualisation of the data. As the information we were transferring became more complex, so did Query. Each decaqubit we added to the quantum calculation space refined the vis-"

"Hold on," he mentally and physically struggled to keep pace with her, "You mean you have your *own* quantum-state computer? Here?"

She waved away the question.

"A necessary evil. The sort of data we're processing can't be represented as ones and zeroes," she shook her head, "Anyway, as the qubits increased, Query's mapping resolution got better. We could represent objects with greater fidelity during the transportation process. It was this ongoing quest for greater descriptive data that eventually highlighted an error that we'd been unaware of."

She slowed her pace and then stopped outside a door.

"It was this error that took QRI and teleportation in a new direction," she took hold of the door handle, "Let me introduce you to the others."

As Ryan took a deep breath, she opened the door and walked into a meeting room.

One wall was occupied by a fairly old-fashioned whiteboard and geography globe, but he could see other pieces of audio visual equipment that were more up to date. Walking further into the room, he saw three people sitting at a round table. They were all about his age, and they were all looking at him.

"Everyone, this is Ryan," said Diane, and then began introducing each of the others, starting with the copper-haired man on the left, "This is Alec Wright, Theo Reinhardt, and you've already met Petra Defaye."

The woman's duffle coat was now draped over a chair, but her characteristic glasses were still in place. It was odd, but in these distinctly unfamiliar circumstances, Ryan was actually glad there was someone here that he recognised.

"Not Patricia," he nodded.

Petra raised an eyebrow, then handed something to Diane.

As Diane stuck it to the whiteboard, he could see it was the photo from the cafe.

"I know you're already aware of some aspects of McCairn's life," she said, "but I want to quickly tell you about the years that led up to his death."

2020

Diane kept her attention focused on the screen. Each pixel was made up from the internal motions of ten thousand atoms. If all went well, in a matter of minutes another milestone would soon fly past them at speed.

The quantum resonance image began to emerge from the static.

"Theo," she spoke into her microphone, "Can you check outer shell coherence? I'm seeing electron shear."

"I see it," came his reply, *"Is that any better now?"*

"Yep," she saw a positive shift in the data, "QRI two running."

Over the next few seconds, she watched the black-and-white static coalesce into recognisable shapes. Although it was constructed from fizzing noise, she could easily discern the flat disc area on the floor of Lab Two.

"Target zone stable and clear," she reported, "Alec can you confirm?"

"Confirmed," Alec replied, *"Exiting space."*

There was a brief pause, then an indicator lit up on her console and Alec continued.

"Lab Two door sealed," he said, *"Isolation complete. Top hat is ready."*

Smiling at the analogy that Alec had chosen to run with, she looked at the screen on her left: a video coming from Petra's headcam in Lab One. There was a little bit of interference, but this was only to be expected: Lab One was fifty metres further away, and contained an array of electromagnetic sources.

"Everything alright, Petra?" she looked at the video feed, "How's Roger's lucky charm?"

Petra's hand moved into shot and checked the rubidium-quartz crystal that glinted in the collar.

"All good," she said, *"Looking super stylish... goes well with the fur."*

As Petra backed away from the hexagonal-patterned floor disc, Diane could see the white rabbit at the centre was still asleep. It was blissfully unaware that it was about to make history.

The video feed panned left and right around the space, then Petra backed out of Lab One.

"Departure zone clear. Exiting space."

In the video feed, the lab door swung shut. A second indicator lit up on her console.

"Lab One door sealed," Petra reported, *"Isolation complete."*

"OK then," said Diane, "Switching to QRI one."

The wireless video feed was rapidly replaced by a screen of fizzling static. But as she watched, curves and contours began to distort the chaotic noise. A moment later, the rippling settled into a stable form.

In front of her now were two displays. The left screen showed a gently breathing rabbit made from black-and-white static. The right screen still featured the empty area that Alec had called the top hat.

At the heart of the machinery, a magic trick was about to unfold.

The quantum covariant field that underpinned everything from mass to spatial dimensions would be rewritten. With a wave of a figurative physics wand, the complex information that described the rabbit's atomic state would be transfered to a point that was fifty metres away.

"We're at sync," said Theo.

"Thanks," she started recording the sensor data that was coming in from both labs, "Petra are you still recording video?"

"I am," came her reply, *"Should I start walking now?"*

"Yes," she told her, "Let's do this."

Typing the commands into her keyboard, Diane brought the phase shift coils out of standby, and watched the on-screen capacitor gauge rise: a distinctly boring representation of what was actually unfolding in Lab One.

"Ladies and Gentlemen," Alec spoke, *"As you will observe, there is nothing up my sleeves…"*

She couldn't help smiling, but she heard Petra telling him to shut up.

As the gauge passed through the ninety-five percent mark, a tone sounded on the console. Reaching out, she pushed the auto-commit button, and the charge continued to rise. Leaning back from the microphone, she kept a keen eye on the displays and spoke quietly to herself.

"Abracadabra."

The gauge peaked and instantly discharged. Both of the QRI displays collapsed into a churning mass of static: a momentary occlusion where physics and nature collaborated to generate and heal the quantum scar.

Almost immediately, the occlusion cleared. The swirling noise on the displays puckered and bent into the previous familiar shapes.

On the left screen, she could see that the floor of Lab One was now empty. The right-hand screen, similarly shaped from bright static, showed the flat disc in Lab Two. At its centre was an organic-looking shape.

She quickly sat forward and switched the other screen to show her the view from Petra's headcam.

Alec was in vision, his hand poised on the door-release mechanism of Lab Two. As Petra got closer to him, he pulled the handle and opened the door for her.

The video feed swept inside the room and headed straight toward the target disc on the floor. It was occupied by a small white rabbit. As the camera got closer, she saw Petra's hand examining the collar and the creature itself.

"He's still breathing!" she reported, *"He's alive!"*

Wearing a matching headcam, Alec was openly grinning at Petra's camera.

"And that, Ladies and Gentlemen, is how to pull a rabbit from a hat!"

In the celebrations that evening, Roger was kept in his large cage, but the cage itself was given pride of place on the meeting room table.

Diane poked another sliver of carrot through the mesh, but Roger seemed more interested in drinking from his water bowl. Perhaps teleportation induced mild dehydration, she made a mental note.

At the side of the whiteboard, Alec was again grinning at the video that Petra had recorded: a long, single shot that clearly showed the rabbit being locked in Lab One, only to be found inside the other locked lab a few seconds later.

Petra herself was at the other side of the meeting room. Beer bottle in hand, she was talking with teetotal Theo as she sketched what looked like a Faraday cage diagram on the whiteboard. Evidently, the two of them were discussing some new innovation.

"Diane," Alec walked over, holding up his bottle, "To progress."

After a clink of glass, Diane nodded, "To progress."

"Instantaneous transportation," he smiled and shook his head.

Diane hesitated only a fraction of a second before smiling back, but the minor delay was apparently enough to raise Alec's suspicions.

"Er," he briefly glanced at the rabbit, "what's up Doc?"

Smiling at the old cartoon reference, she picked at the label on her bottle, unsure if she should even raise her concerns yet.

"It may be nothing," she shrugged.

"Then tell me the nothing that's on your mind," he insisted.

She put her bottle down on the table.

"This was our first test with the upgraded QRI imaging algorithm."

"Another leap," he nodded, "Is there a problem?"

"The additional scanning resolution..." she said, "It's highlighted a discrepancy. One that the old version couldn't see, because it had insufficient qubits to describe the transport process."

"What do you mean?"

"Alec, I've reviewed the data," she glanced at the rabbit, "The transport was less than instant."

He seemed suddenly relieved, "It's still *way* faster than any-"

"No," she interrupted, "By less than instant, I mean that the interval between departure and arrival was *negative*."

"What?"

"The new scanning resolution was able to detect a *negative* arrival time. Roger arrived in Lab Two *before* he departed from Lab One."

His frown was instant.

"But my headcam video," he said, "If Roger had been in Lab Two, I'd have seen him on the arrival disc before I sealed the room."

Diane shook her head.

"The negative arrival time was only about six milliseconds. Nobody was in the room to witness it, but the QRI occlusion period is a precise match. For those six milliseconds, the event was unobservable."

Alec now set down his bottle.

"The negative offset has always been there?" he said, "We just couldn't detect it before today?"

Diane nodded and looked at the cage on the table.

"If it's true," she said, "it would mean that our humble rabbit here has travelled six milliseconds into his own past."

2021

Alec stretched his legs out in front of him, then tucked them back underneath the plastic chair.

He'd been in this corridor almost twelve months ago, wearing the same headcam, and waiting to open the same door. This time though, his main focus was to verify that Lab Two remained sealed before the test began.

Watching the seconds tick by on the digital wall clock, he shook his head. So much had happened over the past year.

Roger's temporal trip duration had been verified, and then doubled. Then quadrupled. At that point, testing had reverted to inanimate objects, and they'd developed the 'Schrödinger's Box' protocol.

The paradox-avoiding logic was simple but effective.

An object arrives from the future.

You don't see it because it arrives inside a locked empty room.

You now choose an object, target the locked room, and send the object to the past.

You open the locked room.

If the room isn't empty, and if the room contains your sent object, then your time travel experiment has worked.

As Diane had once put it, 'A controllable, time-limited envelope, that sidesteps the issue of future knowledge.'

Alec took a deep breath and re-folded his arms.

Over the past year they'd moved easily beyond Roger's six millisecond trip. For reasons of practicality alone, the current envelope was an hour.

For the last fifty-eight minutes, isolated and unobserved, a video camera inside Lab Two had been recording any activity. When the experiment was complete, the video could be reviewed and the moment of arrival could then be analysed.

He still found it odd to think that, on the other side of the door, the outcome of the experiment had already happened. Until the door was unlocked though, the state of the room remained unknown. Right now, Schrödinger's Box was both empty and occupied.

The seconds on the wall clock ticked away.

They'd now conducted this kind of test on dozens of occasions. They'd varied the exact arrival location inside the room. They'd even varied how far back in time to send the objects. But today's test was different. There were no rubidium-quartz cubes, ostrich eggs, or rabbits.

He didn't know how Diane had managed to procure the Death Row prisoner from the British justice system, and he didn't *want* to know.

As far as the world was concerned, a lethal injection had been administered to McCairn, but the cold truth was that the injection had just been a powerful sedative. If McCairn survived both of the intended teleport experiments, then an *actual* lethal injection would ensure that the mass murderer never woke again.

As the wall clock ticked off the last few seconds, Alec stood from his chair and moved it away from the door.

On cue, he saw Petra approaching from the far end of the corridor. Like him, she was wearing a headcam and a serious expression. Unlike him, she was in the middle of a radio conversation with Theo.

"I don't know, Tee!" she shouted, and immediately broke into a run, "Alec, get it open!"

He turned and jabbed his four digits into the digital lock. The instant that the green light came on, he pulled the heavy door open and followed Petra into Lab Two.

The video camera was recording an empty piece of floor.

FRAME OF REFERENCE

Ryan looked at the clusters of graphs and photos that had now been stuck to Diane's whiteboard timeline.

"So until I put my Brixton article online," he said, "You had no idea where... when... McCairn had gone to?"

"Like I told you before," Diane clicked the cap on her marker pen, "History is a big place."

"But what about your Query imaging thing?" he said, "Couldn't you have just searched for him?"

"The transmitter pad was ruined in the accident," she said, "All we knew was that the temporal offset had a negative vector. He had to be somewhere in the past."

"But how did you *know* that?"

Alec leaned forward.

"Because the video from Lab Two recorded only empty floor. He didn't turn up in the present, like a normal teleport operation."

Ryan's mind again boggled at the casual use of the words normal and teleport.

"The search problem was also geographical," Theo stood.

He walked over to the antique-looking globe in the corner of the room, and placed his finger down on the British Isles.

"McCairn's transit time would've been under a second, but during that time, the Earth moved," he lifted his finger from the curved surface, then rotated the globe underneath it, "He was no longer locked to that location, or that time."

With a twist of his hand, he set the globe spinning backwards.

"The polar coordinate system and Earth's gravity well, combined with the influence of the Sun's more massive gravitational field, meant that he didn't just end up in space. But, even knowing all that, he could have ended up anywhere."

"Or any-when," Ryan now began to understand the scale of how truly lost McCairn had been.

He looked over at the printouts stuck to Diane's timeline, and saw the gruesome 2011 photos of the wrecked chimney: an event that had happened a whole *four years* before Diane had even met her students. The consequences of McCairn's trip had unfolded long before its cause had even been set in motion.

"McCairn's departure," he glanced over at the video screen near the whiteboard, "Can I see it again?"

Diane tapped at her tablet and the video clip of McCairn's final moments began to play on the screen. This time around, Ryan picked up more of the details.

The photo that Petra had shown him in the cafe had clearly been extracted from this high-resolution video. At the centre of frame, surrounded by all manner of tubes and metalwork, was the sedated convict.

Ryan watched the terrifying moment again.

As lights turned on around McCairn, the sedation suddenly wore off. As if waking into a nightmare, the initial disorientation became anxiety, and then aggressive panic. Eyes wide open, the convict desperately struggled against the straps that were holding him to the upright stretcher. As the surrounding lights brightened even more, his flailing arms broke free of the straps. There was a flash and, yelling out in pain, he thrust out his hands.

For a split second, the arms flickered; flesh and brick patterns occupying the same space. There was a bright-blue arc of electrical discharge, then the surrounding machinery crumpled in on itself and the video cut out.

Ryan instantly pictured McCairn's arrival in the past: the body intersecting the atoms of the boarded-up chimney, and the increase in matter explosively blowing out the weak plaster board.

"Took us six months to rebuild the components," said Diane, "Even when repairs were complete, we were still no closer to working out where he'd gone."

Ryan pointed at the screen.

"If your machine was so badly damaged, why did he *go* anywhere at all?"

Diane nodded.

"Ideally, his quantum tether should have kept him anchored to the present before transport…" she rewound the video then paused it at the point when McCairn had struggled free, "You can see the moment when his wristband impacts the side of the chamber. We think he broke his tether just before the transport."

"So the tether was like a guide rope?" Ryan guessed, "It was supposed to keep him in place, but it got snapped?"

"That's actually a really good analogy," said Alec, then quietly exchanged a look with Diane.

She appeared to weigh something up, then gave him a nod of permission.

Alec pointed at the screen.

"There were supposed to be *two* tests that day," he said, "The first one was the standard Schrödinger's Box. Send someone back and wait the hour before opening the box to check."

"And the second one?" Ryan rubbed at his temples.

Alec cast a glance at the others before replying.

"The Schrö-Yo," he smirked, "It's the same sealed room test, but the time traveller doesn't stay for the hour. He drops into the past, spins for a while at the end of the tether, then returns like a yo-yo."

Ryan could easily imagine the process, but he couldn't immediately see what the benefit would be.

"Why not just wait the hour, then have the traveller leave the room?"

Diane looked directly at him.

"Because we knew we'd eventually want the capability to go back much further than one hour. Waiting around in the past for days wouldn't be an option," she held his gaze, "The locked room is just a convenient representation of an unobserved place in history… Like an occlusion."

In a moment of blinding recognition, all the separate pieces he'd been seeing now slammed together.

The McCairn tests had ended two years ago, but Diane and the others must have succeeded in their goal. These people were able to 'Query' blind spots in the past, then yo-yo in and out of them while masked by so-called temporal occlusions. Their destinations were places and times that had, for whatever reason, gone unobserved by history

Judging by their relaxed expressions, he could tell that these trips back and forth through time were a regular part of their daily lives.

Still stunned, he faced Diane and felt the incredible phrase leave his mouth.

"You're commuting… to the past."

"Not just commuting," she said, "Retrieving."

Petra, who had left the room a few minutes ago, now returned carrying a small, framed picture. As she placed it on the table, the picture caught the light, and he saw the intricate brush strokes in its surface.

"Until three days ago," said Petra, "this was in an early twentieth century monastery."

He stared at the oil painting.

The metal detector and treasure analogy, along with Diane's comment about building a spade, now made perfect sense. He was looking at something that had been dug up from the past. Or rather, pulled out *from* it.

"You don't recognise it?" Diane was studying him.

"No," he looked at the sailboat on the calm sunset lake, "But wasn't it in your office?"

The others at the table were now exchanging glances.

"It *was* in my office," she said, "I put it there to see if it caught your eye."

Ryan looked at the painting again, but drew a blank.

"Is it supposed to mean something to me?" he frowned.

Diane sighed, "I guess not."

He now looked at the people around the table.

They could have just erased the Fortean Eye from the web, but they'd surgically removed only a page. They'd politely abducted him without making attention-grabbing ripples. They'd told him detailed information about their extraordinary operation, and yet they still hadn't told him how he was involved in all of this.

He turned to look directly at Diane.

"You promised you'd tell me why I'm here."

She nodded and slid the old oil painting across the table. When it was directly in front of him, she quietly pointed to the bottom right corner.

A signature, carefully inscribed in dark oil paint, read 'Ryan Pryce'.

All he could do was stare.

Like everything he'd experienced this morning, he couldn't immediately process what was in front of him. His name was on an antique, and the implication was that he'd signed it.

It soon became clear to him that the simple act of staring wasn't forcing it to yield its secret, so his mind now adopted the next best approach: rejection.

"That's not my signature," he pointed at the lettering.

"If pens weren't around," said Diane, "don't you think your signature would look different if you could only use a brush?"

He pushed himself away from the painting.

"It's a hoax," he desperately tried to rationalise the irrational, "A coincidence."

"A coincidence?" Diane seemed to find the idea amusing.

Even as he spoke, he knew he was trying to convince himself rather than her.

"Someone else had the same name as me," he now sensed an opportunity to use Diane's earlier words against her, "Like you just said, history's a big place."

"It *is* a big place," she nodded, "which makes it all the more unlikely that we'd find it by accident."

"By accident?"

There was a further exchange of glances.

After Diane gave another confirmatory nod, Alec looked directly at him.

"Time is always short," he said, "The yo-yo doesn't spin for longer than a minute."

"What do you mean?"

Alec leaned forward and explained what had happened three days ago...

THREE DAYS AGO

Alec reviewed the query data on the screen again.

The shifting black-and-white static representing the target environment was overlaid with a false-colour topology map. Resembling the view from a grainy infrared camera, the atomic momentum of particles was now readable as elements and compounds.

Complex objects that were made from multiple materials were a dense swirling mix of rainbow-coloured dots, but simpler objects, fashioned from fewer materials, shone out as solid-toned geometry.

Looking carefully, he could see some of the items were already changing shape. The effect wasn't a distortion within the QRI system; it was an accurate representation of the fact that the room was about to succumb to the blaze on the other side of the wall.

He froze the moment on the screen.

The room was a treasure trove.

Although the British Government was financing the QRI system, it still had no clue that objects could be retrieved from the past. Thanks to the McCairn debacle, and Diane's ongoing concealments, they also still thought that teleportation was a disastrous and expensive failure. That aside, they knew the value of what they *did* have access to.

With QRI, history was literally an open book. Nobody could stop you reading it. The people of the past weren't even aware that you were watching them, and there was no defence against it. Not even quantum cryptography was safe if you could review the very moment that data was encoded. By definition, the ability to retrospectively analyse the topology of any given situation, anywhere on Earth, made it the perfect espionage tool.

In terms of intelligence gathering, QRI's retro-topology system had already been used to detect the atomic structure and location of hidden nuclear stockpiles. It had even helped to stop present-day terrorist plots, just by analysing the past movements of people and materials.

Diane had once told him that the anonymous line item in the Government's yearly defence budget was tiny in comparison to the spending on conventional intelligence methods. As far as the Ministry of Defence was concerned, each page of a QRI report was worth more than its weight in gold.

And they knew nothing of the literal gold.

Alec unfroze the treasure trove room and allowed time to move forward.

As he'd seen before, a wave of chaotic static swamped the view: the telltale sign that the current query was overlapping a temporal occlusion event. He was looking at evidence of their, as yet untaken, retrostep to the past.

Moving the virtual indicator forward, he saw the static eventually clear, then the outlines of the room reappeared. The flames weren't visible, of course, but the widespread conversion of matter into carbon was. The fire had been all-consuming.

He heard Petra let out a whistle.

"What's the event radius?" she said.

He checked the metrics and saw that the occlusion event occupied a spherical space that ended just inside the walls of the target room.

"Occlusion radius is about three metres," he said, "Our sphere of influence doesn't spread beyond the room."

She pointed at the fire's after-effects.

"I think anyone *outside* the room is going to be a little too busy to notice our arrival anyway."

As ever, history would remain self-consistent: the arrival of two time travellers had, in a sense, already gone unnoticed.

Petra pointed at the occlusion data.

"One minute, sixteen seconds."

"Same as before," Alec gave a nod, "By the time the tether's in place, we'll have about a minute."

She frowned at the screen.

"Wind it back," she said, "Pause it before the occlusion."

Alec restored the room to its unburnt state and let the software reinterpret the spectrum of elements.

"These ones," Petra pointed at several of the shapes, "They look like they're gold."

"Or platinum," he shrugged, "The whole room's a valuable haul."

"Then what's that?" she pointed to a duller rectangle.

Alec checked the colour against the element chart.

"Well that can't be right," he found himself mirroring Petra's frown, "Neodymium?"

"The chroma lookup has got to be off," she shook her head, "That element can't *be* there."

He knew she was right. It didn't belong in the early 20th Century, or in a French monastery.

Alec refreshed the false-colour overlay, but the rectangular shimmer persisted.

"Damned if I know what it is," he looked at the orange shape.

"If there's room in the Faraday bag," she checked her watch, "we'll bring it back with us."

Diane strode over the limestone floor of the British Museum's Great Court. Overhead, the masterpiece of interlocking glazed triangles in the roof kept out the continuous grey drizzle.

She really didn't have time to be away from the team during their temporal preparations, but if she was to maintain her deception then she had to answer the Government's calls, no matter how inconvenient they might be.

She swiftly made her way past the gift shop, where the last of the day's tourists were choosing which pencil sharpener best represented ten thousand years of history, then she turned left.

Ahead of her, stooped and peering at the glass-encased Rosetta Stone, was the somewhat rotund Bernard Holroyd.

"Diane," he turned and beamed at her, "How's the team doing?"

She resisted the urge to check her watch.

"Working every second," she smiled. "I know you said it was urgent, but if there's any way that we could -"

"Of course, of course," he affably interrupted her, "I just thought you might want to hear it from me first."

"Hear what?"

Rounded shoulders hunched, he checked that no-one was nearby, then appeared to challenge gravity by leaning forward on his polished shoes.

"It's all a bit hush-hush," he lowered his voice, "but I'll be part of a new... department."

"You're not leaving, are you?" she quietly hoped.

"Quite the opposite," he raised his eyebrows, "I'll be the new head of Mort."

She quickly forced herself not to react negatively.

The so-called 'Ministry Of Retro Topology' was a parallel arm of the Ministry of Defence that would focus on the long-term capabilities of Query. Not only had the deathly-sounding Mort been given the green light, it would now bring in additional unwanted attention. The only positive aspect of the news was that she wouldn't be dealing with a complete stranger.

Doing her best to sound pleased, she extended her hand to him.

"Better the devil you know!" she forced a laugh, "Congratulations."

"Thank you, thank you," he laughed and shook her hand, "It'll make additional funding a breeze."

"Ha," she managed, "Great."

He now seemed to spot the bag that she was holding.

"Ooh," his eyes widened, "Is that for me?"

Remembering why she'd brought it, she nodded and handed it over to him.

He looked inside and prodded at the plastic-wrapped package.

"Another negative result?" he guessed.

"Afraid so."

"Oh," his shoulders sagged, "What *should* it have been?"

She'd prepared the fake sample several hours ago, so she knew exactly which trace elements were in the bag of ashes.

"It was supposed to be another kilo of soil from the seventeenth century," she let out a disappointed breath and then delivered the lie, "We can view things in the past, but we still can't accurately transport them back to the present."

He smiled and raised an encouraging finger, "Yet!"

She smiled, "We'll keep trying."

Bernard closed the bag and shrugged.

"Still," he said, "From next month, at least you won't need

to parcel things up for me. With Mort in place, I'll be working right alongside you."

She delivered a delighted-looking smile.

"Bernie, I'm already counting the hours."

With another jovial laugh, he nodded his thanks for the bag, and wandered off toward the exit. As soon as he was clear of the Great Court, Diane turned on her heels and dashed away.

The query had clinically shown Petra the layout of the room, and its assembled treasures, but the realities of being in the past were always an assault on the senses.

Even though the fire was on the other side of a closed door, she could feel the approaching heat, hear the crackle of the burning wood, and smell the hot air that was forcing its way into the room. She'd been in the room for less than a minute, but already the sweat was pouring down her neck.

The reason nobody travelled back alone was abundantly clear: if something went wrong, at least your partner was there to get you home.

"Twenty seconds!" Alec was calling out.

She turned and saw him stuff an ornate chalice into his Faraday bag. When the moment came, its contents would become part of the returning mass. Some items though, like the one she was dealing with, were too large to fit into bags.

She pressed a tag onto one end of an ornamental mace, unwound the sync cable, and stuck the other tag to the opposite end. She quickly lowered it to the floor and whipped around to check the back wall.

She'd seen a neodymium rectangle when they'd queried the scene, but it wasn't here now.

"Alec," she called above the rumble of the flames, "I can't see it!"

Pushing a shallow silvery bowl into his bag, he dashed back across the creaking oak floor.

"It's gotta be here," he coughed, "We saw it!"

Desperately trying to recall the spatial reconstruction, she stared at the wall, then turned to face the door. Smoke was pouring under it and crawling across the floor. The small window to her right was black and she could see orange flecks of hot ash zooming up into the night sky. The monastery was in full blaze. Muted by distance and stone, she could hear vows of silence breaking into painful cries.

Refocus, she told herself.

Comparing her position to her recollection of the plan, she turned again and faced the wall. She was definitely in the right place, but there were no signs of a metallic rectangle. The only vaguely similar shape was a wooden framed picture.

"How can a -"

Alec interrupted her by grabbing the picture off the wall.

"Let's check it later," he pushed it into his bag, "Four seconds."

He pulled the bag's drawstring closed and its recall tag lit up. The tags on the items at their feet now lit up in unison.

As the last second evaporated, she felt the peculiar stomach-dropping pull of the quantum tether going taut.

All sound disappeared. The flecks of hot ash beyond the window, and the smoke crawling under the door, both drifted to a perfect halt. Then history fell away.

OUT OF PLACE

Ryan could see they were studying him, looking for signs of reaction. His first thoughts were no longer about the signature on the oil painting.

"So, basically," he stared at them in disbelief, "The Government bankrolled *all* of this, but it doesn't know you've already cracked human teleportation, or that you're using the tech to steal precious stuff from the past. You're flat-out lying to them?"

Diane leaned forward and steepled her fingers.

"I prefer to think of it as slowing the flow of information," she said, "Bernard Holroyd will be informed about everything in due course."

"Yeah," Ryan recalled, "In less than a month."

"I would've liked longer," she admitted, "but we've been inventing a new technology. Before anyone else gets to discover its workings, it's essential that we know how to safeguard and control it."

"And you can't do that," Ryan now understood, "if someone's watching its development."

Diane nodded.

"We're not lying to Holroyd," she said, "We're just telling him the truth… later."

Imagining the fantastical machinery that must consume huge amounts of power, Ryan could understand Diane's drip-feeding of the truth: as long as Holroyd thought that work wasn't complete, he'd keep paying the exorbitant electricity bills.

"So is all of this costly to run?"

Theo cleared his throat.

"Actually, observation through Query is relatively cheap," he said, "Less than a hundred sterling per second. But teleporting *matter*, either present-to-present or past-to-present, is energy expensive."

"How expensive?"

"About a thousand times the material worth of the item," said Diane, "To put it into perspective, it would have been cheaper to buy an authentic Fabergé Egg than to move our ostrich egg fifty metres. On a purely financial basis, teleportation will never become a commercial reality."

Picturing the Government's displeasure upon learning the news, Ryan shook his head.

"And your man, Holroyd, knows this?"

"Like us," Diane said, "he knows the long-term game."

She got up from the table and walked over to the old-looking globe. As she began turning it on its axis, he couldn't help wondering if it had been bought from a store, or snatched from an ill-fated nineteenth century library.

"The past," she said, "Its information. Its lost resources. They're huge and untapped. Holroyd knows this. That's why we've been given such a long leash."

He pictured the treasure haul that Petra had spoken about.

"I get why rescuing lost gold might raise a large amount of cash," he shrugged, "But -"

"Think smaller," she turned to him.

He pictured the bejewelled chalice that Alec had described.

"Rare gemstones?"

"Smaller," she told him, "Rare elements. Elements that are hopelessly depleted in the present day. Elements that were more abundant in the deep past, or only lasted for a very short time. We can extract them from obscurity and bring them forward to the present day. That's the long-term goal."

"So, all this raiding of history is what? Target practice for finding precious elements?"

"A crude way of describing it," she said, "but fair."

He leaned toward the framed oil painting.

"I know we've cut down the rainforests," he said, "but I'm pretty sure that wood isn't a precious element."

"Like I told you," Alec said, "our retro-topology tagged it as noteworthy."

Looking at the frame, Ryan began to have the same feeling that he'd had earlier: a vague sense that he was looking at a solution, but the pieces of the puzzle weren't quite aligned.

He looked back at the painting.

"You only became aware of the signature *after* you got it back here?"

"Yes," Diane nodded.

"And have you analysed anything else about the painting yet?"

She shook her head.

"No. It's taking a while to go through all the recovered artifacts. We've only had it a few days. Before you were on our radar, we had no reason to prioritise it."

Petra rubbed at her forehead.

"If it hadn't shown up in the query," she glanced at the frame, "we would've missed it. It would've just disappeared into the background."

Disappeared, he thought.

The word now seemed to connect with something else he'd heard earlier: a rabbit from a hat.

"The magician's flourish," his thought emerged aloud.

"What?" said Alec.

Ryan pulled the painting closer.

"A misdirection. A decoration," he said, "Something that focuses attention away from where the real trick is happening."

"Go on," Alec frowned.

Ryan picked up the frame and examined the dull wood.

"In the past, the painting would've blended in with the surroundings. If anyone had tried to raid that room, they would have just gone for the other gold items."

"But we *did* raid the room," Petra leaned forward.

"Sorry, I meant anyone already part of the past. Any potential thieves at the time would have ignored the boring picture and grabbed the valuable stuff. It was a way of protecting the painting from theft. *You* only looked for it because your query tech told you it was neodymium."

Alec folded his arms.

"We only *looked* for it," he shot a glance at Theo, "because neodymium was completely out of place for the era."

"I've already apologised," Theo held up his hands, "I still don't know why the chroma display got it so wrong."

"I'm not sure it did," Ryan looked more closely at the frame, "I think this may be an *actual* oop-art."

"A what?" Diane frowned at him.

"An out-of-place artifact," he turned the frame, "An item that's supposedly in the wrong time or place. Typically they get debunked as hoaxes."

He heard Petra give a light snort.

"More fringe stuff?"

He tilted the edge of the frame toward the light and saw the faintest discontinuity in the grain of the wood. He paused. The craftsmanship and precision were outstanding.

"Most oops aren't this well hidden," he followed the discontinuity to the corner of the frame, "Usually, hoaxers *want* them to be found and talked about."

"But...?" Diane prompted him.

He lay the painting face down on the table, then took hold of the frame's left-hand edge. Gripping the wood tightly, he pushed forward on the lower left corner.

"What are you doing?" Theo was on his feet.

With a slight click, the left edge slid along parallel to the frame, then stopped. Adjusting his grip, he took hold of the displaced edge and pushed it away from the frame. The entire back panel slid with it, exposing a silvery rectangular plate.

The query had been right, but the chronology was all wrong.

A modern piece of shiny metalwork was staring at them.

"Ryan," Diane was quiet and motionless, "How did you know how to open it?"

He honestly didn't know.

A lifetime of looking at unexplained occurrences, secret rooms and trinkets, along with his appetite for mystery, had obviously left some kind of imprint on him. It was possible that he'd once seen something about hand-crafted puzzle boxes and had absorbed it unintentionally.

"Have you *made* one of these before?" Theo was studying both him and the open picture frame.

Ryan shook his head and glanced down at his torn trouser leg.

"I don't even have the craft skills to loosen a ladder bolt," he admitted.

Diane nodded.

"The attic hatch."

"Yeah, I..." he stopped, "Wait, how did you know about that?"

The others just stared at him. Clearly, they were waiting for him to work it out.

"Of course," he realised, "You queried me."

"We had to check where you were," said Petra.

He recalled sitting in the attic amid the boxes, and the uneasy chill he'd felt just before her call. He now pictured Diane and the others looking down on a grainy version of the attic scene: they'd been viewing his own past.

"Walking over my grave," he quietly murmured to himself.

"What was that?" Diane frowned.

"Nothing," he shook his head, "Listen, you don't know *why* I'm involved in any of this, and neither do I. But if all of this is about the past, and odd connections, then I can think of one place to start looking for answers."

He told them about the hundreds of Fortean Eye back issues that were stored in his attic, and how he'd been planning to scan them into an online resource. When he explained how long it might actually take to complete, Diane told him that they may be able to speed up the process.

She escorted him from the room and, accompanied by Alec, they began taking zigzag turns through the building. She tapped a card against a door's reader panel, and they climbed a boxy stairwell. He hadn't been brought in this way earlier, but as Diane unlocked another door, he slowly recognised where he was.

An inscription on the limestone floor read *'And let thy path - millennia hence - be set in depth of knowledge'*.

High above his head, interlocking glass triangles filled the cavernous white space with light. Not for the first time today, he found his thoughts reeling.

"You're running all this," he stared, "from the British Museum?"

Diane didn't stop walking.

"Can you think of a better place to hide things that come from the past?"

In his present state, he couldn't.

"Wait a minute," he lowered his voice, "If QRI is used to gather military intelligence, why isn't this place crawling with security?"

"The only security I have around here is the private firm you met at the cafe, but they're nothing to do with the Ministry of Defence."

What she was suggesting was astonishing.

"You mean the MOD doesn't know the query reports are coming from here?"

She nodded.

"Only Holroyd and the PM know," she said, "Holroyd passes on the data to the MOD, a security separation layer that they seem happy to accept... Well, for the moment at least."

He walked on, agog.

When the British Museum had been closed temporarily, several years ago, he'd assumed that it was only in connection with the installation of the feature roof. It seemed that the roof was not the only feature to have been installed while the building had been closed to the public.

He became aware that Alec was talking to him.

"When we've loaded up the van with your boxes," he was saying, "we'll get them back here and run them through the document scanner upstairs."

Ryan turned to look up at the glazed roof and the massive central Reading Room cylinder that supported it. Like fragments of a DNA helix, two spiral staircases wound around it in opposite directions to reach its summit.

"Up there?" he said, "But isn't that a public space?"

Alec looked at him just long enough to raise an eyebrow.

"Closed for 'renovation' since twenty-sixteen."

Ryan couldn't tell if Alec was joking.

"Seriously?"

Alec smiled, but before he could answer, Diane brought them to a stop.

"OK," she said, "No detours, Alec. Straight there and back."

"Understood," he gave a stern nod.

Ryan looked at her.

"Anything else you should be telling me?"

"Pack a suitcase," she told him, "You may be with us for a while."

MORT

Traffic was once again moving at a snail's pace over Westminster Bridge.

Beyond the tinted glass of his car windows, Bernard saw the other self-driving vehicles that were inching their way through the morning fog. He could tell that the various transports were occupied because of the blurs of light that were emanating from their opaqued windows. Judging by the synchronised changing of the colourful patterns, it seemed that most people had their screens set to the morning news. He'd already seen the headlines, so he was using his commute to catch up on the spectral analysis report.

Displayed on the interior of the windshield were various stats and graphs, each one detailing some aspect of the attempted teleport of seventeenth-century soil.

As far as he could tell, it confirmed all of Diane's findings. Amid the worthless ash, there were traces of ferrous oxide and woody fibres. It was a far cry from the caesium or platinum that they were ultimately aiming for, but transporting a whisper of iron *did* count as progress. Eventually, Diane and her team would succeed. In a field with no current competition, that would mean they were ahead of the game.

"Display clear," he spoke aloud.

The facts and figures faded, leaving only the tinted view of his immediate surroundings. The car had now cleared the bridge and was drawing alongside Memorial Gardens.

Jutting up through the dense fog were the sand-coloured remnants of the old Houses of Parliament; the truncated sections of masonry standing like the gravestones of a bygone era.

As the car continued its slow track along the north side of the wide memorial site, a childhood rhyme drifted through his mind, *'Remember, remember, the fifth of November…'*

He felt a chill run down his spine. The course of a nation had shifted on that fateful day. If Mort succeeded though, this country would again be a superpower to be reckoned with.

A triple-toned harp sound accompanied an on-window notification:

'Incoming Call - Miranda May.'

He sat up straight and faced the windshield, "Answer call."

The glass turned opaque, and the video call connected.

"Morning Bernard."

"Prime Minister," he checked the time, "Sorry, I'm late. I think the fog must be playing havoc with the smartgrid's collision-detection systems."

"I know," she rubbed at her temples, *"I think we're looking at another gridlock."*

Bernard couldn't help exhaling a deep sigh. The digital gridlock last year hadn't been weather related, but the fault had brought the entire city to a complete halt. It had taken the emergency services a whole day to clear the outermost streets and then free up the gridlocked centre.

"We could switch to a secure video link," Bernard shrugged, "I could give you my Mort briefing from here."

There was more temple rubbing.

"Seven eleven," she checked her watch, then puffed out her cheeks in frustration, *"A live link's not ideal, but OK. Looks like it's going to be one of those days."*

"OK," he nodded, "It'll take me a moment to get set up."

She looked off to one side and didn't reply.

As the car rocked to another standstill, he spotted that the video feed had actually frozen. It seemed that she'd hung up.

The windscreen became semi-transparent again and, in the distance, he saw that the morning fog was stained a fiery orange.

A PERFECT STORM

For the past few days, Ryan had been using the scanning rig in the upper section of the Reading Room. He'd been manually digitising each page of the Fortean Eye back issues, and allowing the rig's machine-learning algorithm to catalogue and analyse the hundreds of articles. But an hour ago, he'd been forced to set the whole process to automatic: the breaking news was saturating his attention.

Facing the room's small TV screen, he blankly watched the aerial camera drone images of the Westminster area. At his side, Diane seemed equally quiet and stunned.

There was a ping sound and he saw her check her phone.

"He's here," she sighed.

She started walking toward the door, but then quickly retraced her steps. Grabbing a pile of loose paper, she covered up the sailboat oil painting that was at the side of the scanner. After a swift glance around the room, she returned to the door and opened it.

The large man outside bustled his way in and, from the way that Diane had described him earlier, Ryan immediately recognised who it was.

"Bernard," she closed the door behind him, "Are you

alright?"

"Had to abandon the car," he mopped his brow with a handkerchief, "Nothing's moving out there."

"I know," she closed the door behind him, "We're just watching it."

As Bernard came further into the room, he spotted Ryan and froze.

"Who's the stranger?" he stared.

Diane turned her back on Bernard and gave Ryan a covert wink.

"This is Ryan Pryce," she said, "A specialist in random influence within complex historic systems."

It wasn't a lie, but it was the first time that Ryan had heard someone describe his writing job in such an abstract manner.

"And who authorised him?"

"I did," Diane walked away.

"You…" Bernard broke his stare to focus on her instead, "I wasn't even consulted."

Diane casually added a few more pieces of paper to the pile.

"I still have autonomy here."

"Diane, Mort isn't just -"

"Bernie," she interrupted but then her tone quickly became one of pacification, "how would you have assessed the technical requirements of the role, let alone the chaotic criteria that the potential candidate needed to fulfil?"

Bernard folded his arms.

"And you ran the background checks?"

"The QRI sessions revealed no security issues," she replied, "They proved he was uniquely suited to the task. He also passed the waiting room chair test."

Ryan hadn't even been aware that the presence of a chair was a means of assessment. Perhaps his walking around had somehow demonstrated his ability to behave independently of his environment.

"The chair," Ryan did his best to give a casual-looking nod of confirmation.

Bernard continued to scrutinise him for a moment, then he seemed to give up all hope of controlling the conversation, and sat down heavily in the nearest chair.

"It was the perfect storm," he said, "The fog caused a gridlock, so when the earthquake hit, it was just chaos. Emergency services couldn't get in."

Ryan looked at the devastating aerial shots on the screen.

The Thames had changed shape. A widening pool of brown river water was slowly inundating the ruined streets. Where the water intersected the raging fires, great plumes of smoke and steam rose into the air.

Bernard rubbed at his eyes.

"She..." he trailed off, "Downing Street's gone. If I'd been there..."

Although Ryan didn't much care for the politicians that formed the Government, he wouldn't have wished this horrific fate on any of them. The fact was that they weren't the only victims of the disaster. By the latest estimates, over three hundred people had already lost their lives.

He watched the water slowly swallowing the streets. An unrecognisable archipelago was emerging: tiny islands made from broken buildings, submerged crushed vehicles, and woefully inadequate rescue boats. Within hours, the water would probably reach the lake in St. James's Park, and then spread out even faster.

"One of those days," Bernard was muttering to himself.

"Pardon?" Diane frowned.

"It was the last thing that Miranda said," Bernard shook his head, "I was *literally* about to do my Mort update from the car, and then all of this happened."

Perhaps influenced by the Fortean Eye conspiracies he'd been re-reading and scanning, Ryan now felt a faint theory trying to emerge from the mist. These days, minor earth tremors weren't uncommon, but what were the chances of a full earthquake occurring at the same time as a gridlocked Westminster, dense fog, *and* a Mort briefing? A perfect storm, he recalled Bernard's words: the odds were against it.

He knew he wasn't on first-name terms with Bernard, so he addressed him more formally.

"Excuse me, Mr. Holroyd," he raised his hand, "When you say you were *literally* about to give your update, how much time are we talking about? Five, ten minutes?"

Again Bernard was shaking his head.

"Seconds," he said, "I can still picture her face. All I had to do was switch to a secure link."

"So the events could almost be considered simultaneous?"

"Ryan?" Diane was frowning at him, "Where are you going with this?"

He wasn't sure how to phrase the vague notion that was forming in his mind, so he pointed at the news on the television.

"Could you use QRI to look at the event?"

Bernard gave a mocking laugh.

"I'm sorry," he looked at the devastation on the screen, "You want to *query* an Act of God?"

"What if it wasn't?" Ryan shrugged.

Bernard exhaled a derisive laugh, but then his brow buckled and his eyes darted across the images of destruction.

"Are you suggesting this was done… deliberately?" his eyes were wide as he cast his hand over the screen, "Like a spread of stealth missiles? Or, heaven forbid, low-yield tactical -"

The desk phone near the scanning rig rang out.

Without pause, Diane reached out and pushed the phone's speaker button.

"Give me some good news," she said.

"The seismic sensors are reset," Petra's voice came through, *"We're back online."*

SEVEN ELEVEN

Standing with the others in front of Diane's curved projection wall, Ryan watched the conventional TV video feed of the slowly unfolding destruction.

The more Alec talked, the more he began to understand that running a QRI on the London earthquake was not going to be as simple as watching the feed from an aerial camera drone.

"Imagine looking through a cardboard tube," Alec mimed holding a tube up to one eye, "but the circular view at the other end is made up of, say, a thousand pixels. I could use those thousand pixels to look at a grain of sand, or I could use them to look at a wide landscape."

Ryan thought he understood.

"The resolution falls as the field of view gets wider."

"Yep," Alec nodded at the screen, "You can't query a square mile of London at sand-grain definition."

"Because the resolution would be too great," he nodded.

"No," Theo now answered, "It's because the number of possible quantum states needed to represent the scene would be greater than the number of atoms that make up London."

"Ah..." Ryan stared at the devastation, "So we have to look at smaller pieces and put them together?"

"Something like that," Petra adjusted her glasses, then consulted her phone screen, "The news channels have conflicting start times. They range from seven oh nine, to seven thirteen a.m."

Bernard wiped his brow and cleared his throat.

"It was seven eleven," he said, "I saw Miranda check her watch."

"Only one way to know for sure," Diane cleared the TV images off the screen.

As she continued to tap at her tablet, Ryan saw the curved wall fill with shifting static.

"Adding geometric orbit," Diane worked her screen.

The noise on the wall started to shift and he saw formations beginning to emerge from the sea of static. It seemed that the human eye could more easily detect perspective and shapes if they were in motion. A moment later, he realised that the perspective view he was looking at was a blocky representation of the Westminster area of London.

He quietly turned to Alec.

"I thought you just said we couldn't image something this size?"

Alec again mimed a tube in front of his eye.

"At this resolution," he said, "a hundred pixels is a city block. We can't read anything meaningful."

"Bernard," Diane didn't look up, "Where were you at the time?"

"In my car."

"Geographically?" she corrected him.

"Sorry," he shook his head, "I'd just passed Memorial Gardens. North side."

The view on the screen tilted to show an almost plan view

of the area: a grid arrangement of streets filled with stationary rectangles.

"Er, I don't know," Bernard moved closer to the wall and circled an area with his finger, "Maybe about here?"

The view dropped to street level and Ryan saw blocky versions of identical-looking cars.

"Refocusing," said Diane.

Each clump of pixels on the wall seemed to blister and then the scene took on greater definition. Unstopped by the presence of physical matter, the point of view now pushed forward through the side of a self-driving car and began to orbit the interior.

Although the scene was still a grey-scale representation, there was no mistaking what they were seeing. Sat astride the thighs of a semi-naked man, an equally topless woman was frozen in a moment of sensual abandon.

"That's not me!" Bernard spluttered, his cheeks bright red.

In front of them, the urgent-looking tableau continued its sedate rotation. It was perfectly clear from the muscular proportions of the man that it wasn't Bernard in the throes of passion, but that didn't stop Alec from commenting.

"Ladies and Gentlemen," he was grinning, "I think we've found the source of the earth-shaking event."

"That's never been my experience," Petra smirked.

Alec grinned, "Obviously you've not been in the back of Bernie's car."

Ryan now stifled a smile.

"I must protest!" Bernard's discomfort was clear.

Face deadpan, Theo pointed at the screen.

"I'm not seeing a lot of protesting."

Ryan swiftly turned his exhaled laugh into a cough and covered his mouth.

"Enough, please," Diane was frowning at her tablet, "I'll check the cars closer to Parliament Street."

"Sorry, Bernard," Alec brought his grin under control, "It's not like we haven't seen this sort of thing before in a query. I guess it beats just sitting in traffic."

A few moments later, the wall was displaying the interior of Bernard Holroyd's car. The windshield, which had apparently been displaying a video call, only appeared as a featureless surface, presumably because images didn't register as three-dimensional geometry. The grainy, large-proportioned man was very clear though. He was shrugging and moving his mouth.

"Why's there never any sound?" Ryan frowned.

"Sound waves don't have atomic structure," Diane quickly dismissed the question.

The self-driving car rocked back and forth slightly.

"Was that it?" Theo pointed.

Bernard frowned, "Don't know. I thought it was just the car stopping."

"I've been watching," said Theo, "The car was already stationary."

The view froze and then rewound.

Diane pulled the viewpoint outside the car and then replayed the moment. Bernard's car jostled in place, as did the other vehicles around it. But they didn't all move at the same time: those that were further away moved a little later.

Ryan knew he'd seen a similar effect in stadium crowds at sports events.

"Mexican wave," he thought aloud.

"Or a circular ripple," Theo moved his hand in an arc.

Over the next few minutes, Diane repeated the query process for several streets in the area. Looking at the timing of the vehicle movements, she slowly built up a set of construction lines that pointed toward the middle of a rough circle.

"The epicentre," she said, "Back-calculating from the timing of the other motions, the quake must have struck at seven eleven, plus seventeen seconds."

The construction lines met in the middle of Downing Street.

Bernard quietly moved toward the small office sofa.

"Query it," he sat down.

Diane cleared the diagrams from the screen and then tapped at her tablet. A timestamp appeared in the upper right corner: '7.11.17'.

Again, the curved wall became a scramble of static.

"Adding five-second pre-roll," said Diane, "Adding geometric orbit."

A blocky, aerial view of Downing Street and the nearby River Thames emerged from the monochrome noise. Apart from the fact that the morning traffic was moving sluggishly, nothing seemed out of place.

Suddenly, the middle of the scene collapsed into waves of chaotic static.

"What happened?" Bernard took a step toward the screen.

Ryan could see Diane staring at her tablet and glancing at the wall of randomly shifting pixels. The shape within the static wasn't like the sphere of influence that Alec had once told him about. It was elongated, as though a long party balloon was following a fault line.

"Diane?" Bernard faced her.

"Wait," she instructed him, "Scanning forward."

The noise continued to fizz.

And fizz.

There were no fast-arriving missiles. No succession of car bombs. There was just a blank in the static.

Although he was new to all of this, Ryan could think of only one reason why there would be impenetrable noise in the middle of a query. They were looking at an occlusion. A moment where time had been overwritten. Or would be.

The others clearly understood and started looking in Diane's direction. Diane, however, remained focused on her tablet.

Ryan watched the timestamp on the screen advancing through the passing seconds.

"I don't understand," Bernard was frowning at the screen, "Isn't it working?"

As the timestamp hit 7.11.29, the static suddenly leapt back into geometric formations.

A craggy, Y-shaped chasm now dominated the screen: a geological tear that ran though the urban landscape to the meet a new waterfall at the edge of the Thames.

Bernard shook his head and swore under his breath.

"OK," he exhaled loudly, "At least you've got it working again. Rewind the damn thing."

Diane paused the QRI.

"I don't think it will help."

Bernard squared his shoulders and faced her.

"I'm not asking," he stared.

Over the next fifteen minutes, they viewed the event from multiple angles and perspectives.

Whether they viewed things in wide overview, or in detailed closeup, the conclusion was the same: the occlusion was still present, and the banal moments surrounding the earthquake suggested that it was nothing more than an untimely natural event.

The lack of answers didn't ease the tension in the room.

Bernard turned away from the screen, his face thunderous.

"You're trying to tell me," he pinned Diane with a stare, "that for twelve whole seconds, our QRI capability was completely and utterly blind?"

"Bernie," Diane began, "I think -"

"From a defence position," he spoke over her, "we have absolutely no idea if we've just been attacked."

"Earthquakes release a lot of energy," Theo was clearly trying to deflect attention, "Our own seismic sensors were disturbed, so the QRI may not have -"

Bernard silenced him with a raised finger.

"You all look at me like I'm some sort of simpleton," he faced Diane, "but I can read the room. What aren't you telling me?"

Ryan didn't know where to look.

Despite being the financial conduit of the operation, Bernard Holroyd knew nothing of temporal transport or occlusions; a fact that seemed to be freezing Diane to the spot.

She glanced at Bernard, then quietly faced everyone else.

"Would you mind giving us the room?"

WAITING ROOM

The conflict began barely five seconds after they'd all left Diane's office.

Although Theo couldn't hear the words, he could hear the machine-gun exchange of aggressive tones being fired between Diane and Bernard on the other side of the closed door.

It seemed that the friction was contagious. Standing in the middle of the waiting room, Theo suddenly became aware that Petra was raising her voice at Alec.

"Well why don't you ask *him?*" she was saying.

From the chair in the corner of the room, Ryan looked up at her.

"Me?" he frowned.

"Come on, Duff," Alec was clearly trying to pacify her.

"No," she jabbed a finger in Ryan's direction, "This is on him."

"What?" Ryan's stunned expression deepened.

Petra glanced between Theo and Alec.

"We were doing just fine," she insisted, "Retrievals were going well, we knew what we were doing, and then *he* shows up."

"I didn't show up," Ryan defended himself, "I was *brought* here by you and your heavies."

Theo knew he was talking about Diane's private security team, and completely understood how Ryan must have felt. The last thing they needed right now though, was more conflict.

"There's enough arguing going on in *there*," Theo pointed to the door, "Can we please just -"

"What Theo? Stay calm?" she shook her head, "We've just seen the signs that we're about to jump back to the site of a bloody earthquake!"

"We don't *know* that," Theo attempted to correct her, "the twelve second occ-"

"Tee," she cut in, "All of this started after *he* arrived!"

"Hey," Ryan now fought back, "You're the ones who started this."

"What?"

Ryan levelled a finger at Alec.

"If *he* hadn't stolen that painting, nobody would've seen the signature, and I'd be living my normal life right now."

"OK, stop," Alec pointed back, "If *you* hadn't published your spooky blather about McCairn, none of us would have found out your name in the first place."

Ryan suddenly stood, his tone incredulous.

"In the *first* place?! It wasn't me who *teleported* a convict into the damn past!" he turned on Theo, "And it wasn't *my* colour-coding that got you all looking for a piece of metal!"

"There was nothing wrong with my coding," Theo shot back.

"So you said," Petra shook her head.

Theo looked away but couldn't stop himself rising to her passive taunt.

"Well I'm not the one who chose to bring it back."

"So this is *my* fault?" Alec stared.

"You could have left it there," said Ryan, "No metal, no mystery."

Alec coughed a hollow laugh, "Says the man who knew how to get the metal plate out of the frame."

"I didn't know that it was in there, did I?"

"Didn't you?" Petra folded her arms, "Why'd you sign your name on it then?"

"For the *tenth* time," Ryan now shouted, "that's not my signature! You guys built all of this, but I've been dragged into it! Ever since I got here, I've been scanning things in the hope it'll help, but I haven't got a clue why any of this is happening!"

The waiting room fell quiet.

Suddenly it felt like none of them wanted to add any more fuel to the fire.

After a few seconds, Theo realised that the argument in Diane's office had also stopped; something that the others seemed to notice too.

As they began exchanging glances and shrugs, the door opened and Bernard Holroyd exited the office, muttering something about needing to get some air.

He brushed past Theo and managed to clumsily clip Petra in the shoulder, causing her to stumble back a step. Bernard physically hesitated for the briefest of moments, as though he was about to apologise, but then he kept going. A second later he was gone.

Diane now joined them in the waiting room, her expression as blank as the walls.

"Well that went well," she delivered flatly.

Theo looked around at the others.

For a long while, they'd managed to hide their activities from the Government by a complex superposition of knowns and unknowns. But now, he could almost feel those unseen probability waveforms collapsing. Their untold truths and deflective omissions had just resolved themselves into one single observable state: Bernard Holroyd now knew about quantum occlusions.

"Do you want me to go after him?" Theo volunteered.

Diane shook her head, "He'll be back soon enough."

"How d'you know?" Petra rubbed at her shoulder.

Diane stared back into her office.

"Given what's just happened, he wants to fully brief the Ministry of Defence about -"

"What?" Alec cut in.

"He can't do that," Petra swiftly followed.

"Unfortunately, he *can* do that," Diane nodded, "Longer term, it was always part of the development conditions."

Theo knew she was right.

QRI, teleportation, and quantum tethering; any single one of these required the highest level of defensive protection. Bernard had just found all *three* under one neatly glazed roof. The next step was both predictable and unavoidable: the project they'd been working on would be taken from them.

Diane sighed.

"Bernie won't want to send defensive troops to our doorstep straight away."

"Why not?" Ryan shrugged.

"London's still reeling from the aftermath of the quake," she said, "Military resources will be stretched thin for a while."

Alec was nodding.

"From an international point of view, adding a brute force defence cordon to a public museum would attract too much attention."

"It'll take him time to get a soft defence perimeter in place," said Petra.

"A what?" said Ryan.

"You know," she replied, "Like adding a civilian-looking bag check area to the entrance."

Theo looked at Diane, who appeared to be deep in concentration.

"Diane," he said, "how long do you think we have?"

She checked her watch.

"Difficult," she said, "but I'd say no longer than forty-eight hours."

"That's... pretty specific," Ryan frowned, "Why do you think it'll take Holroyd that long?"

Diane shook her head.

"You misunderstand," she said, "Forty-eight hours is when we run out of power."

"Hold on," Ryan was shaking his head, "I thought all of this ran on the National Grid."

"It does," she said, "but in an emergency, we can run everything from our own independent backup supply."

"Wait Diane," Theo now realised what she was suggesting, "You want to switch to emergency mode... on purpose?"

"Holroyd's instructed me to stop all operations," she gave a shrug, "He can easily check our power consumption through the National Grid load database. If we switch to internal power, he won't know."

"You're serious?" said Alec.

"The way I see it, the longer we delay, the sooner the Ministry of Defence will be breathing down our necks. So we should make use of the time we have left," she looked at Ryan, then glanced back at her office display wall, "I think we're looking at some kind of temporal jigsaw puzzle, but we don't know the overall picture yet."

"So," Theo pointed at the screen, "we keep gathering pieces and assemble the picture later."

Diane nodded.

"If necessary," she said, "We'll use tethering to -"

"Whoa," he cut in, "Deliberately running the tether on reserve power is risky."

"Ordinarily, I'd agree with you Theo."

"But?"

"While we were arguing in there," she now held up her phone, "I got a notification from the Reading Room scanner algorithm."

Ryan noticeably took a step forward.

"The Fortean scans," he said, "It found a link between articles?"

Diane shook her head.

"It found a link to the oil painting."

APPLETON

Lonny reset the keypad lock, then swung the door shut on the rear of the box truck.

"OK," he turned his back, "You can put your new code in now. Push the asterisk when you're done."

He heard the four keys being pushed, followed by a final one.

Turning back to the primly dressed woman, he handed her a clipboard which she duly inspected.

"Nobody else has access?"

He pointed at the lock.

"That box is a sealed unit," he said, "I can't even get into it from the cab. So until you phone that combination through to your guy, you're the only one who can open it."

She signed the clipboard and handed it back to him.

"Send me regular updates."

He looked at the checklist of times.

"Of course."

Nodding to herself, she turned and headed back across the gravelled driveway.

He clipped the pen back in place, then walked to the front

of the truck. He gave the tyres a quick kick, then climbed up into the cab and started the engine.

After double-checking the map, he eased the truck forward over the satisfyingly crunchy gravel, and gave the woman a cheerful wave. Her only response was to check her watch.

Her mood was perhaps understandable: the cargo was valuable. Her job, and his, were on the line if anything went wrong. Hoping to drown out the unhelpful thought, he turned the radio on and rhythmically tapped the steering wheel in time to the synthetic beat.

The town centre passed in a blur of street signs and traffic lights, and soon he was at the outskirts. The left and right turns transitioned into long straight roads that seemed to stretch to the horizon.

As time wore on, the horizon failed to get any closer, and the steering wheel drumming sessions became an occasional solo.

Eventually, the monotonous rumble of tyres on road was only interrupted by the mildly diverting thump of small potholes passing under the truck. Once or twice, the holes had been deep enough to force him to swerve or slow down a little, but the excitement was short lived: the road ahead was in much better condition.

As he continued heading west, only the drone of smooth tarmac accompanied his drumming fingers.

PIECES

Ryan sat at the table in the meeting room. To his right, the whiteboard was still occupied by timeline diagrams and photos from different years. To his left, Theo sat down and examined the metal that had once been concealed within a wooden frame.

Now separated from its historic hiding place, the rectangular plate was easier to see; its mercury-smooth finish and chamfered corners seemingly at odds with the fact that it had been discovered in an old monastery.

As Alec and Petra took their seats at the table, he saw Diane sync her tablet with the room's display monitor. A moment later, the screen was showing the Fortean Eye article that the AI algorithm had found.

Diane pointed at the screen.

"This is a portrait by Mr. Jean Metzinger," she said, "A French artist, noted for his cubist works."

Ryan looked at the image that was surrounded by text.

Unlike the articles that he'd manually scanned page-by-page, this one must have been digitised automatically by the rig. The old typesetting and fonts were familiar, but the story itself only rang a very distant bell. He'd probably last seen the article when he was in his teens.

The black-and-white portrait was a collage of superimposed, multi-sized rectangles, each one depicting a unique facet of a suited man.

As though viewed through a monochrome kaleidoscope, details were displaced and oddly magnified, giving the impression that the segments had been painted according to what the artist had found most interesting.

Checkered cloth framed a truncated shirt cuff and tie, an angular eye peered through a light curl of smoke, and a tobacco pipe sat within a grey rectangle. All the elements combined to give a fractured portrait of a man with folded arms.

"Sorry," said Alec, "but what has this got to do with the painting that we brought back?"

"Take a look at this small area," Diane now zoomed in on the top left corner of the image.

Ryan now saw why the scanning rig's AI had found a connection.

Within the portrait, the artist had painted a smaller *inset* painting. A sailboat on a calm sunset lake. The simple scene looked just like the oil painting that Alec had rescued from the monastery fire.

Diane now displayed the recent scan of the rescued painting. She overlaid the sailboat scene onto the inset version that was within the main portrait.

Ryan watched as she toggled the overlaid image on and off.

The 'Ryan Pryce' signature appeared and disappeared with each toggle, but everything else remained in place. With the exception of minor differences in scan quality, the geometry and brush strokes were an exact match for each other.

As Diane separated the two images and zoomed out to

show the whole magazine article, he began to recall why the story had been included in the Fortean Eye.

"Didn't the main portrait go missing?" he said, "Something about it mysteriously vanishing while on loan?"

Diane nodded.

"Two years after this catalogue photograph was taken," she read from the article, "the Mysterious Metzinger portrait, and several other items, disappeared in a puff of cubist smoke."

Looking at the rectangular segments in the blocky portrait, and the rectangular shape of the fire-rescued oil painting, Ryan imagined the small sailboat section being neatly cut from the original portrait and then signed.

When he mentioned this to the others, it triggered a line of conversation that resulted in them discussing a curious piece of logic: if the small portrait section and the piece of neodymium had both found their way to the *past*, then they must have been *taken* there for some reason.

"That can't be right though," said Alec, "We only take empty Faraday bags with us so that we don't pollute the past."

"So," Ryan eyed him sceptically, "you've never left behind anything modern by accident?"

"No," Alec seemed mortified by the idea, "But even if we did, it wouldn't matter."

"Because?"

Diane raised a finger.

"By definition, the temporal occlusion sites we *take* from, are never observed by history. Any occlusion site is either permanently lost or destroyed."

Petra, who had been quiet for a while, now spoke up.

"Like Downing Street."

"What do you mean?" said Theo.

"Well," she gave a shrug, "A massive occlusion site like

that? You have to wonder what was so important that we would risk travelling back to it."

Alec shot a nervous glance at her.

"I guess we'll find out soon."

"No," said Diane, "we won't."

"What do you mean, we won't?" Alec frowned, "There's just been an earthquake and a matching occlusion. Why *wouldn't* we be looking into it as soon as possible?"

Diane rubbed at her temples.

"Because unfortunately we're about to lose our autonomy," she sighed, "I want answers as much as you, but we have to face the facts. When Holroyd returns, quite possibly with the MOD, the first thing he'll want to do is investigate the quake. At that point, we won't be the ones who are making the decisions. Right now, I think we need to stay focused on the painting and the metalwork."

For a moment, the room became quiet, then Theo gave a nod. He leaned forward and picked up the rectangular piece of metal from the table.

"OK. By today's standards, it's a fairly ordinary alloy of neodymium, iron, and boron," he turned it over in his hands, "It's magnetic throughout."

Ryan saw Theo run his fingers over the metalwork. Although the majority of the metal was as smooth as glass, one edge was rougher than the others.

"There's a part number," Theo tapped at the edge.

"Anything you recognise?" Alec frowned.

Theo shook his head, "Afraid not."

"What about the neodymium itself?"

"No leads there either," said Theo, "It's the same type that's used in every modern-day electric motor. The size of the plate is -"

"We're wasting time," Petra cut in.

Theo gave a shrug.

"If you've got anything that will speed things up, I'm all ears."

Petra pointed to the cubist image on the screen.

"If the portrait vanished without a trace," she said, "let's just query the event. If there's a blank, then we'll know that we were the ones who took it."

Cross-referencing the Fortean Eye article with online literary sources from the art world, they determined that Metzinger had created 'Man with a Pipe' around 1911. It had been displayed at various locations around the world before finding a home at a university art gallery in Wisconsin. A further forty years had passed before it was next sent out on loan.

According to historic records, a secure transit company in Appleton had handled the transportation of the painting. By all accounts, the box truck had remained locked during its journey: a trip that had begun on July 27th 1998.

As they queried the first few hours of the journey, it revealed what they'd already grown to suspect: a static-filled sphere that lasted one minute.

WALK

Bernard knew he'd lived his life in accordance with certain basic assumptions: the ground underfoot was solid, and time ran in one direction. The devastating Downing Street quake and the subsequent meeting at the British Museum had shattered both of those illusions.

The deluge of Diane Sellick's terminology washed through his head. Pockets of self-consistent causality. Temporal occlusions. Rubidium-quartz yo-yos flying on quantum tethers.

Walk and think, he told himself, let the morning air cool the thoughts.

Immediately he pictured Diane's QRI wall and being the butt of everyone's joke.

He dug his heels down harder as he walked. Diane and the others had kept everything from him. Even the document-scanning new guy had known more than him.

Diane hadn't just concealed things, she'd actively deceived him. Over the course of months, she'd knowingly placed bagged soil samples in his hand and told him that there was little progress.

What made matters worse was that she'd prepared the

bags so well: each one showing a slight improvement on the last, each one showing perhaps a ten milligram increase in the traces of elements. She'd purposefully placed the traces for him to verify.

He hadn't seen any of the equipment that supposedly achieved the feat of temporal displacement, but one thing was certain: vast sums of government money had poured into the project. Whatever shape the equipment was, it lay somewhere beneath the museum floors.

He slammed down another heel and kept walking.

The project had been an arms-length arrangement, so that it could avoid public scrutiny and accountability. All of which made sense: with the best will in the world, accidental government leaks could have fallen into foreign hands. On the world stage, even the *suggestion* that temporal manipulation was being researched would have been enough to trigger a new arms race.

The museum solution had sidestepped all of that. In fact, it had done it so well that he should perhaps be *thanking* Diane for her deception instead of blaming her. Thanks to her efforts, only Diane's team, he himself, and the Prime Minister knew about QRI.

A helicopter thundered by overhead.

Unbidden, Miranda's last moments flashed into his mind: the oak panelled wall, her desk laden with documents, and the insignificant sideways glance that had been her final action.

He'd known her since their college days.

Both of them had entered politics, but she'd had the drive that had eventually propelled her to the top. Fiercely intellectual, but possessing an uncanny flair for diplomacy, she'd been pivotal in negotiating the 2010 peace treaty with France, and stabilising the sterling: a fact not forgotten by the British public during the following two general elections.

In her treaty speech, she'd proposed greater

understanding through stronger cultural ties. As Culture Secretary, he'd stood at her side as she'd signed the accords and shaken hands with the French delegation. Shortly afterwards, she'd overseen the presentation of the commemorative lapel pins.

He could still remember the moment when she'd pinned the roman numerals to his lapel, and the look that she'd given him. The three gold letters denoted the year of the treaty but, in something of a private joke, they also represented her initials and a shorthand kiss.

The loss hit him again.

The earthquake had swallowed and crushed her in an instant. In the space of twelve unobservable seconds, his oldest friend had been taken away.

He walked on.

Eventually, he was on the approach to Westminster Bridge and saw that the scene had changed since the early hours of the morning. There were now more camera drones hovering over the area, either assisting the rescue efforts or just relaying the images to the rest of the world.

The long lines of self-driving vehicles were at a standstill. Their auto navigation lights were off, and their roof-mounted scanners were no longer spinning. The two facts combined meant that there were no occupants present. Looking further along the bridge, he could guess why.

Work crews in hard hats were inspecting a crack in the stonework, and further drones were being used to inspect the underside of the bridge. In front of a tape barrier, a solitary police car was parked across both lanes, presumably to deter anyone from trying to cross the bridge. Clearly, resources were already stretched thin.

Continuing to walk along the east side of the river, he glanced to his right and again saw the impossible sight. He'd seen it several times from the perspective of aerial news drones, but experiencing it in person at street level made it feel more real.

The flow of the Thames wasn't heading north or south, it was simply pouring west through the breach in the riverbank. Even with the noise of overhead helicopters chopping at the air, he could hear the rush of water and see the spray that was splashing off the wrecked buildings nearby. As he watched, an empty rowing boat got caught in a fast-moving eddy and was dragged through the breach, never to be seen again.

Further along the bank were the government offices of Portcullis House. Or rather, what remained of them. The quake had destroyed the entire south-east corner, so an operation was underway to set up temporary offices in the old London County Hall building.

Closed just before the turn of the century, largely because the modernisation costs couldn't be met, the old building was to be given a second chance. The office premises wouldn't be ideal, but they would be sufficient to house the emergency government that was about to be assembled.

At the very least, it would provide a worldwide symbol that a beating heart was still present in the centre of London.

At the centre of the crescent-shaped entrance, military personnel were unloading jeeps and carrying equipment inside, and he could see a basic security perimeter was being constructed.

Once he entered the building, his life would become even more complicated than it was at the moment. With his close friends and colleagues gone, he didn't yet know who he'd be able to trust with matters relating to Mort.

He walked on along the bank, and headed up the steps to the bridge. There was one last thing he wanted to do before returning to County Hall.

As he set foot on the bridge, the officer near the police car homed in on him.

"The bridge is closed."

"For some," Bernard held up his ID card.

The policeman glanced at it and hesitated.

"Sir," he said, "They're checking the bridge for stability."

Bernard stepped to one side.

"I'm sorry, but I need to get across."

"For your safety," the policeman moved to block his path, "I can't let -"

Bernard now held up his hand.

"Listen," he said, "I count at least eight people on the bridge already, one more will make zero difference to its stability. I *will* be walking across. You don't have a choice in the matter."

"Oh?" the officer gave a patient frown, "And why's that?"

Bernard looked directly at him.

"Because," he lied, "government files were left on a car's data storage space when the quake hit. Unless you want to be the one who's responsible for a devastating breach in national defence, you'll step out of my way."

A little under ten minutes later, he'd crossed the bridge without incident and was standing outside his car. He presented his phone to the door handle and the car unlocked itself.

The scanner on the roof began rotating in anticipation of a journey, but Bernard knew he wouldn't be travelling anywhere. He wouldn't even be accessing the onboard computer. He was only here for one thing.

He didn't know for sure, but he suspected that when he'd hastily left the car earlier, he'd caught his coat on an armrest and lost something valuable. Hoping his instincts were right, he began searching the floor and seats of the car.

Sure enough, at the side of the seat, there was a gleam of light-yellow metal: the lapel pin that Miranda had given him. Reaching into the narrow gap, he grasped it with two fingers and pulled it free.

With the precious item now safely in his hand, he relocked the car and walked into the nearby Memorial Gardens.

To his left and right, slabs of stonework jutted up from the ground; their chaotic angles arranged to frame a more ordered avenue of stones.

He wiped a smudge off her shiny lapel pin.

It was here that she'd first introduced him to Diane Sellick. Walking between these stones, he'd first learnt the basic theory of quantum resonance imaging, and where it could lead.

The finer technicalities had been beyond him, but with his extensive education in matters historical, he'd seen the extraordinary potential of being able to tap into the wealth of the forgotten past.

The pairing had been the perfect fit: he knew which eras of history to search for valuable resources, and the technology would eventually be able to image and retrieve them.

He put the lapel pin in his jacket pocket and zipped it closed.

She'd wanted him to work closely with Diane.

So that's what he'd do.

He didn't particularly like the way that Diane had under-reported her progress, but he had to admit that she'd kept the project out of the public eye. More importantly, the project had worked. It had worked in a way that far exceeded the original intentions.

He looked up at a grey sky dotted with rescue helicopters and drones. Rebuilding a fractured London would be costly, but the solution was within his grasp.

What the future required, he thought, the past would provide.

MINUTE MEN

Standing on the transmitter pad, Alec looked at the displacement coils that were surrounding him. Although he couldn't yet hear it, he knew that charge must be starting to build up. Above him, what Petra called the doughnut was starting to rotate.

A few feet away, at the other side of the wide departure pad, Theo was looking back at him, a tight-lipped smile superimposed on his face.

Alec returned the smile and gave a nod.

Both of them had made temporal trips before, often together, but this one felt different. Running a retrostep on reserve power should be indistinguishable from running it on the conventional power grid, but if the reserve failed, then there would be no backup option.

There were also the technical aspects of the trip to deal with.

Although Diane had thoroughly checked the non-static reference frames and the spatial confinement limitations, he knew that retrostepping hadn't been used this way before.

Theo nodded back.

Both of them turned on their jacket-mounted LED

flashlights; where they were going, there would be no lighting.

There was a minor crackle from the nearby loudspeaker, then Petra's voice came through.

"System check," she said, *"Ready Tee?"*

"Ready," Theo replied.

"Alec?"

"Ready as I'll ever be, Duffy."

"OK chaps," she said, *"Standby for tracer."*

None of them liked the tracer, but it was a necessity.

One-way trips, like a rabbit's one-hour journey into the past, didn't need a tracer. The trip was short enough that it could just hop around in its cage while it passed through the same hour all over again. *Human* trips typically had timeline destinations that were much further away than an hour. Twiddling your thumbs might eventually get you back to the present day, but you'd grow much older while doing so.

The rubidium-82 tracer had provided a solution. It maintained the temporal link and allowed the journey to be two way: there and back in one convenient yo-yo trip. This convenience came with time limitations, of course.

Alec presented his wrist to the pneumatic injector nozzle at the side of the rig, and tried not to tense his forearm. He'd learnt from previous trips that it was best to keep his muscles relaxed when the tracer was injected.

He took a deep breath and tried to focus on the timings.

The half-life of the tracer isotope was only 76 seconds. By the time that tissue absorption had been verified, only 65 seconds would remain before the tracer degraded. A few seconds were always lost while the transport field permeated the space, and then there was the inevitable moment of disorientation that would follow the discontinuity.

Despite undertaking several of these trips, and knowing what to expect, he knew that the yo-yo's effective limit was 60 seconds.

A single minute.

It was this limit that had given rise to Petra's nickname for their covert team.

Named after the small teams of adaptable militia in the American Revolution, the 'Minute Men' could mobilise at short notice, and be in and out of a target site at speed, while leaving no lasting impression.

He found himself smiling. Petra had later admitted that she'd only suggested the male-skewed nickname because of a more vulgar interpretation of being quickly in-and-out while leaving no lasting impression.

The injector nozzle delivered its shot.

"Ow," he reported.

"It's just a little prick," Petra's smile was audible, *"You'll get over it."*

Typically, he was the one who joked in stressful situations, but it seemed that Petra was also finding their present circumstances difficult to deal with. Rather than joke back, he gave her something to focus her attention on.

"Is the catcher mitt in place?"

In the pause that followed, he heard the capacitor banks reaching the upper limits of their charge.

"Mitt's ready and standing by," Petra replied.

"Tracer absorption confirmed," Diane's voice now came through the speaker, *"Retrostep imaging is clear. Alec, Theo, are you good to go?"*

He exchanged a glance with Theo.

They'd both studied the plan in great detail and knew exactly what needed to be done. Now it was time to put theory and preparation into practice. Above the steadily increasing noise, they both called out.

"Go!"

Lights came on around the transmitter pad, and a hum vibrated the air.

"Auto-commit locked in," said Diane, *"Safe trip."*

Alec placed a finger in each ear, closed his eyes, and murmured to himself.

"We're history."

On the other side of his eyelids, there was a rapid strobing of light. It was followed by a void that, by definition, lasted no time at all.

1998

Theo pictured the Appleton transport truck.

Relative to his current state, it would be moving at over fifty miles an hour.

Once he and Alec were inside the box compartment, the frame of reference would become stationary again. The transition was the tricky part.

Although the straight road and the truck's constant velocity had simplified the vector offset calculations, the timings were more critical than previous trips. Separated by a fraction of a second, he and Alec would soon be arriving into the same sealed space.

After Diane wished them a safe trip, he placed his fingers in his ears, then breathed out and closed his eyes.

In a disorienting swirl of strobing light, the departure pad separated from his feet. He felt the familiar drop sensation, then the dark void became physical surroundings.

His feet made contact with the floor, and he immediately realised that his arrival velocity wasn't a perfect match for the moving vehicle. Although the truck was only going slightly slower than they'd calculated, the difference was enough to tip him forward.

As he instantly threw out a hand to steady himself, a thick blast of air accompanied Alec's arrival. In the close confines of the sealed volume, the resulting pressure increase slammed against his exposed eardrum and he felt it burst.

Yelling out in pain, he felt Alec trip into him: a victim of the same velocity mismatch. They both landed awkwardly on the floor of the moving truck.

With flashlight beams scattering randomly around the enclosed space, they both struggled to get back on their feet. From the continuous rumble that filled the air, it was clear that the truck must still be moving at a constant speed. The driver may have slowed, but he wasn't stopping.

As far as Theo could tell, they were still undetected.

When they'd queried the scene before and after the occlusion event, they'd seen that the truck's artworks had been disturbed for some reason. Looking at the scene in front of him now, he could see why. Their own arrival had been the cause of the disarray.

"Not the best of starts," his voice sounded weirdly muted.

Feeling at his damaged ear, he checked his wristband and saw there were barely fifty seconds left on the timer.

"Which one is it?" Alec stared at the randomly arranged packages.

As they'd seen in the QRI, each of the artworks had been carefully wrapped for transportation. Some were still secured to the side walls, but others had been toppled a few seconds after their arrival.

The whole space rattled. Evidently, the truck had driven over one of the potholes that had shown up on the QRI.

Picturing the static-toned scene that had been on Diane's curved wall, Theo tried to visualise where things had been positioned.

There had been a package that was wrapped like a right-angled triangle, and a small polythene-fronted crate of metallic modern art sculptures. Both had been stacked next to the Metzinger portrait, but their positions had now obviously shifted.

Although the truck driver was isolated in his cab, and therefore well out of earshot, Theo couldn't help lowering his voice.

"That triangle one," he thought aloud, "wasn't it over on the right?"

Alec turned, and his flashlight lit the side wall and floor.

"Yeah," he nodded and pointed at the plastic-wrapped crate, "which would make *this* one..."

"The one that was next to the portrait!" Theo cut in.

Stepping around toppled boxes, Alec quickly manoeuvred himself to the other side of the shallow crate, then began checking a large, cardboard-wrapped package near the side wall.

A double-beep came from Theo's wristband. They had less than thirty seconds left, but Alec was grinning.

He tapped at the reference label on the side of the package, "This is it!"

As they'd expected, the item was too large for a Faraday bag, but they'd come prepared. Theo pulled four recall tags from his pocket and unwound the sync cable that connected them together. On the far side of the portrait, Alec was doing the same with his own set of tags.

Working with practised speed, they began attaching the tags to the corners. With each new corner that was tagged, a cuboid of space was being defined that would envelop the target object.

As Alec stretched out the sync cable and lined up the last tag, a triple-beep came from his wrist.

"Fifteen seconds," Theo stood up.

The truck jolted.

"Bloody potholes!" Alec steadied himself again, "If the driver could just avoid -"

The whole space suddenly jarred to the left.

Theo fell sideways and managed to brace himself against the side wall, but Alec stumbled back, dragging the sync cable with him as he hit the floor.

Mind racing, Theo knew that the truck must have swerved.

The display on his wristband tether was now flashing.

Ten seconds remained.

Lunging forward, he knelt on the crate and dragged Alec back to his feet. Theo held the portrait still, and Alec pushed the last tag into place on the corner. The eight recall tags lit up around the portrait.

"Five seconds," Alec shook his head, "I mean, I knew it was gonna be a close one, but -"

He saw Alec physically pause, and then a look of wide-eyed anxiety filled his face.

At the other side of the portrait, struck silent, Alec was staring at the sync cable that was stretched between two of the recall tags. Somehow, in his fall, the cable had got tangled around his wristband.

Everything seemed to unfold in slow motion: Alec desperately struggling with the cable... The lower tag popping free of the cuboid package and swinging like a pendulum... The final second arriving... The flashlight illuminating Alec's panic-stricken face.

Theo felt the tug of the quantum tether around his wrist, but he could see that Alec's wristband was still tangled in the cable.

And then it happened.

As though evaporating from within, Alec simply disintegrated, then the world went black.

For one timeless instant, it felt like the universe had blinked, then Theo felt himself falling through the air of Lab Two.

Spanning the room beneath him, the elastic netting of the

catcher mitt broke his fall, but he was still moving with considerable speed.

Feeling like he was turning head over heels, he heard the mitt's pneumatic support rods hiss as they absorbed the net's momentum. Tumbling sideways, he could already feel the net lowering itself to the floor.

As he rolled to a halt, solid ground arrived underneath him. Sitting bolt upright, he whipped around to see that the outer part of the net was making contact with the floor. At the centre of the net, he could see the package they'd tagged, but there was movement behind it.

"Alec!" he was on his feet.

He found himself running and slipping on the smooth mesh that now lay flat on the ground.

As the tagged package loomed into view, he was confronted with the stark truth of the matter. The movements he'd seen were actually just fragments of wooden crate and sculpted artifacts coming to rest in the collapsing net.

Dropping to his knees, he cried out at the sight that now greeted him.

Fused with the sync cable were the smoking remains of a wristband tether, and Alec's severed hand.

PRESENT

Standing near the door of Lab Two, Ryan watched in stunned silence.

At the centre of the large empty room, Diane, Petra and Theo stood motionless and staring at the small collection of things that lay in the collapsed mesh net.

Alec was gone.

In his place were lifeless, inanimate artifacts: a broken crate, a wrapped painting, and pointless golden sculptures that supposedly explored the human condition.

In the space of one minute, a man's life had been exchanged for planks of wood and pieces of gold.

In Ryan's mind, the exchange echoed something vaguely biblical, but the only thing he could remember was that there had been an element of betrayal involved.

He felt another wave of guilt pass through him. From the moment that Ryan had arrived here, Alec had been destined to die.

Inevitably, the thought occurred that if they could revisit the moment and change the outcome, then Alec could be saved. But time didn't work that way. There were pockets of occlusions, but their outcomes were always final and unchangeable. Alec's death was now an immutable part of history.

Ryan looked over at Theo, who was still staring at the floor.

From the tone of the quiet murmur that was coming from the centre of the room, Ryan knew he must be recounting the whole trip again; endlessly retelling the events to anyone who would listen, until the memory had lost its cutting edge. He didn't know Theo very well, but he knew that this sort of mental trauma didn't dull itself overnight.

He now saw that Petra was walking in his direction, her face expressionless.

He braced himself for her sharp words of blame, or a piercing stare, but neither arrived. Although she made eye contact, her fire was gone: stolen by the shock and grief of the event.

"Petra," he began, but then didn't know what else to say.

Still walking, she shook her head and passed him.

"We shouldn't have looked," her voice was flat.

Ryan turned to see her quietly leaving the room.

It had been her idea to query the box truck scene, but none of them had countered it. Using the most powerful set of tools on the planet, they'd all let curiosity lead them down a dark and dead-end street.

The cafe flashed into his head.

If he hadn't met Petra, then none of this would have happened. As fast as the thought arrived, another part of his mind reminded him that Alec himself had retrieved the small oil painting because of Theo's colour-coding data. Without those events, Petra wouldn't have gone to the cafe.

The whole situation was a dense loop of impenetrable circular causality. None of them, and all of them, were to blame for the circumstances that had led to Alec's death.

Hearing footsteps behind him, he turned to see that Theo was also heading for the door. Features blank and drawn, he looked back at the package that still lay at the centre of the net.

"Unwrap your damn present," Theo's voice was low, "Alec paid enough for it."

Without a backward glance, Theo quietly left the room. The door clicked closed behind him, sending hollow echoes around the empty space.

He heard Diane clear her throat.

"No one blames you."

"Of course they do," he faced her.

She shook her head.

"They know it was my fault," she walked over to him, "I'm the one who sent Petra to bring you in. None of this would have happened if I hadn't tried to shut down your story."

He knew he'd only written it to increase online subscriptions.

"So if I hadn't *written* it…" he found himself caught in the same mental loop again.

"Ryan," she stopped his line of thought, "Holroyd gave me a total dressing down in my own office. It was *my* idea to do all this behind his back. It was *me* who wanted one last temporal hurrah before he brought the MOD crashing in on our private party. Forty-eight hours… what the hell was I thinking?"

He knew that ten of those hours had already gone, but the remaining time was irrelevant. One of the team had lost their life. The project was over.

He found himself staring at the centre of the net.

"Diane… I'm sorry."

She sighed.

"Alec was always the one who would jump into things feet first, and ask questions later. This trip was no different. He wanted to go."

"What about Theo though?"

She seemed to take a long moment before replying.

"Theo's like a... protective brother," she said, "He wanted to be there for him."

Ryan stared at the floor, "Of course."

Diane took a deep breath and looked at the door.

"I should check on them both. Will you be alright?"

Ryan nodded.

He didn't feel alright at all, but he knew he was the outsider here. Diane and the others needed time together without him being in the way.

After she'd left, he found himself drawn to the middle of the room. A small piece of cloth had been draped over the remains of Alec's hand, hiding it from view, but the wrapped package now lay on its own; its wide, flat surface staring up at him.

Theo's words echoed through his mind.

Alec had paid the ultimate price to retrieve this artifact. Leaving it wrapped would mean that he'd died for nothing. If an answer lay inside the padded layers of cardboard, then he owed it to Alec to uncover it.

He knelt down and pulled his pen from his pocket.

Working carefully, he pushed the tip of the pen through the dense cardboard and worked the hole wider. With the papery surface breached, it became easier to tear it away.

SUMMATION

Alone with her thoughts and still in a daze, Petra found herself wandering into the workshop.

She just wanted the room to stay in comfortable darkness, but the helpful energy-saving detectors turned on the bright lights and showed her the space that Alec would never occupy again.

Filling every wall and workbench was an eclectic mix of the tools they'd used over the years. Racks of screwdrivers and drawers of electronics framed a multi-headed drill stand. Soldering irons, circuit boards, and reels of brightly coloured plastic lay scattered around their 3D printer. Half-disassembled VR equipment, oscilloscopes, and bundles of wire peeked out from under sheets of blueprints.

A room of half-made projects and inanimate things were all that remained of Alec: a pitiful, inadequate summation of his life.

In every direction she looked, she was given a fresh reminder of the times they'd all spent here: their late nights, their problem solving, the things they'd invented to research retrostepping, the things they'd invented for specific trips.

It was all in the past.

Nothing could be invented that would bring him back.

The view in front of her misted up with condensation.

Taking off her glasses, she wiped at her eyes and slowly breathed out, but it didn't expel the tight knot that pulled within her chest.

Looking at the plastic-framed glasses in her hands, another series of memories flickered through her mind.

Alec had designed the built-in micro cameras to record and transmit their stereoscopic view over long distances. In that respect, because the glasses had elements of spectacles and binoculars, Alec had modestly called them 'spectaculars'.

She could still picture his pleased-looking grin.

In time, the frames had been adapted to carry her standard lens prescription, and slowly they'd become an indispensable, invisible part of her life.

Looking down at the wide glass lenses, she stood still and watched the condensation evaporate; a shrinking, immaterial mist that disappeared far too quickly.

She quietly folded the arms of the glasses and put them in the pocket of her hoodie, then the empty workshop became a watery blur.

WESTMINSTER FALLS

In dusty old rooms, packed with political predators, Bernard could see that the manoeuvring had begun in earnest.

In the wake of the Downing Street disaster, the power vacuum had sucked in the most treacherous elements of the Westminster elite. Remorseless self-serving sharks, who cared nothing for his grief, had shaken his hand and grinned their teeth before swimming off to another part of the room.

During the ceaseless conversations that swirled around the requirements of forming an emergency government, he politely excused himself from the feeding frenzy and walked away.

He found the nearest stairs and began climbing. He realised that, literally and figuratively, he must be trying to distance himself from the corruption-tainted air below. The heavy feeling of general decay followed him though; the empty floors and peeling decor failed to provide any sense of relief.

Perhaps he was naive, he thought, but he was one of the few people who were still trying to hold fast to their moral standards. Many of his colleagues had long since succumbed to the temptation of corporate influence: a fact that made him almost ashamed to be called a government minister.

Soon there were no more stairs left to climb.

In front of him was the door to the roof. He was as far from the ground floor as it was possible to be. Almost. He put his hands on the emergency exit bar and pushed.

Stepping out onto the open flat roof of London County Hall, he gratefully breathed in the cold air and looked out at the orange-tinted night sky.

Taking out his handkerchief, he mopped the film of sweat from his brow.

It was now ten hours since the quake.

In the distance, fleets of air ambulances and heavy-lift military helicopters hammered out stuttering walls of noise. Closer by, the newly formed Thames breach was still adding its low background hiss to the busy air.

People were already calling it the Westminster Waterfall, but on social media platforms, the more ominous ampertag *'&WestminsterFalls'* was rising in popularity.

As ever, in the digital world, tragedy was spreading faster than hope.

Although this was a disastrous geological event, he knew it was a *local* one. The rest of the country was unaffected and was still going about its business. Of course, it hadn't stopped the country reacting to the news.

For a lot of people, the idea of wiping the political slate clean was a very appealing one. In fact, there had already been public calls for new systems of government to be considered: systems that were free of historical bias, or systems that were a wholly digital democracy.

He was educated enough to know that there was no such thing as a perfect democracy. For time immemorial, disagreements had always required a resolution to be found. Moving beyond the caveman's club had been an advancement, but democracy carried its own limitations. At best, it was a method of determining how many people agreed with a proposition, but it didn't placate those who still disagreed. In the modern day, where disagreement was shared at the push of a button, it was easy for any number of opinions to wash back into the political waters and churn up the debates that had supposedly already been settled.

There was no perfect system.

Water continued to flow through the Thames breach.

For a moment, he thought he felt dizzy: his body had moved slightly from side to side, and yet his head was completely clear.

The sensation hit him again, and it suddenly dawned on him what was happening. He was stationary, but the old building was shifting underneath him. It was an aftershock.

The lights in the surrounding streets flickered, then a deep low rumble pushed him off his feet. As the lights failed, he fell forward and threw out his hands.

AFTERSHOCK

He hit the ground hard, his knees and shins taking the full blow of his weight. Still toppling, his shoulder took the next hit and he felt the air being physically knocked out of him.

He could hear the thud of things impacting the ground, and he instinctively covered his head as he rolled to a stop.

Everything became quiet and dark.

Mind still racing, he desperately tried to get his bearings and recall the last few seconds.

He'd felt the pit of his stomach drop, a white-hot burning sensation had sliced at his wrist, then a perfect darkness had engulfed the space.

The darkness that now surrounded him wasn't as dense. There were stars above him, damp ground beneath him, and he could smell moist soil.

He put out his hand to lever himself upright, but found that the ground level next to him must have been lower than he'd thought. As he twisted further over, to place his hand down, his fingers failed to meet the ground.

Turning quickly, Alec saw why. Caught in the glare of his chest-mounted flashlight was his truncated hand. Yelling out in shock, he pulled it close and cradled it with his other hand. Head swimming and stars swirling above him, he felt faint and lay back on the cold ground.

Pulse pounding in his ears, he closed his eyes and willed away the horrific sight, but the vision persisted in his mind's eye. Heart hammering, and yelling his denial of the cold facts, he probed at his injury. He could feel the void where the palm of his hand should be.

The last few seconds before the discontinuity flashed through his mind. He'd been desperately trying to pull his hand free of the tangled sync cable, but it had only tightened around his wristband.

He recalled the lower tag popping off the package and swinging out. In that fraction of a second, the volume of the returning mass had been redefined. It had been expanded. His hand had been caught within it.

There was no direct pain, but a thick ache throbbed at his wrist.

Risking another glance, he saw that it wasn't bleeding. It was in fact cauterised: the injury presumably sealed shut by the light-speed retreat of the temporal envelope. At least he wouldn't bleed to death, the dark thought fled through his mind.

Still cradling his wrist, he eased himself into a sitting position and experimented with breathing slowly. In the flashlight beam, his breath misted out in front of him. It was cold here.

Wherever here was.

The cold of the ground started to seep through his woefully thin clothing. If he wanted to avoid dying of shock and exposure, he knew he'd have to get to a phone quickly. At the very least, he'd have to find shelter against the jet black sky.

As he twisted to one side, his flashlight picked out a pinprick of light reflecting back at him from the darkness. A primal reaction seemed to kick in. Fearing that a wild animal was staring at him, he froze and held his breath.

Ears straining to listen for movement, he felt the pulse in his throbbing wrist marking off the seconds. The glint of light didn't move an inch. It didn't even blink.

Unable to hold his breath any longer, he slowly exhaled. The flashlight on his chest dipped. The pinprick of light disappeared, and then reappeared as Alec took his next tentative breath.

Eyes now adapting to the light, he cautiously leaned to one side to get a better view of his potential foe.

With a huge sigh of relief, he realised that the reflective circle was actually lying on the ground. It wasn't an animal. It was something artificial. And familiar.

Manoeuvring himself on one hand and knees, he kept the item in the light beam and crawled over to it. Reaching down, he picked up the remains of a severed wristband.

Most of the timer dial was as absent as his hand, but the rubidium-quartz crystal seemed to be intact; its diamond-like qualities reflecting and refracting the light on his chest.

It was only now that the cold facts of the matter started to hit him.

His quantum tether was broken.

He had no idea where, or when, he was.

Diane and the others had no way of knowing either.

He was as lost as the ill-fated McCairn.

Still processing the thoughts, he cast his flashlight around the general area.

It seemed that when the imperfectly tagged volume had flared wider, it had affected more than just his hand. Strewn across the cold ground were pieces of things that had been inside the transport truck.

The heavy thuds he'd heard when he'd arrived here now made sense. In addition to fragments of wooden crate, there were small pieces of modern art sculptures lying in the dirt.

The chunks of precious gold gleamed in the flashlight, but they were all worthless to him. They couldn't keep him warm, or provide sustenance.

He gripped his throbbing wrist.

He was as good as dead.

LOGIC

Kneeling at the side of the wrapped portrait, Ryan slowly tore away the papery surface.

Layers of cardboard gave way to a light framework of protective wooden slats, but these too had been built for disassembly. The frame came apart easily, exposing a painting that had last seen the light of day twenty-five years ago.

He stared at the black-and-white canvas.

The fractured man stared back at him through an offset curl of cubist smoke.

He suppressed a shiver. Metzinger's portrait had skipped forward through a quarter of a century, only to be unwrapped at this exact date and time.

Alone in the empty room, it almost felt like the moment was meant for him.

The portrait looked exactly like the one they'd seen in the Fortean Eye article. The upper left rectangle contained the same sailboat scene, but unlike its wooden-framed counterpart, there was no 'Ryan Pryce' signature.

The physical evidence before him confirmed the theory: the signature hadn't been added to the main portrait, yet.

Recalling Diane's meeting room screen, and the signature

toggling on and off, the further logic now locked into place. This portrait, or at least a rectangular part of it, *must* eventually find its way to the past with a piece of magnetic metal.

In his mind, the dark signature toggled on and off; isolated from everything else, but somehow attracted to the neodymium-backed painting.

Magnetic, the thought occurred.

As he stared at the range of black tones that covered the canvas, he felt his thoughts begin to crystallise into an idea. The more he looked at the cubist man, the faster the idea emerged.

He knew he had to find Diane.

RIPPLE

Alec kept walking.

Three days ago, he'd been faced with a choice. Either die of exposure and have no effect on the timeline, or save himself by interacting with the era that he'd found himself in.

He'd known that his presence here in the past was problematic. Every one of his actions could influence the timeline. Every little thing he did could create a ripple that would travel forward and influence the future he'd left behind.

He'd rationalised his decision to keep living, through analogy alone.

Like a ripple on a pond, he'd reasoned, the strength of the radiating wave diminished with distance and time. When the consequences of his actions reached the future, it was possible that the ripple would have become lost in the background noise of other people's lives.

He glanced behind him and walked on.

He remembered day one.

As the first light of dawn had crept into the dark sky, he'd walked up to higher ground. His intention had been to get an idea of his surroundings and work out where to go next, but on reaching the top of a shallow hill, he'd stopped dead in his tracks. Beneath him had been a city. Although it hadn't been well lit, he'd recognised a distinctive silhouette on the horizon: built for the 1889 World's Fair, the iconic tower of iron had been clearly visible above the Parisian landscape.

He recalled the elation he'd felt. His life could so easily have been ended by arriving here in the middle of a tree, or under solid ground, but he'd arrived on the outskirts of a civilisation. As it later turned out, that civilisation was over a century in the past, but he was no longer lost.

He remembered dashing back down the hill and collecting the fragments of gold sculpture from the ground: universal currency for his stay in the past. He hadn't taken all of it though. He'd hastily buried a few pieces in the soil, just in case future-Theo was able to isolate their position in time.

Alec shook his head at the memory.

The first day had been the hardest. Arguably, it would have been considerably harder if he hadn't learnt French during his school years.

In his early teenage years, an air of optimism over the French peace treaty had bolstered the drive to educate the young and prepare them for opportunities on the continent. Like every other teenager, he'd hated learning the vocabulary, but three days ago it had paid dividends. When he'd walked into a small 'boutique de tailleur', covered in dried mud and missing a hand, he'd been able to hold a basic conversation.

Of course, the tailor's comprehension and patience had risen sharply after Alec had placed a nugget of gold on the counter. The man had quickly closed the shop and had made sure that all his clothing needs were fully met. In exchange for the nugget, he'd even provided a generous amount of local currency. Two hours later, wearing clothes that blended in with the era, Alec had left the shop with a wallet of French francs and the beginnings of a plan.

After securing accommodation in a cheap hotel on the outskirts of the city, he'd kept a low profile by day and moved by night.

This was night number three.

Changing his pace, he left the path and began retracing the steps he'd made on the two previous nights. Walking up the hill, he headed back toward the site of his first arrival.

In his heart, he knew that the plan was a long shot, but he had to try it. If Theo was somehow able to scan for the *specific* concentrations of gold that had gone missing from the box truck, he'd find a repeating pattern.

The gold buried at the arrival site would remain stationary, but the gold in Alec's pockets would converge on it every twenty-four hours. The effect would register as a flashing beacon in any QRI scan. All he had to do was return every day to the same deserted spot.

Assuming they got the message, they'd know when and where to find him.

He could picture Theo arriving with a replacement wristband and an isotope injector. Within a minute, the yo-yo would go taut and they'd disappear from this remote, unobserved place.

He massaged the stump on his left wrist. His hand would still be gone, but at least he would be home.

As he approached the top of the hill, he heard the thumping of rapid footsteps. Looking up, he was surprised to see someone running toward him; their handheld light swinging from side to side.

His heart skipped a beat at the thought that his plan had worked. But as the person ran closer, he saw that the light was an oil lantern. The man holding it was a complete stranger and he was showing no signs of slowing down. At the last moment, he veered around Alec.

"L'or!" he ran past, his expression one of glee, "Il y a de l'or!"

Unsure what was happening, Alec slowed his pace and checked ahead. The hilltop was dark, but he thought he saw movement against the night sky. Another lantern now appeared over the hilltop and illuminated a small gathering of people. Carried on the light wind, he could hear the excited tone of their voices.

Moving more cautiously, he passed the top of the hill. A bright patch of light came into view below. Four or five lanterns, and more silhouettes, were moving back and forth over the exact spot where he'd arrived.

Now given context, the running man's words returned to Alec in perfect English: Gold, there's gold.

He froze.

His buried fragments had been discovered and were being looted.

Theo would never discover a repeating pattern.

As he watched the silhouettes excitedly weaving between the lanterns, the realisation hit him: as word spread about the gold, more people would descend on the area.

His arrival site would no longer be one of history's unobserved locations.

An occlusion point couldn't form here.

Nobody would be coming to rescue him.

The cold, isolating sensation that he'd felt three days ago, seeped back into his bones.

He was actually stranded here.

He backed away from the scene, but the dark logic pursued him. If he could never return home, then he'd live out the remainder of his days in this time. Already, he was embedded in the past. Part of history. He would die before Theo and the others had even been born.

While terminal thoughts continued to rattle through his head, he saw a lantern bobbing toward him. Caught in its yellow light was a familiar-looking man who was studying something in the palm of his hand. When he was only a few feet away, the man looked up.

They both recognised each other.

Alec saw the tailor close his hand around a large piece of gold.

There was a moment of silence, then the tailor looked at the ground and gave an awkward-looking shrug.

"Désolé Monsieur," he mumbled a quiet apology and then hurried away.

Too late, Alec understood.

Intrigued by a mud-covered man with a nugget of gold, the tailor had decided to follow him during his night-time excursions. For two nights in a row, Alec had led the way to the site, unaware that he was being watched. On this third night, the tailor had reached the site first. By the looks of it, he'd also invited others to try their luck in a new gold rush.

Hearing their excitable voices drifting through the cold night air, Alec backed away. The truth of the matter was drowning out every other thought: his attempt to engineer a way home had created the very mechanism of its failure.

Still in a horrified daze, he let his feet carry him away from the hill.

As the city lights grew brighter around him, he pictured the circular pond ripple spreading out and meeting other ripples; their peaks and troughs colliding, reinforcing or cancelling each other out. Apparent randomness resulting from an ordered input.

Drifting on through the busy Parisian streets, he watched the random motion of the night-time crowd; each person contributing their own personal intent to the resulting chaotic effect. They moved and sometimes bumped into each other, but the crowd adjusted and remained the same crowd.

He was no longer a visitor here. He was now part of it. As if to prove his own point, a man jostled into him and tipped his top hat in apology.

"Pardon," a rich cloud of alcohol fumes slurred from his mouth, then he meandered off into the busy street.

Alec stopped walking.

Perhaps influenced by the smell of the alcohol, and definitely influenced by his own stranded status, he knew he wanted a stiff drink.

He didn't have to look very far for the solution.

Despite the late hour, the brightly lit city was as lively as it had been during the day. Bicycles weaved between horse-drawn carriages. Tall motorcars and buses trundled along on tyres that looked more like cartwheels. All around him, the pavements were lined with the chattering buzz of restaurants and bars.

He found the nearest bar and made his way inside.

The cool clear air of the street was replaced by thick, beige layers of warm fog. Laughing and talking animatedly, customers at tiny tables faded into the distance amid the mist of cigar and pipe smoke. Permeating the entire space was the smell and promise of readily available liquor. In every sense, spirits were high.

Taking a vacant space at the bar, he placed his good arm on the counter and looked at the range of bottles on the shelf.

It seemed that none of the brands of this era had lasted long enough to reach the century he was familiar with. Floral, slanted fonts decorated every label, but gave him little clue what the bottles actually contained.

The bartender finished serving the man to his left and turned to him.

"Oui Monsieur?"

Hastily recalling the French lessons of his youth, Alec mentally assembled a sentence and hoped for the best.

"Un cognac, s'il vous plait," he managed, "Double."

The bartender pulled a brown-labelled bottle from the shelf and poured the double measure. He placed the glass on the counter, then walked away to serve another customer.

Alec picked up the cognac and stared at the liquid for a moment. Picturing the faces he'd never see again, he held his drink a little higher and quietly bid them farewell.

"Gonna miss you," he drank.

The mouthful of alcohol delivered the required warmth, and he set the glass down again.

Letting himself fall into a slump of contemplation, he watched the cognac shift as he tipped the glass from side to side. Tip: if he'd been faster with the sync cable, he'd still have his hand. Tip: if he'd looked more carefully at the query of the potholed road, he may not have fallen. Tip: if he'd identified the package quicker, he wouldn't be here.

Things could have been so different.

"Excusez-moi," a voice came from his right.

Alec sighed into his glass, but didn't look up, "Oui."

The man began a sentence in French, but then tutted to himself and restarted in English: each vowel seeming to come from the back of his throat.

"You are… American?"

Alec exhaled a short laugh. In his own time, he'd had the experience of foreigners deftly switching to English after they'd heard his attempt to speak their language. It seemed the past was no different.

"Sure," Alec didn't have the energy to correct him, "How did you know?"

The man raised his own glass.

"Gunna miss you," he faintly imitated Alec's toast, "It is American phrase, non?"

He didn't really know the answer. Over a century of linguistic shifts separated him from the man. What were common words for Alec, were perhaps still geography-locked phrases in this time.

A century, the historical distance hit him again.

He took another drink, "Yeah."

The man seemed pleased with his deduction.

"Bon," he drank.

"No," Alec contemplated the bottom of his glass again, "Not bon."

For a few seconds the man frowned, but then his eyebrows lifted. It seemed that another deduction was about to be made.

"Ah, you are sad," he pointed to Alec's glass, "because your friend is depart to the America?"

"My friend..." he had no words to describe the feelings of the situation and ended up illustrating a large gap between his outstretched arms, "My friend, is far away."

The man now noticed that the gap was imperfectly framed.

"Your hand..." he glanced at the empty space before looking acutely embarrassed.

Suddenly, Alec felt self-conscious and uncomfortable. Quickly dropping his arm out of view, he brought the conversation to a swift close.

"Bonsoir Monsieur," Alec downed the rest of his drink.

He tapped the glass on the counter a few times to get the bartender's attention, then put his one functional hand into his pocket to retrieve his money.

The man was now desperately trying to apologise.

"I have *grand* sorry!"

Alec impatiently dug around inside his coat, willing the wallet to meet his fingers. This had been a bad idea. All he now wanted to do was pay and leave. Continuing his search, he began patting at a different pocket.

Suddenly, he remembered the man in the top hat who'd blundered into him. It hadn't been a blunder, he now realised. It had been a theft.

With a sickening sense of dread rising from his stomach, he knew he wouldn't be able to pay for the drink he'd just gulped. He didn't know what the laws were like here in 1911, but the involvement of the French police was unlikely to end well.

"I bloody hate the past," he shook his head in disbelief.

"Monsieur?" the man frowned.

"My wallet," he pulled his coat pocket inside out, "Er… a thief."

He saw the man's expression shift. The apologetic look of social embarrassment faded, and he glanced between Alec and the bartender. The man had clearly had an idea.

"I will pay," he placed his hand on his chest, "My sorry."

The man was trying to apologise for any offence he'd caused by offering to pay for the drink.

Alec didn't know what to say, but the man interpreted his hesitation as acceptance, and began a conversation with the bartender that was too fast for Alec to follow.

After a few glances in his direction, the dialogue ended and the bartender thanked the man.

"Mercy, Monsieur Metzinger."

As another glass was filled and set down on the bar top, all Alec could do was stare.

THEORY

Standing in the meeting room, Ryan finished explaining his theory to the others. As he'd expected, they looked at him with a mixture of incredulity and contempt.

"I saw him die," Theo stared at him.

Ryan turned to Diane.

"Isn't it worth trying?"

"Have you any idea," she stared, "how utterly unlikely all of that would be?"

"But that's exactly what I'm saying," he insisted, "We're not looking at a coincidence."

"Then what *are* we looking at?" Petra folded her arms.

"I think we're looking at an event that was already part of history," he said, "Alec didn't *coincidentally* arrive at the location where Metzinger made the painting."

Diane narrowed her eyes.

"You're saying Metzinger made the painting *because* Alec arrived?"

"I don't know about the 'because' bit," he admitted, "but I think the timing works, and artists *did* experiment with all sorts of pigments. Please… What have we got to lose? Run the element scan on the painting."

"We ran it before the Appleton trip," Theo rubbed at his ear, "Any elements would have shown -"

"No they wouldn't," Ryan cut in, but then raised his hands in apology, "Sorry… We queried the Appleton gallery *room* to get the general layout of the space, but we *confirmed* the portrait's position using old photos from the nineties. We watched a QRI of the portrait getting packaged and loaded onto the truck, but *everything* was a wide-area scan."

"Wide area," Petra was nodding, "Lower resolution."

"It's like Alec told me," Ryan nodded back, "You can only have detailed scans of small areas."

He saw a glimmer of hope flicker over Theo's face.

"You mean we didn't look closely enough?"

Ryan nodded.

"I know nothing can change the fact that he's gone," he said, "but I think he may have lived out his life in the past."

The room became quiet as all eyes turned to Diane.

"Even if it were true," she said, "what makes you so convinced that there's anything to scan for in that painting?"

Ryan looked back at her.

"If you had *one* opportunity to send a message forward through time," he pointed at the portrait, "wouldn't you try to write it on the *one* thing that was already in your friends' possession?"

FOCUS POINT

Alec could feel he was approaching consciousness. Part dreaming, part recollecting, he let himself drift wherever his thoughts took him.

He'd been at home, or he'd been in a place that had felt like home. Either way, there had been a feeling of safety involved. Or perhaps it had been a feeling of trust. Comfortable.

There had been a time before that though, his mind swam and took in the sights.

Accordion music floated through a fuzzy memory. There had been music and talking. And drinking. There had definitely been drinking. He'd been sad because someone had taken a wallet.

No, that wasn't it, another part of his brain stirred. He'd been sad because someone had left him behind, or he'd left them. It was all back to front.

There had been smoke and coughing. And more drinking. There had been talk about time and perspective. Again there was a feeling of something being back to front. Inverted.

A dim light started to come in now, along with the gentle drum of an approaching headache; a rhythmic pulse running from his head to his fingertips. And his wrist. A throbbing ache in his wrist.

In an instant, consciousness took hold of him and jarred him awake.

Eyes wide and breathing hard, he found himself sitting in a comfortable armchair.

At one side of the room, sunlight was streaming in through slatted window shutters, sending pale-yellow bars spraying across the walls. At the other side of the room, a cluttered table stood next to a closed wooden door.

He now became aware of the sounds that were drifting in through the window: the trot of horses and the mechanical sounds of motor vehicles. A loud car horn sounded, confirming that his hangover and the previous night's drinks weren't a figment of his imagination.

Still trying to work out where he was, he turned to take in more of the details.

Next to him, the small side table held a pouch of shredded tobacco, a half-glass of beer, and an ashtray. The smell threatened to turn his stomach over, so he quickly stood and was immediately hit with a nauseating reminder that the hangover would be his companion for a while.

Steadying himself on the arm of the chair, he looked round at the walls. From floor to ceiling, they were covered in artistic sketches.

Rendered in everything from colourful paint to monochrome charcoal, the images depicted an array of different objects in an angular, abstract form.

"Of course," he rubbed his pounding head.

This was Jean Metzinger's apartment.

Fragments of their late-night conversation now echoed back to him, and memories started slotting back into place.

Through a patchwork of language and sketched diagrams, they'd talked about cubism: the idea of capturing the essence of a subject from multiple angles and moments, but displaying each of the facets *simultaneously*.

Alec had the vague recollection of Jean insisting that the viewpoint of the artist *himself* was also a key component of the finished result. In terms of its multi-dimensional concept, it was easy to see that cubism had contributed in some way to the development of holography and eventually QRI.

Standing upright, he carefully walked over to the table at the side of the room. Littering its surface were sketches, and segments of his broken wristband.

More memories resurfaced.

He'd told Jean that the band was 'jewellery' from his American friends, and that he wouldn't be seeing them ever again. He recalled removing the rubidium-quartz crystal from the middle of the ruined timer dial.

His memories caught up with the present moment. On a stand at the rear of the table, clamped between an arrangement of lenses and a mirror, was the crystal; its multi-faceted shape reflecting and refracting the sunlight that played across its surface.

Glancing behind the crystal, he saw a hole in the wall, and remembered the camera obscura effect that Jean had talked about.

Focused by a lens arrangement, light from one room would pass through an aperture and into a dark room. The brightly lit scene would then appear as an image on the rear wall of the darkened space. The optical principles *had* been known and used in this era, but it had been Alec's drunken idea to insert the crystal into Jean's setup.

"What were you thinking?" he muttered to himself.

Leaving the table behind, he slowly opened the door and moved into the neighbouring room.

Inside the dark space, a diverging beam of light emerged from the hole, passed through the mote-filled air, and illuminated a circular patch of the opposite wall.

Filling the disc of light was a kaleidoscopic collage of superimposed, multi-sized rectangles; each one a projection of a facet within the rubidium-quartz crystal.

Moving toward the wall, he could see that the light was actually hitting a canvas. The rectangles held additional detail. The closer he got, the more angles he saw, but the structures on the canvas seemed random.

Glancing back, he saw the bright point where light beams were entering the dark room. Of course, he remembered, the beams were being flipped by the lenses and mirror: the projected image was upside down.

Facing the canvas, he carefully bent to one side, tilted his head, and let his mind make sense of the projection.

The sketched outlines of an image were more clearly discernible. Although no paint had yet been applied, a horrible suspicion began to cross his mind.

He felt his head beginning to swirl.

He slowly stood upright again and allowed the sensation to subside. Looking back through the open door, he saw the armchair that he'd been sitting in.

It was placed directly in the path of the lenses.

With his pulse still hammering in his head, he now recalled the moments before he'd passed out.

Jean had been in the dark room and had asked him to sit in the chair. Inhibitions lowered by the night's alcohol, Alec had played along and had even joked around with the pipe that had been next to the tobacco. Jean, however, hadn't come back into the room.

Now staring at the illuminated canvas, Alec knew why.

Metzinger had been busy starting his new cubist work, 'Man with a Pipe'.

The angular portrait was of him.

Or it would be, once it was finished.

Thoughts running riot, he walked back into the brightly lit room.

In their research before the retrostep, they'd found nothing about the exact method that Metzinger had used in the creation of the portrait. Judging by the other paintings on the walls, it seemed that Jean was fully capable of creating stunning works of cubism without the need for a camera obscura. It was therefore possible that the lens arrangement was simply one of the many experimental techniques that artists were exploring at the time.

Rubidium-quartz crystals, however, did *not* belong here.

He looked at the crystal that he'd introduced, and found his thoughts reeling again. It was possible that he'd just rewritten part of history.

Somewhere below, a door closed, and he heard the sound of footsteps climbing stairs.

He didn't know what effects his actions were having, but he suspected that he shouldn't leave fragments of future technology lying around in the past.

Swiftly returning to the table, he collected the pieces of broken wristband, and put them in his pocket: a process that took considerably longer with one hand.

He was just about to start freeing the crystal from the stand, when the apartment door squeaked open.

"Ah!" Jean bustled in through the door, and smiled, "Bonne après-midi!"

Alec quickly turned away from the crystal and rubbed at his head.

"Afternoon? Already?"

"Oui, yes," Jean handed him what looked like a bottle of tomato juice, "For your... er... hangman?"

"Hangover," Alec nodded and accepted it, "Merci."

Jean grinned and took off his coat.

"Much to do!" he pointed at the lenses, then opened the window shutters.

It didn't seem possible, but the room got brighter and the street noise got louder.

Alec winced at the unwanted sensory input, but the artist seemed to find it amusing. Gathering various sketches from around the room, Jean smiled and made pathetic-sounding groans before telling Alec to drink the whole bottle.

Drinking the tomato-red remedy, Alec wasn't sure if its purpose was to cure his hangover, or just distract him from it by burning his tastebuds. If nothing else, it *did* make him feel more alert.

Thinking of the canvas that was hanging inverted in the dark room, his mind began racing again.

Putting aside the disturbing temporal order of things, it seemed extremely likely that his arrival had triggered a chain of events that had brought the portrait into existence. But from this point on, he would be part of history. His actions, however small, would influence its direction.

Which left him with a conundrum.

Was his presence here causing the future to unfold in a different way? Or was he now inside some kind of looped predestination, where seemingly random events actually *generated* the future that he'd already experienced?

Given the unlikely way that the proto-portrait had emerged from the rubidium-quartz crystal, he was rapidly coming to one conclusion: the past, and his presence within it, had always been part of history.

He saw Jean bend down and pick up a pipe from the floor.

"The American smoker," he imitated a cough and grinned again.

Remembering the coughing fit he'd suffered after trying the pipe, Alec couldn't help smiling back. They had both laughed so loudly that it had caused a neighbour to bang on the wall. It had been the first time that he'd felt at home in the past.

Jean placed the pipe back on the side table and wiped his hands on an oily rag. At some point in the future, those hands would complete the portrait. Eighty-seven years from now, it would be aboard a moving box truck. The rest was predestined history.

Drinking from the bottle, Alec sat down in the armchair and contemplated the fact that the remainder of his life would be spent here in the past.

SHIFT

Standing in front of the curved viewing wall, Diane saw Theo take his seat on the viewing sofa. He checked the discreet wad of cotton wool in his injured ear, then seemed to change his mind about his seating position. He shuffled to the other end of the sofa, presumably so that he'd be able to hear whoever sat next to him. Diane knew that, in all likelihood, his perforated eardrum would take weeks to heal properly.

Petra sat down in the space that Theo had left behind, but Ryan remained standing and had his arms folded. It seemed obvious that Ryan still considered himself to be an outsider, but his slightly hunched shoulders told her something else. His concern for Alec was completely genuine. He wanted the scan to prove his theory.

She tried to keep her own hopes in check. Wanting something to be true, and observing the facts of a matter, were two different prospects. More often than not, the two things did not go hand in hand.

"Purging buffer," she tapped at her tablet and watched the projection wall lose its illumination.

The wall lit up again, but the view wasn't one of fizzling static. It was a list of error reports.

"What the hell?" Petra stood, "Seismic sensors are offline *again?"*

She saw Theo swiping at his phone screen.

"Diane," he hesitated, "There's..."

Clearly he was seeing something disturbing, but couldn't summarise it quickly enough.

"Send the link," she pointed at the wall.

A moment later, a news feed dominated the screen, and it quickly became apparent that there had been an aftershock. The dark, aerial shots of London made it difficult to tell which areas had been affected, but Diane could see that at least one building had collapsed.

"We felt the first quake," Petra's face was pale, "Why not this one?"

"Looks like it was much smaller," Ryan pointed at the text that was crawling along the bottom of the screen.

"Damn it," she squinted at the words, then hurriedly put on her glasses, "This was an hour ago."

"Just after I got back from..." Theo's voice trailed off, "That's why we missed it."

The report switched to a recap of the earlier quake. Daytime images of the Thames breach, and scrolling social media tags read 'Westminster Falls' and 'Drown-ing Street'.

She heard Petra groan.

"What?" Theo muted the sound.

"He's going to be back here like a shot, isn't he?"

"Who?" said Ryan.

"Who d'you think?" Petra rubbed at her shoulder, "That pain in the ass Burny Hemorrhoid. He'll want more queries running."

Diane looked at the scrolling political tags and the general notes of public dissent.

"Wherever he is, I think he's probably got his political work cut out for him. But let's not waste time. If we want to check Ryan's theory, we should get things running again as fast as possible."

Petra stood and dashed for the door, "I'll get the seismic sensors back online."

Seeing the vacant seat on the sofa, Diane spotted an opportunity to make Ryan feel like he belonged here.

"Ryan," she gestured to the space next to Theo, "Have a seat. It'll take Petra a while."

Ryan hesitated for a second and then sat down next to Theo. She couldn't help noticing that he was trying to sit in the exact spot that Petra had occupied, so that he didn't encroach on Theo's space.

"So," Ryan looked at her, "how do we check for elements?"

She could have answered him herself, but she thought it might be better if the two men started talking to each other. With a simple turn of her head, she redirected Ryan's question to Theo.

Theo shrugged.

"The same way as a standard query," he replied, "but we use a false colour overlay to identify specific electron states."

"Painting by numbers," Ryan nodded, "Got it. When do we start?"

Theo frowned at him, as though the answer should be obvious.

"Well, we have to wait, don't we?"

"I… don't get it," he said, "What do we have to wait for?"

Theo's frown persisted.

"Petra has to reset the seismic sensors," he shrugged again, "We can't run a query if there's been a shift to the datum."

"But…" Ryan seemed to struggle, "I'm not talking about querying the painting in the past. It's already in the landing net thing. It's right here in the present."

Diane held her tongue, knowing that Theo wouldn't be able to resist correcting Ryan's novice point of view.

"There is no 'present'," Theo turned to him, "For anything to be observable or measurable, anything at all, it's already part of the past."

"Even if you're looking at something that's *directly* in front of you?" Ryan countered.

Theo nodded.

"Case in point," he said, "the speed of light. The fastest thing in the universe still has a travel time. In the time it takes light to move from an object to your eye, the object you were looking at is already in the past."

Ryan gave a cautious nod, "Like the light from the stars."

Diane saw Theo pause slightly. He perhaps hadn't expected him to be so quick with the analogy.

"Exactly," he recovered, "Now consider the other end of the distance scale. The Planck length is the shortest distance we care to define, but light would *still* take time to travel through it."

"How long?"

"In seconds?" Theo seemed to contemplate how best to phrase it, "Picture the number five, then move it *forty-three* decimal places to the right. Tiny. It's that *minuscule* fraction of a microsecond that separates the future from the past. For all practical purposes, 'the present' is actually unaddressable. When you're dealing with quantum resonance imaging, the painting currently on the floor of Lab Two -"

"Is technically in the past," Ryan completed.

Theo's eyebrows relaxed, "Yeah."

Diane could see that Ryan was beginning to make sense of things.

"So… if the aftershock moved things even a fraction of an inch," he said, "then at a microscopic level, the imaging equipment would be *massively* out of registration. The scan would be a garbled mess."

Theo gave him an appraising nod, "Exactly. We have to wait for Petra's reset."

The two of them were quiet for a moment, then Diane saw Theo prod at his ear.

"We can't help Petra," he pushed himself up from the sofa, "but we could optimise the setup for scanning the portrait. It would be quicker with two people."

Ryan immediately stood.

"What can I do?"

As Theo quickly led the way out of her office, she could hear him talking to Ryan about the storage crates in Lab Two. Within a few seconds though, their voices had faded, and she was left alone.

Looking down at the now empty sofa, she felt her eyes quietly fill.

"I'm sorry," she whispered her apology.

But of course, Alec wasn't there to forgive her.

LIFE

A month after his first arrival, Alec felt like he was starting to settle into his new life.

Following the theft of his wallet, he'd been forced to convert another piece of his gold into francs. The bank had offered to open an account for him to store the money, but he'd politely refused; somehow it seemed wrong to inject his name into documents that would eventually become a historical record.

Generally, he was in good health, and his quantum-cauterised wrist hadn't shown any sign of infection; a small mercy given the medical limitations of the era. Occasionally, he suffered tingling, phantom sensations from the hand that was missing, but usually any discomfort was limited to a dull ache.

He was still resident in the same cheap hotel room, but that suited him very well: everyone there kept themselves to themselves. His room was quiet and had a loose floorboard: ideal for storing a separate bundle of cash and the remaining fragments of gold.

He'd continued to carry one of the small nuggets with him every day, in the vague hope that Theo may somehow be able to detect his element beacon and attempt a night-time rescue at the hotel. As time had gone on though, every night seemed to become quieter than the last.

His hopes of rescue had now all but left him. Within another month, he'd have to use the remaining gold just to stay alive. He'd then have to find employment: a task that would be made trickier by the fact that he didn't speak the language fluently.

His French teacher had always maintained that the best way to learn a language was to listen to it as often as possible, so that the brain started to make connections. With that in mind, he now spent his days in the lively parks and cafes.

The past was a different place.

Taking a deep breath from the fresh air, he leaned back in his cafe chair and ate the last morsel of his sandwich.

Food tasted better here, but he knew it wasn't just the quality of the ingredients. It was the whole lifestyle. People were still busy, but they made time to stop and watch the world go by; something that didn't happen in the world he'd left behind.

Overhead, the warm afternoon sun saturated the scene with clean, bright light and made every surface seem to shine with a positive glow. He smiled to himself. It was odd to think that a few billion photons of sunlight could so easily adjust his world view.

Across from the cafe, there was a public garden filled with people who were actually talking to each other. At the edge of a well-tended pond, a boy was carefully lowering a painted wooden sailboat into the water, under the attentive eye of crouching parents.

Alec couldn't help picturing the modern equivalent: all three family members would have been on their phones, taking photos of a completely unused water feature. The further thought occurred that, of course, none of them would even be out for a walk in the first place.

There was a splash, and he saw that the boy had fallen into the pond.

Instantly, Alec felt a quiet surge of anxiety and wondered if he should be trying to help, but nobody else seemed to be concerned at all.

Without fuss, the half-soaked boy got up, calmly righted his boat, and set it sailing again before stepping out of the pond. Although the father took off his coat and put it around the child, neither parent seemed particularly unsettled by the events. In fact, the boy's own laughter was making them smile.

Alec shook his head.

In the future, a similar water feature would probably have had a metal fence surrounding it, along with red signs warning people that the pond contained water.

Here in the past, people just got wet, and learnt from it.

He couldn't put his finger on what it was, but it seemed that the people here in the past were somehow more resilient. Arguably, life was more dangerous here, but people jumped into things with both feet.

Turning away from the pond, Alec picked up his newspaper and continued trying to read the columns of French text.

Sometimes the tenses in sentences still tripped him up, but he knew he must be getting better. For most of the articles, he understood the broad gist of what was being reported.

As he turned a page to a section on world news, a word caught his attention, but it vanished into the sea of surrounding French text. Although he hadn't had chance to read the word, he knew it had been familiar.

He straightened the page and began reading from the top. If this had been a modern web article, the dense blocks of text would have been broken up by pictures or videos, but in this time he'd have to read each and every word to find the one that had just escaped him.

While reading an article about iron and steel production, the word suddenly leapt out at him and triggered a flurry of memories: memories of an event that had yet to unfold for the people of this time.

Feeling an uncomfortable jab of conscience, he put the paper down.

The longer he lived here, he thought, the more this would happen. He would know about things that were preventable, but he wouldn't be able to change a thing. Anything he did to interfere would still result in the same history unfolding. He pictured Diane's meeting room whiteboard: the dots on the timeline would remain in place. Unchanged.

'Unobserved', the thought popped into his head.

Not for the first time, he pictured the last few seconds in the box truck. The tags on the painting. The panic. Theo's stunned expression. The moment of darkness.

He shook his head.

From a certain point of view, Theo would only arrive at the catcher mitt in over a hundred years' time. He could picture the elastic net catching Theo along with the imperfectly tagged contents of the box truck.

From a different perspective, and despite the fact that Metzinger's painting was still here in 1911, Theo and the others must already have the painting in their possession. For all he knew, they could be looking at the portrait right now, and still be trying to work out why Ryan's name wasn't signed on the sailboat sub-picture.

Ahead of him, it seemed that the family's pond trip had come to an end.

Holding his painted sailboat close to him, the boy stood still and let his mother wrap him up. As they walked away, only the tip of the sail was visible. The rest of the boat was occluded by the oversized coat.

Alec stopped and stared.

With gathering intensity, thoughts began fusing together in his mind.

The word in the newspaper. The pond scene. The painting that existed in two time periods. Occlusions. Changes that weren't changes.

He needed to act now.

Standing quickly, he almost toppled his chair. Catching it and setting it upright again, he struggled to pull money from his pocket. A few coins hit the ground, and he gave up trying to work out the cost of his lunch. Dropping a generous handful of change and a few notes on the table, he quickly thanked the bemused waiter and then ran.

PREP

Ryan looked at the centre of the elastic mesh net that covered the floor of Lab Two.

The large painting was exactly where he'd left it. Surrounding it were the objects that had been accidentally transported here from the box truck: a few modern art sculptures, and fragments of the wooden box that they'd been packaged in.

Using a large plastic storage crate, he worked with Theo to collect the debris from the floor.

After tidying away several splintered pieces of wood, he picked up one of the small golden sculptures. Although most of it was curved and globular, a small section was completely flat. He couldn't tell if the flat feature was because of some sort of artistic intent, or because a rounded chunk of gold had got sliced off as it had left the truck.

Either way, the gold in his hand was heavy.

"Must be worth a fortune," he shook his head, "I can see why Holroyd would want the tech so badly."

"Yeah," Theo picked up a wooden slat, "Things will definitely change once he gets back."

Ryan tossed the gold into the plastic crate and moved on. He dreaded to think how the Ministry of Defence might eventually use and abuse the technology.

After a minute or so, most of the pieces had been cleared, and only one item remained on the floor. It was covered by a piece of cloth.

He saw that Theo was just staring at it.

"It's OK," Ryan crouched down, "I'll do it."

"Thanks," he looked away.

Taking a steadying breath, Ryan slowly pulled back the cloth.

Fused with a length of sync cable was Alec's severed left hand. There was no blood or bone. There was just a clean-cut, cauterised oval where the hand simply ended.

He spread the small cloth out on the floor and took hold of the hand. The flesh compressed, and he felt the uncomfortable sensation of the bones shifting as he picked it up. Somehow it didn't seem heavy enough: as if life had a weight, and it was now missing.

He placed it onto the cloth, gathered the attached sync cable, and wrapped everything into a woefully small shroud.

The long-departed Alec no longer had a use for his lifeless hand, but none of them had discussed what should happen to it. The difficult conversation would probably only happen when they considered any memorial service but, for now, Ryan knew he just had to conceal the remains from Theo.

After he'd laid the small bundle in the plastic crate, he put the lid on and clipped it closed.

The sharp click bounced off the walls.

Although Theo didn't say anything, he looked at Ryan and gave him a nod of thanks. They carried the box to the far side of the room and lowered it back to the ground. After an uncomfortably quiet few seconds, Theo took a deep breath and set his eyes on the centre of the net.

"We should probably get started."

They returned to the painting that still lay flat on the floor, and took up positions at opposite ends. Crouching down, they slowly lifted it by its shortest sides. Moving carefully, and stepping sideways so that neither of them had to go backwards, they began to walk it clear of the net.

After a few steps, Ryan risked a look at the black-and-white canvas. From his point of view, the portrait appeared upside down.

For most paintings, if you viewed them the wrong way up, you could probably still guess what the image was about.

He couldn't say the same for this piece of art.

Even knowing that left was flipped right, the segmented nature of the image made it impossible for his brain to see it as a person. He didn't know if it was true for all cubist paintings, but in Metzinger's case, it seemed that the orientation definitely mattered.

They cleared the edge of the net.

"OK," said Theo, "Over there, on the bunny pad."

Ryan recognised the disc and the colloquial term from the test videos of the rabbit.

"If QRI can scan anywhere," he said, "Why do we need to put the canvas down on the pad to scan it?"

"Clarity," said Theo, "During an element scan, we can keep this pad in a very specific electromagnetic state. Because we *know* that state, we can subtract it from the QRI. It leaves us with a crystal-clear image of anything that's on the pad, and we don't get any interference from the ground."

"Seems a lot of effort."

"Of course it is," he said, "But don't forget, this equipment was originally built to handle *teleportation*. Clarity is important. The transmitter pad in Lab One is built the same way."

Ryan still hadn't seen Lab One or the transmitter pad, but

he could imagine someone standing with their feet firmly planted on its surface.

"Ah," he realised, "so that's how you isolate a person from the matter they're standing on. You mathematically remove the floor before transport."

Theo seemed to study him for a moment, then nodded.

"Very good."

Slowing their sideways walk to a halt, they carefully lowered the painting into place at the centre of the pad. As Ryan stepped clear of its surface, a thought occurred to him.

"In the old video," he said, "The rabbit arrived on this pad, so…"

"So why do we use the catcher mitt instead?" Theo preempted his question.

Ryan looked back at the net, "Yeah."

Theo pointed to the wide, open room.

"When anyone returns from a temporal trip," he said, "we're in control of their arrival coordinates."

"OK," said Ryan.

"But we're *not* in control of the surface that was directly under their feet when they left the past," he said, "To get around that, we set their return coordinates to be *above* ground. Any stray atoms that get pulled into the transport field, can only intersect with air."

"Instead of an expensive floor disc," Ryan understood.

"Exactly."

Ryan looked at the net and tried to picture it suspended in the middle of the massive space.

"But if you know the arrival point," he said, "why does the net have to be so big?"

"It was Alec's idea," Theo shrugged, "He says it gives us a large margin of error."

"I guess that makes sense," Ryan nodded.

A weak smile appeared on Theo's face.

"To be honest, I think Alec just liked the idea of a big flying trapeze net. He could be a bit of a showman."

Ryan hadn't known Alec for very long, but he suspected that Theo was right. Over the past few days, Alec had usually been the one who would look for opportunities to entertain.

THE MAGICIAN

Still struggling to get his breath back from the run, Alec looked up at the shuttered window and shouted above the noise of the street traffic.

"Jean!" he called up, "Hey, Jean!"

Most people ignored him, they were too preoccupied with their own lives to notice, but some people frowned as they walked past.

Alec smiled back and gave a casual shrug.

"Un bon ami," he bluffed, then turned away and resumed yelling at the top of his voice, "Jean!"

The shutters remained closed.

He pictured the artist's two rooms, the canvas, and the lens arrangement that had brought everything together.

When he'd first left Jean, he'd decided to leave the rubidium-quartz in his possession; if the crystal had brought the portrait into existence, then removing it from Metzinger's setup was probably the wrong course of action. He'd also reasoned that, without the rest of the wristband pieces, the crystal wasn't readily identifiable as a component of future technology. To the naked eye, it looked like an internally flawed, flat diamond. Should it somehow go missing, then any ripples would be minimal.

He yelled again and banged on Jean's door.

Weeks ago, he'd thought it best to give Metzinger the space to complete the canvas without external influence, so he'd kept his distance and hadn't pursued him.

Circumstances had now changed.

He stepped back from the door and looked up at the closed shutters. He was in the middle of calling out again, when he felt a punch on his arm. Turning to his left, he saw that Jean was standing next to him.

"Tais-toi!" he told Alec to shut up, but there was a look of mild amusement in his eyes.

Smiling, Alec pretended that Jean's punch had hurt him.

"Ow," he held up his left arm, "You punched my hand off."

"Idiot," Jean smirked and put his key in the front door, "Come."

Alec followed him inside and the two of them climbed the wooden stairs to the upper floor.

"Le portrait?" Alec asked, "C'est fini?"

Jean framed a small gap between his fingers.

"Presque fini," he smiled and opened the apartment door, "Nearly finished."

Alec walked in and saw that the furniture had been rearranged. The armchair stood in the corner of the room, covered with a pile of sketches. Standing closer to the light of the window was an easel.

He stopped in his tracks.

On the easel was the portrait he remembered: a collage of mismatched and interposed rectangles, each one depicting a different aspect of the suited man. An angular representation of Alec.

Depth and space echoed through the canvas. In some rectangles, he was facing forward, but in other sections he could see the side of his head. The cubist's concept of time was present within it too. The beer glass he'd drunk from was simultaneously visible as full and half empty. The pipe, which had only been in his mouth for a few humorous seconds, was at the centre of the image accompanied by a curl of smoke.

Alec now saw the folded arms.

When he'd first seen the Fortean Eye image, he'd assumed that the truncated shirt cuff of the man was a mere artistic arrangement. Now he saw the detail for what it was: a representation of his truncated hand, subtly hidden by a time-delayed view of his other arm.

"Jean…" he was lost for words.

The artist actually seemed worried, "You like?"

When Alec considered how things could have turned out, he knew there was only one way to answer.

"It's everything I hoped it would be," he smiled, "Bon."

"Bon," the artist nodded.

It was only now that Alec noticed a quirk.

He'd lost his *left* hand during the retrostep but, owing to the inverting effect of the mirror and lens arrangement, the man in the portrait had his *right* hand missing. In any case, it didn't matter. Mirrored or not, the portrait looked just like the one he remembered seeing in the Fortean Eye article.

Shaking his head in amazement, he recalled the words that Diane had read from the magazine.

"The Mysterious Metzinger," he waved his hand in front of the painting, "Jean, you're a magician."

There was a slight snort of derision.

"Monsieur, please, this is not magic."

Alec looked around at the lens arrangement on the table, and pointed at the pipe in the portrait.

"Smoke and mirrors, mon ami," he smiled, "You *are* a magician."

Standing in front of the easel, Jean explained that in order to protect the portrait from accidental smudges, he hadn't yet filled in the central tie area. Alec couldn't believe that he hadn't spotted the glaring absence. The man's tie was still canvas white, but it needed to be a dense black.

As Jean began preparing the oil paint and easel, Alec quickly reviewed his plan.

On his way here, he'd worked out what he needed to say to Diane and the others, but he hadn't known where to write it.

The unpainted area was the perfect place.

If it was done correctly, then his efficient message would go unobserved for the next one hundred and twelve years. From a certain perspective, Theo already had the painting. Given that the painting had been the focus of so much curiosity, Theo would definitely give it a thorough element scan.

Alec had been wondering how to physically get the message into place without Jean being aware of it, but looking at the missing right hand in the portrait, it gave him an idea. He could encode the short string of characters using a very simple cypher. Jean himself could paint the message for him, and be completely unaware of the future information that it contained. He just had to get the artist on board with the idea.

"Monsieur Magician," he said, "Can you perform one more trick?"

Jean put down the oil paint, "Quoi?"

Alec explained that he wanted to place some random letters and numbers into the tie area, and then paint over them so that they would be masked from view.

"Masquer les lettres?" Jean frowned at the peculiar request, "Why?"

"Cubism," Alec made up a reason, "The viewpoint of the artist is important. Only we will know they are there."

Jean walked away from the canvas, rubbing at his head. Clearly he was unsure about the idea. After a few seconds of slow pacing, he stopped and faced him.

"OK."

Alec couldn't help grinning, "Excellent!"

"But I ask a favour," he looked awkward.

"Sure."

Jean ran his hand over his neck, then walked over to the rubidium-quartz crystal that was still mounted in the lens arrangement.

Although no words were spoken, Alec understood. The artist's infatuation with the cubist properties of the crystal was obvious: it had provided a random spark of inspiration that he didn't want to lose.

Seeing the crystal again, Alec was reminded of home. Part of him wanted to reclaim the shiny object and keep it to himself, but he knew he had to let it go. He couldn't jeopardise his only chance to return to his previous life.

"Jean," he said, "It's yours."

It took them most of the day to source a small pot of iron filings, but the process of mixing them into the black paint was accomplished in minutes. Stroke by stroke, the 11 digits of the message were carefully added to the canvas in iron-rich paint.

Leaving the paint to dry, they talked into the night. Their two languages made conversation slow, but both of them had the time to spare.

When Jean had asked if there was any meaning to the random digits, Alec told him that it was in memory of his distant American friends. When Alec had asked him why he found cubism so captivating, Jean had told him that he considered cubism to be the artistic view of dimensional truth. Given what Alec knew about the painting's forthcoming temporal journey, he was inclined to agree.

Sometime around dawn, the digits were just dry enough to be painted over. Using plain black paint this time, Metzinger carefully began filling in the rest of the tie. Within an hour of sunrise, the numbers and letters were completely obscured, and the heady smell of the oil paint hung in the morning air.

As they stood back from the completed portrait, the message began its journey through one hundred and twelve years.

TEXT

While the others were making preparations to scan the portrait, Diane had taken the opportunity to get some fresher air. Standing in the open space of the Great Court, she tried to gather her thoughts.

Under normal circumstances, the loss of a prime minister and the simultaneous occurrence of an earthquake in London would have been enough to induce a sense of alarm in anyone. But, as she knew very well, these weren't normal circumstances: Downing Street had been surrounded by an occlusion at the same time. She was having to force herself to think more logically.

She took out her phone.

For several seconds, she stared at it and drummed her fingers against the dark screen.

"Focus," she told herself and stilled her fingers.

When Bernard had left this morning, he'd given her strict instructions not to power up the QRI equipment. Despite the day's events, he hadn't been in touch with her for over twelve hours. Which was becoming a source of concern.

Before he'd stormed out, she'd been watching him carefully. When he'd mentioned that he'd have to brief the

Ministry of Defence, he'd subconsciously adjusted his tie. Having known him a long time, she knew that this particular quirk emerged when he was mentally preparing for an imminent and uncomfortable meeting.

The more that time had gone on, the more she'd begun to suspect that talks had already happened and that wheels were in motion to rapidly bring Mort under military control.

Raising her phone again, she composed a short text message to Bernard.

'Trying to reach you. We're using the machine.'

She hoped the semi-impatient opener, and the more provocative close, would be enough to get him to respond quickly. She hit send and began walking in a wide circle around the empty court, her thoughts punishing her with every step.

She'd allowed Bernard's admonishment to influence her critical thinking. Like a petulant toddler, she'd decided to retaliate against the authority figure who'd caught her misbehaving. She'd stamped her foot and used the machine again as fast as she could. Because of her reckless lack of preparation, Alec was gone. Dead before he'd even been born.

By running numerous queries, and making the energy intensive retrostep itself, they'd already burned through forty percent of their reserve power. The preparations that were underway below her would exhaust even more energy, but she owed it to Alec to search for any last words he may have had.

By the time she'd circled back to the floor-inscribed Tennyson quote for the fifth time, she'd come to the conclusion that Bernard hadn't been provoked by her text message.

She could almost picture the coming military intervention: armed soldiers patrolling the halls of a British Museum that was no longer under her control.

She looked up at the interlocking triangles in the high

roof. Beyond the multi-faceted glass, the bright light of day had quietly become darkest night. All she could see was the distant reflection of the white museum floor, and her tiny figure standing in isolation at its centre.

Having already stamped her foot, she knew she had no choice. She had to move quickly before the punishment inevitably arrived.

PAINT BY NUMBERS

For most of her life, Petra had been used to reading things on a screen. Phones, tablets, monitors; the glare of the pixels, and the flash of the advertising had all fought for her attention in an ever-busier world.

Reading the paper copy of the Fortean Eye that was open on her lap, she felt no sense that the information was battling to be seen. Although the magazine didn't have the gravity of some great historical tome, there was a definite sense that the stories on its pages were embedded in the physical world. Somehow, the words were more real. It was almost as if the act of *holding* the information, and seeing the ink on the paper, made everything feel more solid and grounded.

Having seen the actual portrait in real life, the image printed in the Fortean Eye now connected with her more strongly than before.

Leaning back in the office sofa, she couldn't help drawing a deep breath.

"I know you told us before," she looked over at Ryan, "but... you *really* think the portrait is of Alec?"

At the far end of the sofa, next to Theo, Ryan nodded and gave a gentle shrug.

"It's the missing hand," he glanced at the magazine, "Once you see it, you can't unsee it."

She looked back at the image.

When Ryan had first outlined his theory, they'd talked about the left-right discrepancy of the portrait. The biological matter in Lab Two proved that Alec had lost his *left* hand, but the painted man had lost his right.

They'd discussed the idea that Ryan was projecting his personal hopes onto an artistic quirk of cubism, but he'd countered with something that had stuck in her mind: if every picture told a story, then it was remarkable that Metzinger had, by pure coincidence, depicted Alec's story.

She ran her hand over the matte paper.

If the man in the portrait *was* Alec, then he'd survived the accident and had lived out his entire life in the past.

"I hate to think of him growing old back there," she shook her head, "In France, of all places."

Diane walked into the room.

"I don't think tensions were as high back then," she said, "He may have lived a very good life. Hopefully he's left us a clue."

Petra sat upright, and she saw Theo cross his fingers.

Diane tapped at her tablet.

"Purging buffer."

There was a momentary pause, then the curved wall fizzed with black-and-white static.

Petra heard Theo breathe out in relief.

She could see Diane's fingers flying over the tablet screen.

"Query running," she said, "Adding geometric orbit."

A grainy image pulled itself from the noise: a high-perspective, moving view from the corner of Lab Two.

"Reframing," Diane continued to work.

The viewpoint swooped down to one side of the lab, and she saw a rough rectangle surrounded by the circular disc of the bunny pad.

"Is that...?" Ryan pointed, but then stayed quiet.

The viewpoint moved closer to the rectangle.

"Refocusing," Diane glanced between her tablet and the screen.

The broad pixels began to change: each single one becoming a cluster of hundreds. Now framing significantly less than the entirety of Lab Two, the scene took on higher definition.

"Subtracting bunny pad," Diane tapped.

The surrounding noise vanished, leaving behind a thin cuboid with crystal-sharp edges.

Petra had seen this sort of effect before, but she heard Ryan stifle a gasp.

"You weren't kidding," he stared, "I... wow..."

Diane tilted her head from side to side.

"Let's get a better look at you."

The viewpoint shifted again.

In a move that seemed like the lab floor was tilting into a vertical cliff face, the horizontal portrait pivoted upright and presented itself square-on to the screen.

"Theo," Diane handed him the tablet, "You're up."

Petra watched him swiftly reset the tablet interface and bring up his own set of tools.

"Running hydrogen calibration."

"Hydrogen?" said Ryan.

"Periodic table," Petra quickly answered, "Element number one."

The cuboid lit up with a speckled wash of red.

"OK," said Theo, "We've got a baseline."

He tapped at the tablet and the false colouring disappeared.

"Ryan, the paint was oil based, right?"

"Yep," Ryan stood.

"OK, so let's loop in carbon," he tapped, "and see if we can get a trace on hydrocarbons."

As Petra watched the plain cuboid, the static grey shape took on additional detail. In the areas that had the densest concentrations of paint, speckles of blue began fizzling into place. After a few seconds, Metzinger's black-and-white portrait had been re-rendered in speckled blue-and-white hydrocarbon traces.

She saw Ryan take a silent step toward the screen, his expression one of absolute wonder. For a moment, she just watched him. Sometimes it was easy to forget how miraculous the process actually was.

"Adjusting levels," said Theo.

The blue-toned display changed brightness and contrast several times before returning to its original state.

She saw Diane's expression change, as though something had just occurred to her.

"The tie…" Diane was frowning, "That area didn't change."

Petra glanced at the image in the magazine.

"It's the blackest area," she said, "so the contrast couldn't shift."

"Yeah," Theo nodded, "The paint there is so dense that nothing can…"

The room was instantly quiet.

To Petra, it felt like everyone had just had the same idea, but Ryan moved first. He dashed up to the screen and used both hands to frame the tie.

"Look," he spoke quickly, "I don't what I'm asking, but can we concentrate the query's, er, magnification and then -"

"Ahead of you," Theo cut in, his fingers jabbing swiftly at the tablet's interface, "What you told us before about pigments, you're still sure we should be searching for iron?"

"Yes," Ryan looked impatiently at the screen.

As the view zoomed in closer, Petra found herself on her feet and moving to the screen.

"If it doesn't work," she stood next to Ryan, "we'll scan for every other element."

"Whatever it takes," Diane joined them, "How are we doing, Theo?"

"Refocusing," he called out.

The black-and-white pixels blistered again and reformed into finer detail.

"OK that should be it," Theo lowered the tablet, "Scanning for iron."

Petra kept her eyes glued to the screen.

From one side of the curved wall to the other, the grey noise continued to fizzle. Then, as if arriving like the first drops of a rainstorm, orange speckles began to appear on the surface.

The orange dots now arrived faster, and started joining up with each other. Dots spread out to become lines.

Petra felt a chill of anticipation run through her. The lines were reaching out and becoming letters. And numbers. A long chain of digits.

As the orange tone stopped spreading, she felt her sense of wonder stall.

"What the hell is *that* supposed to mean?"

TRACKS

Alec watched the sunny countryside drifting along outside the window of the train carriage.

Fields of sheep, cows, and hay bales swept by, interrupted only by fleeting patches of faint white steam. The rhythmic clack of the track marked the passage of time, and each sway of the carriage induced a delayed sway to his head; a gentle cause and effect that lulled him into a comfortable daze.

He closed his eyes and let the sun warm him.

Months ago, when he'd resigned himself to living in the past, his interactions with people hadn't really affected him. In his mind, he'd found a certain comfort from knowing that his actions were, in a sense, predestined; the ripples of his presence wouldn't alter the way the world worked.

When the idea had struck him about sending a message to Diane and the others, his perspective had literally shifted overnight. As he'd watched Jean painting over the digits, he'd become hyperaware that his own actions *were* having an effect. Every conversation and interaction could influence his own fate.

Leaving Paris had therefore been hard. Not because of any emotional attachment, but because he'd had to leave his hotel.

The room had been basic, but it had been a safe haven for him: a place where he could lock out the outside world, and quieten his thoughts. Within its isolated confines, he hadn't needed to consciously evaluate the causal effects of his actions on the people of the past. Leaving Paris had meant letting go of that safe space. It had meant being more aware of everything he said and did.

He recalled the day he'd said goodbye to Jean.

It hadn't been a big farewell, just a simple 'Au revoir'. He'd delivered it as casually as if he'd see him again soon. In truth, Alec had known he'd never be seeing him again. He'd wanted to say thanks for their interesting time together, or to tell him to look after the portrait, but he'd done neither: it would have raised too many odd questions.

After narrowly missing a moving motorcar, the artist had crossed the street and had disappeared into the crowd.

A whistle blew.

He opened his eyes and saw that the countryside was becoming obscured by the rising blur of a grass bank. Another tunnel was approaching.

During his time in Paris, he'd been frugal with his limited wealth, and had steered away from buying possessions. The notable exception was the wooden hand that now occupied his left glove.

As the grass banks rose up to blot out the view, he checked that the leather straps were still secured to his forearm, and then protected the prosthetic with his right hand.

Thinking of the painting and the occluded digits it held, he took a deep breath. He now had to let history take its course and deliver the portrait to the back of a box truck.

Carrying him on straight tracks toward his own future, the carriage entered the dark tunnel in a rush of noise and steam.

DIGITS

In the hour following the discovery, Ryan had sat on the sofa and watched as the others had run dozens of scans on the portrait.

They'd looked at every square foot of the canvas, including the as yet unsigned picture-in-picture area. They'd scanned for every possible element, even the radioactive ones, but they'd found nothing else of note on the canvas.

All that persisted was an eleven-digit arrangement, formed from iron filings.

He thought back. The idea of scanning for iron had come to him shortly after he'd unwrapped the portrait in Lab Two.

The 'Ryan Pryce' signature had of course been absent from the large canvas, but he'd found himself mentally toggling the words on and off. In his imagination, the thin black lines of the signature were floating free and, like iron filings, they were being attracted to the magnet in the frame of the smaller signed painting.

The dark gritty iron filings, and the dark black shading in the cubist portrait had become connected in his mind. The presence of Alec's detached hand, and the one that was missing in the portrait, only consolidated the idea that a hidden message was a possibility.

"So were the markings *always* under the paint?" Theo was saying, "Or did Alec alter things when he put them there?"

"Possibly both," said Diane.

"What do you mean?" Petra pushed up her glasses.

"When we first queried the art gallery, we weren't looking for markings. Even if Alec *is* the one who ultimately created them, he didn't see the markings before he departed from the present day. It's self-consistent causality, just like every other temporal trip."

Ryan stared at the screen, hoping that something might occur to him, but the digits just twisted back and forth. The message that had remained hidden for over a century wasn't going to give up its meaning that easily.

Petra sighed and read out the numbers and letters.

"Twenty-one Ninety-one C in a tit," she forced a shallow laugh, "I mean, what is that? A massive bra size?"

He exhaled a short laugh, but it was mostly for her benefit; clearly she was as frustrated as he was with their lack of progress.

"If Alec *did* send this," said Diane, "then it should mean something to us personally."

The screen continued its static fizzling, and the highlighted digits kept blaring out their time-delayed message.

Ryan knew that QRI was nothing short of miraculous, but if Alec had created the message, then none of this technology would have been available to him. The world back then was analogue. The solution had to lie in something very simple.

Turning away from the glare of the screen, he picked up the Fortean Eye and looked at the printed image on the page.

Free from element-shader overlays, the cubist man sat with his arms folded and stared at him from a simpler time.

Again, the undeniable discrepancy confronted him: the arm in the foreground was missing the wrong hand.

Maybe the others had been right, he thought.

Like so many of the conspiracy theorists who had contacted the Fortean Eye over the years, perhaps he too had succumbed to finding patterns where none existed.

When he'd carried the canvas across the floor of Lab Two, the upside-down view had made the portrait look like a random collection of lines. Perhaps, like the inverted portrait, he'd been getting everything back to front.

The cubist man stared at him, arms folded.

No, not back to front, the realisation dawned.

"Left is right," he looked at the missing right hand.

"Huh?" Petra turned around, "What did you -"

"The portrait was a mirror image," he thought out loud.

Looking up, he double-checked the digits on the screen:

'2 1 9 1 c i n a t i t'

"We're supposed to read it right to left!" he laughed, "He's telling us where to find him!"

TITANIC1912

With the deck swaying beneath his feet, Alec looked out over the undulating water. There was no going back now, he thought. This was his only shot.

Months ago, when gold seekers had swarmed his original arrival site in Paris, the location had immediately become a very observed space. The chances of any temporal rescue occurring in that historical spot had dropped to zero because an occlusion spot wouldn't have been able to form.

For a long while, he'd given up hope and had assumed that he was here to stay. The inspiration to seek an *alternative* rescue spot had only come along about a month or so later.

While reading a newspaper, he'd seen that a Belfast shipyard was causing a local shortage of iron and steel. The resources were being completely absorbed by the construction of a new ship called RMS Titanic. He'd recalled the historic disaster, along with the sobering fact that he was the only one who knew it was coming.

He could still remember the lightning bolt zigzag of thoughts that had given him the inspiration.

The pond-soaked boy with a sailboat. The tip of its white sail peeking out from his father's coat, like an iceberg above water. The Titanic on the open sea. The sailing boat in the frame that he'd rescued from the monastery. The identical boat that would appear in Metzinger's portrait. The portrait that would end up in a box truck. The thought that, amid the chaos of a sinking ship, corners would go unobserved. The idea of sending a message via the portrait that was already in Theo's hands. The possibility of rescue.

The coastal wind blew at his hair, and he looked ahead.

Years ago, they'd all discussed the possibility of a traveller's yo-yo tether breaking in the middle of a retrostep.

They'd talked through the idea of querying the surrounding moments to locate the traveller, or performing a limited search for the elements in their wristband. But, as he himself had pointed out, the more time that elapsed after the tether loss, the wider the search area became.

In theory, they knew it was technically possible for another person to travel back carrying a rescue wristband. In practice though, they wouldn't be able to go to the original occlusion point because that moment was already occupied.

Even if the team found a *different* occlusion point nearby, either in time or in space, then they would have no way to notify the stranded team member. With no communication method, there would be no way to coordinate a common meeting point.

From his position in the past, he'd now given them a place to begin their search.

If he could find an unobserved place on the ship, then when the time came, any occlusion point would form around him: a side-effect of them searching for him. Unobserved by history, they'd be able to pinpoint and rescue him.

He hoped.

There may have been other recent disasters that held the possibility of an occlusion envelope, ones that had been closer to Paris, or had been closer in time, but his historical knowledge was far from encyclopedic. All that had stuck in his mind was a year and an old movie that he'd once seen.

He took one last look behind him.

The harbour at Cherbourg hadn't been deep enough to hold the 'unsinkable' ship, so he and the other passengers were being ferried across the water in a much smaller vessel.

Leaving the port behind, the SS Traffic headed out into deeper water. As it pitched up and down, ripples of laughter washed back and forth between the swaying passengers on the deck; each of them excited for the journey ahead.

He felt the breath in his chest becoming colder, but it wasn't in reaction to his own troubled thoughts. Turning away from land, he understood why. The temperature had dropped because something massive was absorbing any available heat from the air.

The Titanic's near-vertical wall of black steel towered above him.

NEWS

After closing down the QRI portrait scan, Diane cleared the curved wall and put it to use as a four-way display space that they all could share.

Using separate devices, the four of them were scouring websites, historical archives, and online exhibitions for any information about the Titanic's fateful journey.

Slowly, a scrapbook of verified information was being built up.

Diane displayed a 1912 shipping route map on her corner of the screen.

"Departs from Southampton, midday, April tenth," she said, "Arrives Cherbourg, just under seven hours later."

"You think he got aboard in France?" said Theo.

"It would make sense," she nodded, "If he'd been living there, it would have been the closest. It seems less likely that he'd have tried for Belfast or Southampton."

"Wait a sec," Petra stopped work and switched to a separate website, "I think I spotted something about that. Hold on…"

Diane saw Ryan shake his head.

"What?"

"Nothing," he said, "It's just the thought that Alec may show up in some of these photos. It's mind blowing."

Diane still remembered Alec's ginger hair and modern clothes, but of course any photos from the era were monochrome and featured people in very different fashion. She could already have seen Alec and not even realised it.

"OK," Petra called out, "Here we go. Two Cherbourg passenger manifests."

"Two?"

"Yep," she said, "Apparently the Titanic was too big to dock, so they used two smaller ships to ferry people. SS Nomadic and SS Traffic."

She separated the images and placed one on her screen.

"I'll take Nomadic," she flicked the other image over to Ryan, "and you can get stuck in Traffic."

"Funny," Ryan started zooming into the handwritten list, "Third-class passengers."

Diane returned to the shipping routes.

"The ship left Cherbourg just after eight p.m., and arrived in Queenstown the next day."

"What?" Theo frowned, "New Zealand? Doesn't seem right."

Diane typed at her tablet keyboard, and soon found the source of the confusion.

"OK," she said, "It's the older name for Cobh, Ireland… It then departed on April eleventh, around two p.m., and began the Atlantic crossing."

Diane switched information sources and saw the cold facts displayed before her. On April fourteenth, the Titanic collided with an iceberg, sank within three hours, and left 711 survivors.

When she highlighted the number for the others and told them the details, the room became a little quieter. For everyone, the facts were becoming less like historical documents, and more like recent news. From a certain perspective, she thought, this catastrophe was happening to real people at this very moment.

"Er..." Ryan hesitantly broke the silence and looked away from the documents he'd been studying.

"What's up?" Petra frowned.

"Just checking," he said, "Alec's surname is *Wright*, isn't it?"

Diane felt cold.

"What have you found?"

"It's..." he stopped and expanded a photo to fill the width of the screen.

Sandwiched between the other names on a handwritten list, was an entry that read 'Alec Dexter'.

"Dexter," Ryan pointed, "As in right-handed."

"As in Alec Wright," Petra stared.

Diane wasn't sure if she actually wanted it to be Alec, but she knew she had to look at things with a cooler logic than when they'd studied the Appleton gallery.

"It may not be him," she said, "We could be making the details fit into what we want to see."

"That's what I thought," said Ryan, "but check out the guy's occupation details."

He moved the image over, so that the neighbouring columns became visible. Amid the list of welders, carpenters and labourers, one profession looked distinctly out of place.

"Magician," Diane started laughing, which made the others start too.

In the next column, under specialist work skills, was the word 'Escapology'.

"He was there!" Ryan was beaming.

"This is perfect!" Petra's eyes were alive and she spoke quickly, "Now we query the hell out of the sinking."

Theo nodded.

"We narrow down the exact time and coordinates," he spoke with similar speed, "Then set up a wide area query -"

"We'd need to factor tidal drift," Petra cut in.

"Of course," Theo began pacing, "but it wouldn't be anywhere near as fast as a moving truck."

"But the ground level," Ryan mimed a wave with his hand, "It won't be constant."

"Good point," Petra nodded, "but once we get a motion lock -"

"You can do the er... inertial remap?" Ryan checked his terminology with Theo.

"Like the box truck," he nodded, "but with... well... wavier maths."

Ryan shook his head and looked back at the passenger manifest.

"I know he ended up in nineteen-twelve," he said, "but why *that* specific year?"

It was a question that had been bothering Diane.

"I still don't know," she admitted, "But when the tether's containment failed, there would have been severe quantum interference effects. Like the McCairn incident, the year and location might be random, or there could be variables that we're not even aware of yet."

While they were working to determine the ship's last documented position, she felt her phone vibrate. Taking it out of her pocket, she looked at the message on the screen.

'Message not delivered: out of network failure.'

Bernard hadn't been ignoring her text, she realised. The text had never reached his phone. These days, this sort of network report was exceptionally rare.

The news images of the aftershock slammed into her mind.

The collapsed buildings.

She'd been so preoccupied with studying the past, that she'd ignored the present.

"Damn it," she shook her head.

"Diane?" Theo looked at her, "What's wrong?"

Within a minute, they'd filled the wall with news channels.

She felt cold.

She'd seen the news earlier when the seismic sensor had tripped, but she hadn't been giving it her full attention: the dimly lit shots of partially collapsed buildings had just been a collage of unidentifiable ruins.

In the intervening time, it appeared that the news channels had been racing each other to neatly package the disaster. The channels had recreated the sequence of events using a combination of their own sources and people's amateur phone videos, then pumped it out for the story-hungry world to consume.

It seemed that the aftershock had been captured on phones almost by accident. Interior shots of shuddering rooms and falling shelves segued into exterior night shots of the stationary vehicles on Westminster Bridge. In a whip pan shot that found its target a little too late, a section of the bridge cracked and sent ornate sections of masonry tumbling into the Thames. Another phone tried to video the crumbling bridge, but instead succeeded in capturing the building in the background.

Diane watched as one side of London County Hall shrugged and slumped slightly at one end. More shaky phone videos recorded the confusion as government ministers were evacuated from the ground floor of the same building.

Smooth-moving aerial drone videos now entered the mix; their attention focusing back on the bridge where one end had begun to disintegrate.

As though unzipping down the middle, the bridge started dropping chunks of concrete into the Thames. Every few seconds, parked cars plunged backward into the growing split and were submerged under frothing water.

At ground level, a handheld phone was capturing the same falling cars, but then the frame shook. There was a confused blur of motion while the camera was quickly pointed in the opposite direction, and then the framing settled on its target.

Although the beginning of the collapse had been missed, the ending hadn't. Still crumbling and fracturing apart, the London County Hall building folded into a growing plume of dust.

The multiple aerial cameras that had been so intensely focused on the spectacle of the bridge now hastily turned their attention to the building collapse, but only succeeded in capturing the expanding dust cloud.

Over images of dust-covered people fleeing the area, left-scrolling text relayed the news that several government employees were still unaccounted for.

Bernard, the thought hit her.

She rapidly ran through her options.

She hadn't told the others about the text that she'd sent to Bernard, or the fact that it had failed to reach him. She knew there was only one way to confirm what had happened: she'd have to query the County Hall scene and check if he'd been one of the victims. The problem was that they'd already used almost half of their reserve power on element scans, historical queries, and the Appleton retrostep. Querying the scene of the collapse would deplete even more power, which meant that she'd have to make a decision.

Logically, there was only one choice she could make.

"We have to stop work on Alec."

"What? No," Theo's reply was instant, "We can't just *leave* him. He's stuck back there in the past."

"And that past isn't going anywhere," she said, "It will wait for us."

Theo opened his mouth to reply, but then closed it again.

"Why stop?" Petra frowned, "We're making progress."

Diane knew this was going to be difficult.

"We thought we'd researched Appleton and the truck scene, but we *still* missed critical details. We can't make the same mistake when we start looking at the Titanic. The analysis will *definitely* be more detailed, and that's before we even consider the complications of attempting any rescue. We can't, shouldn't, try to do all that on reserve power."

Theo threw his arms out.

"So we turn the damn power back on!" he said, "Let Holroyd get mad. What's he gonna do? Fire us? We're the only ones who know how all this works!"

"Maybe not," Diane told him.

"What?" Petra looked at her.

"With the Prime Minister gone, we don't know if Holroyd has discussed QRI with anyone else. Restoring main power could alert them to what we're doing. If the Ministry of Defence shows up, they could shut us down."

"How?" Petra gave a snort, "By sending some stiff in a suit with a strongly worded letter?"

"By sending soldiers."

"What?" Ryan actually took a step back.

"Look at what's happening two miles away," she pointed at the news, "Military helicopters are already assisting the relief effort. How hard do you think it would be to send armed troops to our front door? We know the *power* of this place. If they *physically* take over control, we won't even get the opportunity to save Alec. He'll just die in nineteen-twelve."

Theo pointed at the news.

"Why has *this* suddenly got you so worried?"

Diane pulled out her phone and showed them the failed message.

"I think Bernard was in the building when it collapsed."

"But we saw people being evacuated," said Ryan.

Petra pointed at the scrolling lines of news text.

"Some are still missing..." she exhaled and then rolled her eyes, "Damn it, Diane... You want to use the reserve power to query the collapse."

Diane nodded.

"If Bernard's still alive, we can tell the rescue crews exactly where to focus their effort. That's why we have to do this right now. We'll still have to run things on reserve power -"

"Because if Bernard *isn't* in the ruins," Ryan completed, "then he would know we're using main power and might show up with soldiers."

"But, if we saved his *life*," Petra nodded, "he'd owe us. He'd keep the MOD away long enough for us to get Alec."

Theo rubbed at his temples.

"What if we *can't* save Bernard?"

Diane knew that if that happened, then the facility here at the British Museum could rapidly pass out of her control. At that point, they would have nothing left to lose.

"If that happens,"she said, "we'll switch focus back to Alec. We'll keep running things on reserve for as long as possible, then turn the main power back on anyway. Whatever it takes to get him back."

In the minutes that followed, familiar viewpoints emerged from the black-and-white static on the screen.

Small fizzling cubes toppled from the strip of noise that made up Westminster Bridge and were then absorbed by the effervescent Thames.

Like a grey sandcastle slumping under its own weight, the grainy London County Hall shifted at one side and caused chaotic-moving pixels to evacuate themselves from the building.

Reviewing the event several times, it became apparent that one pixel wasn't with the others. It moved across the rooftop and stopped. After the partial collapse occurred, the pixel's position became stationary.

Each time they looked beyond this event, the same thing happened: a spherical mass of impenetrable static intersected the rooftop. A minute later, the grainy view always returned to show the sandcastle collapsing into the water.

THE SANDCASTLE

For a moment, Bernard thought he felt dizzy: his body had moved slightly from side to side, and yet his head was completely clear.

As the sensation hit him again, he realised that it wasn't him that was moving, but the rooftop itself. The lights in the surrounding streets flickered and a deep, low rumble pushed him off his feet. As the lights failed, he fell forward and threw out his hands.

Even as he was falling, he realised that the rooftop was dropping underneath him. Almost immediately though, he caught up with the concrete and landed hard. Rolling to a stop on his back, he felt the continuing vibration. In terror, he froze.

Ryan had watched the rooftop query being run. In grainy static close up, he'd seen a rotund man mop at his forehead with a handkerchief.

While he himself hadn't been so sure, the others had made the identification almost immediately. To them, it was as clear as day that the stature and mannerisms could only belong to Bernard Holroyd.

As the query had continued, Ryan had seen the flat rooftop shift from side to side, and then drop by a few feet. Unsurprisingly, Bernard had been knocked down by the first part of the aftershock, and in the moments that followed he'd remained deathly still.

When Petra had been concerned that Bernard may have suffered a cardiac arrest, Diane had reframed the query. Resembling the view of a pregnancy sonogram, pulsating grey pixels had confirmed that his heart was still beating. If nothing else, it had shown them that he was alive just before the occlusion event had obscured the rooftop.

After closing down the query, Diane and Theo had left the office talking in technical terms that were beyond him. Having nowhere else to go, he accompanied Petra back to the meeting room. As they walked, she leafed through the pages of the Fortean Eye.

"So, do you get a lot of readers?"

"A few thousand, maybe," he shrugged, "but since it moved online, it's got harder to reach new people."

She nodded and turned a page.

"I guess you're competing for screen space with every vaguely 'spooky' ampertag out there."

He couldn't help sighing.

"The fact is that most people haven't got the time to visit the site," he said, "When they're online, they want their entertainment pre-filtered and delivered to them. People don't have time to sit and read things that aren't in their bubble."

She continued flipping through the pages.

"People don't come across things randomly anymore."

"You know," he said, "there's probably some truth to that."

They entered the meeting room and she put the magazine

down next to the framed picture on the table. As before, the watery sunset scene and the 'Ryan Pryce' signature seemed to glare at him.

"We should probably element scan this one too," he thought aloud.

Petra raised an eyebrow.

"And see if there's anything 'spooky'?" she walked over to the busy whiteboard, "Help me clear space?"

Piece by piece, Ryan helped to take down the material that had been put up for his benefit a few days earlier. Gruesome images of the wrecked chimney, video stills of McCairn, and polar coordinate graphs all ended up in a pile on the table. Soon, all that remained on the whiteboard were marker pen lines: clusters of arrows, blocks of annotation, and dates that stemmed off a long horizontal line.

Looking at the timeline, he thought about what they'd just seen in the query.

"Do you think we save Bernard?" he asked.

For a moment, she stayed very quiet and still.

"I don't know," she said, "It's... problematic."

When he asked if she could explain, she walked back to the whiteboard and began wiping a space clear.

"Before a transport," she said, "the quantum tether entangles with the isotope tracer that's in the body tissue. Later, when the yo-yo returns, the tracer comes back with it."

"OK," Ryan nodded, "But the tracer degrades within a minute, doesn't it? How were we expecting to bring back *Alec* if his tracer's faded?"

Petra picked up a pen and started drawing a vertical red line down the board.

"Each tracer is tuned to the individual..." she drew a disc at the base of the red line, "It's like painting a yo-yo and its string with a unique colour. It's one of the ways we keep patterns separate from each other during transport. The idea was to go back and hit Alec with a booster of his own tracer..."

She filled the disc with red ink.

"... and then we pull the tether -"

"Alec comes back with it," he understood, "So why can't we do the same for Holroyd?"

Petra picked up a black pen and drew an empty circle.

"Holroyd doesn't have any tracer in his body."

"No, I mean why couldn't you just travel back and then hit him with a tracer?"

Petra shook her head, picked up a green pen, and began filling in the empty circle.

"That would be like painting the yo-yo," she then pointed above it, "but there's no string. No link back to the present."

"Ah," he said, "So the transmitter pad needs to have a record of the pattern before it can send stuff to the past, or pull it back."

Petra put the cap on the pen.

"Sort of," she said, "but..."

"But what?"

She wiped another section of the board and picked up a black pen.

"OK, here's our traveller," she drew a stick man, "and here's the transmitter pad..."

She drew a line underneath the man, but left a slight gap under his feet.

"...The pad *does* use the tracer to create a personal pattern, but it also defines a volume *around* the traveller, including any airspace."

She picked up the red pen again and drew a dotted box around the man.

"So..." Ryan looked at the dotted space, "it's like a safety buffer around the traveller?"

"Yep," she nodded, "The airspace goes with them."

Ryan pictured Theo and a large volume of air arriving inside the sealed box truck.

"That's what burst Theo's eardrum?"

With a loud exhale, she stared at the board, "How dumb was that? So avoidable…"

Looking at the stick man, Ryan felt a faint idea start to form.

"Can I borrow your pen?"

"Knock yourself out," she handed it to him.

After clearing a small area, he drew two stick figures that were standing on either side of a small rectangle.

"Theo… portrait… Alec," he tapped each in turn, "All three, in the truck."

"OK," Petra straightened her glasses.

He drew a dotted box around Theo.

"Time runs out and Theo returns…"

He rubbed out the figure on the left, leaving only the rectangle and the other stick man. Adding an extra line, he extended Alec's arm until it touched the portrait.

"Alec's isotope was still active…" Ryan drew a dotted line around the man, but made sure it followed the stick profile closely, "Now… the tags on Theo's side of the portrait stayed fixed in place…"

He added some dots to the left side of the rectangle.

"… but the tags on Alec's side got jolted loose."

"So this is where it started to go wrong," Petra nodded, "Theo thinks he saw the tags swing wide, and define a larger envelope."

"OK," Ryan added some dots on Alec's side of the rectangle, but positioned them further away.

Connecting the dots, Ryan drew a skewed box shape that contained the portrait, but it was clear that the area overlapped with Alec's extended arm.

"Alec's hand came back because it was inside the, er, *tagged* volume?"

Petra exhaled again, "Yeah."

Ryan's rough idea started to take shape.

"The tagged volume," he said, "You don't define it before you go back in time, do you?"

"No," she said, "The tags know where each other are. We just place them at the vertexes of a cuboid, and the corners define the volume."

"And when the yo-yo returns -"

"The contents of that volume joins the returning mass," she frowned, "Where are you going with this?"

He circled the area where the portrait box and the stick man's hand overlapped.

"Alec's hand was *alive* at the moment of transport," he said, "The tagged volume accurately brought back *organic* matter. The only reason it didn't survive was because Alec wasn't attached to it."

Petra stared at the diagram.

Ryan sketched another stick man, placed four dots around it, and connected them into a box that surrounded the figure.

"If we tagged a space around Bernard," he said, "could we bring him back?"

Pinned to the rumbling rooftop by sheer fear, Bernard looked up at the cloudy night sky; each hammering heartbeat pulsing pictures through his terrified mind.

He was going to die. Alone on a cold rooftop, his life was about to end. Crushed under concrete, or buried alive. Never found. A grey statistic in the footnotes of a book that nobody would read.

Over and over, the thoughts paralysed him.

Run, he told himself, but his body wouldn't comply.

Petra looked at the scrawls that covered the meeting room whiteboard.

The timeline that Diane had first sketched for Ryan was now interrupted by rubbed out patches; each one populated by stick men, dotted boxes, and yo-yo diagrams.

She watched Diane looking at the sketches as she considered the idea. After what seemed like many seconds of silence, Diane turned to Ryan.

"I can see what you were going for," she said, "And for what it's worth, it's a good theory."

"Thanks," he replied, "But…?"

Diane now turned away from Ryan and faced her.

"But, we both know that the tag volume technique hasn't been tested on live subjects."

Petra knew this was true: by the time they'd reached the testing of live subjects, they'd switched to using the isotope technique to enhance their targeting. The volume tags had been demoted to non-organic use. Even so, she wasn't about to give up on Ryan's idea.

"Diane," she said, "Compared to when we first started with the tags, our imaging method has got to be at least ten thousand times better by now, right?"

"That may well be, but -"

"And Theo," Petra continued, "Didn't you say you found a way to mathematically boost that by a factor of ten?"

"In theory, yes," he hesitantly tapped at his temples, "but it's untested and -"

Diane cut short the discussion by holding up a hand.

"All of this may be true, but we have no guarantee that Bernard would survive the trip. As you said, Theo, it's untested. We still need to look at options."

Theo shook his head at the yo-yo diagrams.

"Isotope tethering's out of the question. I can't think of anything else."

"Listen," Diane looked at them all, "I think we need to query the aftermath even further, find his position, and get it to the rescue crews."

Ryan's growing frustration was clear.

"We've already *seen* the occlusion," he said, "Isn't it obvious that we go back there to save him?"

"We may have seen the occlusion," said Diane, "but it doesn't mean that we bring him *back.*"

"So you've got another idea then?" Theo folded his arms.

Diane picked up a pen.

Using multiple strokes, she built up a thick-lined box around one of the stick figures.

"What if the purpose of us going back there was to take a strongbox," she pointed to the man, "We put Bernard inside it -"

"Oh come on!" Petra couldn't help herself, "You're not seriously suggesting that he should ride out the building collapse inside a box, and then wait to be dug up?"

Diane capped the pen.

"That's why I want to query the aftermath," she said, "If we find evidence of a protective box, then we'll have our answer."

Theo was vehemently shaking his head.

"But if we *find* a box, that would be future knowledge -"

"No it wouldn't," Diane quickly countered, "because I didn't *get* the idea from the future. I came up with it just now."

A sudden, loud slap came from the whiteboard.

Petra and the others turned to see that Ryan had banged his hand on the surface to get their attention.

"Bernard's dead or dying," he said, "And he's doing it *right now*. We don't have *time* to build a quake-proof box."

Bernard told himself to run, but his body wouldn't comply.

Suddenly he felt cold, as though a shiver was suspended in his spine. The rooftop shuddered underneath his back, and he felt a jolt.

This was it, he thought.

But then came the sound of running footsteps. And voices. Voices that were shouting at him.

He turned to see two figures, each wearing smog masks and dressed head to toe in black. Against the night sky, they were barely visible. One of them was busy doing something that he couldn't see, but the other was now crouched at his side and was shaking him.

"Move!" the man was hauling at his hand, "Get up!"

The more the man shouted, the more the cold rooftop seemed to hold onto him. He was aware of his own confused attempts to speak, but words weren't forming. A slap arrived at his cheek.

Stunned, he looked up at the man in the smog mask.

"Bernard!" the muffled voice was forceful, "Get up! We're getting you out of here!"

The confusion left him.

He could hear the wider world again.

"Forty-five seconds!" a woman's voice called out, "Come on!"

Still not knowing what was happening, he did as he'd been told. He grabbed the man's hand and, a few uncomfortable seconds later, he was on his feet. The man pushed him in the direction of the woman, and he found himself running.

Seemingly in the space of a few heartbeats, the distance to the woman disappeared. Like the man, her features were obscured by a dark pollution mask.

"Get in!" she shouted.

"What?"

"We don't have time for this!" she pointed, "Get in!"

He looked down and saw a dark grey box.

"You want me to…" he struggled.

"Do it!" the man shook him, "Thirty seconds!"

The ground shuddered.

Hoping that these military types knew what they were doing, he leaned on the man and manoeuvred his left leg over the rim of the box. As soon as his foot made contact with the floor of the box, he could feel that the interior was padded. Taking a deep breath, he transferred his weight onto it and lifted his other foot from the rooftop. As he moved his right leg over the rim, the man kept him upright and spoke to him.

"Lie down, and whatever happens…" he looked directly at him, "Do. Not. Move."

He complied as quickly as he could. The box was quite short, so he lay on his side and bent his knees. Outside the walls of the box, the woman was calling out that fifteen seconds remained.

"OK," the man briefly looked down at him, "This will get rough."

For a few seconds, all he could see was the rim of the box and the night sky beyond. The low-level rumbling continued, as did the urgent voices. Without warning, they lifted a dark rectangle above him and placed it on top of the box. Before he could say anything, he was in total darkness and he could hear things being clicked into place.

Raising his hands, he felt that the surface above him was as padded as the floor. As were the sides. The thought of being buried alive flashed into his mind again.

"Hey!" he called out.

Through the top of the box, he could just hear the man's muffled voice.

"Five seconds!" he said, "Bernard! Don't move!"

The floor underneath him shook.

The voices outside went quiet, and again he felt alone.

He could almost feel the walls of the box pressing in on him.

Taking a deep breath, he clamped his eyes shut. The darkness got darker and he felt a huge jolt. The roof of London County Hall must have given way, he thought, because he could feel the box was falling.

NET EFFECT

Ryan paced back and forth.

Regardless of how things turned out for Bernard, it was the others who were again risking their lives. Although everyone had agreed on the final course of action, he couldn't help feeling that *his* contribution to the discussion had sent things in this general direction.

Theo and Petra were now ten hours in the past, their return dependent on the wristbands that they were wearing.

If this had been a trip to a safe area, a broken tether wouldn't matter so much: they could just sit out their time, then walk back into the British Museum ten hours and one minute later.

But everyone knew this wasn't an 'ordinary' trip. Theo and Petra were arriving onto the rooftop of a building during an aftershock, while carrying luggage. Their safety wasn't guaranteed. As Diane had unhelpfully pointed out, *seeing* an occlusion isn't evidence of a successful outcome.

Tightly gripping the handle of his own luggage, he kept pacing.

A single tone rang out, and he immediately stood still.

There was a slight crackle and then Diane's voice echoed out from the loudspeaker.

"Precursor spike!"

He looked out across the vast space and trained his eye on the area that was just above the room-wide net.

During their preparations, Theo had told him about the differences in air density, the light diffraction, and the volumetric effects that would accompany the moment of their return. In every respect, it had been an understatement.

With a deep percussive thump, a pinpoint of light wrenched itself into a wide, glassy bubble. Which expanded. In the blink of an eye, the light-twisting sphere dominated the space above the net. Then, as though a heat distortion mirage was condensing into solid shapes, the bubble evaporated to leave matter suspended in the air.

Ryan actually saw the moment that gravity noticed the new arrivals.

As though some invisible platform had just been removed from under their feet, Theo and Petra fell. Between them, now also affected by gravity's pull, a large plastic crate began its fall.

All three hit the net.

The catcher mitt's pneumatic support rods recoiled, absorbing the momentum and lowering the net toward the ground.

With the defibrillator case still gripped tightly in his hand, Ryan ran out across the floor of Lab Two.

As the elastic material made contact with the ground, he saw Theo and Petra were struggling to stand up. They were alive though. A moment later, the outer part of the net had almost reached the flat floor. He hurdled the edge and ran on toward the box at the centre.

Theo and Petra were now on their feet and pulling off their face masks.

"Turn it over!" Theo was yelling.

As Ryan skidded to a halt and set down the case, he saw that the plastic crate had come to rest upside down. He quickly set the defibrillator charging and joined the others in pushing the heavy box onto one side. As soon as the lid was exposed, they snatched away the corner recall tags and hastily pulled at the securing clips.

Like a drawbridge dropping open, the lid fell and clattered to the floor of Lab Two.

Lying within the plastic crate, Bernard was on his back, knees bent. He wasn't moving.

Ryan turned and quickly crawled back over to the defibrillator case.

"Get him out!" he yelled to the others.

He could hear the plastic lid being scraped aside and the shuffling sounds of Bernard being pulled from the box, but he kept his eyes focused on the charging display. They'd just pulled a man out of time to save his life, but if he died now then the net effect would be the same.

As the double tone on the case sounded, Ryan heard the others go quiet.

He turned to see that they were kneeling next to the box. Petra's mouth was open in shock, but he could see that Theo was smiling.

Ryan crawled forward until he could see Bernard again.

The suited man was still lying on his back, but his eyes were now wide open, his expression one of utter confusion. As both Theo and Petra laughed out loud, Bernard quietly stammered a hesitant question.

"Can… I move now?"

DEBRIEF

Sitting on the sofa, with his hands clamped around a large mug of hot, sweet tea, Bernard looked at the videos on Diane's curved wall.

The news channels continued to replay the moment of the County Hall collapse. For the tenth time, he gripped the mug a little tighter as one side of the building disappeared into a cloud of debris. He'd been at that very spot just twenty minutes ago.

He shook his head and tried to correct his thinking. From the perspective of everyone else, this was an event that had happened ten hours ago. He'd been hooked out of history like a fish out of water.

The reports were now showing an enormous pile of rubble that ran into the banks of the Thames. Under harsh emergency lighting, people walked over the site wearing hard hats and blank expressions. The police car that he'd passed earlier was perched with its rear half hanging over the rushing river; a consequence of the Westminster Bridge collapse.

When he'd been on the roof, it was on the side that faced away from the bridge, so he'd observed none of the drama.

Presumably, the thought now occurred, this meant that his own personal drama had gone similarly unobserved by those who'd been below.

He looked at the other side of the curved wall.

Video stills, taken from a grainy QRI image, were marked with distance measurements and timings, and he could see his own static-filled silhouette lying on the roof. This would have been mere seconds before Theo and Petra had arrived wearing their face masks.

Again he shook his head, and looked at them all.

"And you're saying that you did all this on reserve power?"

There were quiet nods.

He drank from his warm mug and looked at the grainy man on the screen.

"All this time," he said, "I didn't even know you *had* reserve power."

"Again, Bernard," Diane bowed her head, "I owe you an apology for not -"

"You don't owe me," he cut in, "I, on the other hand, owe each of you my life."

He felt his phone vibrate, so he pulled it out of his pocket. The screen was cracked, probably from his initial fall, but he could see that a message had just arrived.

"Oh," he looked over at Diane, "It's from you."

"That was *hours* ago," she frowned, "I thought the message failed."

The text on the screen read *'Trying to reach you. We're using the machine.'*

He glanced at the image of the grainy man on the rooftop, and thought he understood. Diane had been trying to let him know that help was on the way. She'd been trying to tell him that they were going to use the machine to rescue him from his terminal predicament. Presumably the cell networks had been overwhelmed at the time and the message hadn't got through.

"I'm glad that you *did* reach me," he smiled at them all and held up his phone, "I'm also glad 'the machine' is speedier than the message service."

"Ah," Diane's frown now lifted, "of course."

"Of course, what?" said Ryan.

"The message delay," she said, "I think I know what happened."

Bernard nodded, "The disaster put too much strain on London's cell network."

"No," she smiled, "You've just jumped through ten hours. For those ten hours, as far as the network was concerned, your phone wasn't *anywhere* on the planet. You're only getting the message now because the device started existing again."

"Incredible," he looked over at Theo and Petra, "Then I'm doubly glad you both turned up when you did!"

Although they both smiled, he saw that Diane was idly tapping at the side of her phone. It looked like something was on her mind.

"Diane?"

She looked up at him.

"Bernard," she said, "I'm so sorry, but I only sent that message *after* County Hall had already fallen."

"After?"

"At the time," she said, "we were preoccupied with... something else."

Bernard tried to reframe the timings. They hadn't known that he was gone until much later.

"So, the message you sent me...?"

She took a deep breath.

"I was trying to get your attention," she said, "When the text failed to get to you..."

"That's when you feared the worst?" he understood and pointed at the screen, "That's when you started looking."

Slowly, he tried to wrap his head around the twisted chronology that was at work.

"So… the occlusion *caused* by my rescue," he rubbed at his head, "is the very thing that stopped your message from reaching me."

"I think so," she nodded.

He just stared in amazement.

"Wild," he laughed.

For some reason, the others found this funny. Unlike the previous time that they'd laughed in his presence, he knew they were all laughing *with* him.

Picturing the earlier scene, it now occurred to him that Alec wasn't actually here. Bernard realised that he'd been so wrapped up in his own affairs that he hadn't even noticed. He'd thanked everyone else for the rooftop rescue, but had completely failed to recognise any part that Alec may have played. Berating himself, he shook his head.

"I should've thanked Alec," he glanced around, "Where is he?"

Diane looked slightly awkward for a moment.

"There are details that I haven't told you."

"At this point," he smiled, "I'm not exactly surprised."

When he looked at the others, he could see that their smiles were fading. Something was wrong.

"What?"

Diane glanced at the others, before looking back at him.

"Bernard," she said, "We were faced with an impossible choice."

He now saw the looks being exchanged between Theo, Petra and Ryan.

"What happened?" he hardly dared to ask, "Where's Alec?"

There were more deflected glances before Diane continued.

"You won't like what I have to tell you, but I need you to

remember that, in the end, we made the choice to save *your* life."

It now dawned on him what she was implying.

Something had happened, and Alec's life *hadn't* been saved. The warm mug of tea in his hands now felt like an utterly obscene luxury. Ice-cold guilt began to spread through his veins.

"Diane," he put the mug on the floor, "What *happened?"*

They told him everything.

Over the course of an hour, they left out no detail.

The 'Minute Men' approach and the monastery painting. The Fortean Eye article, and Ryan's arrival. The cubist portrait, and the unexplainable picture-in-picture. The box truck accident, and Alec's century-old message. Finally, they told him of their suspicion that the Ministry of Defence may have been briefed about QRI.

Diane's decision to run his rooftop rescue on reserve power had been based on the premise that energy consumption could be monitored externally. Once more, her behaviour had demonstrated that she'd done everything in her power to keep QRI and its various offshoots hidden from the outside world. Thanks to her efforts, their covert London operation had remained exactly that.

When she asked him if he'd briefed anyone yet about QRI, he told her the truth: none of the desperate, hand-shaking sharks he'd met at County Hall could have been trusted with the knowledge.

"Beware allegiances that are forged in tragedy," he recalled his college history lectures, "Strength may be in numbers, but the treacherous will seek strength for themselves."

The room was quiet for a moment, then Diane looked at him.

"So, no-one knows?" she said, "You didn't contact the MOD?"

He shook his head, which seemed to trigger several sighs of relief.

"I was *sorely* tempted," he confessed, "I was furious. Yesterday, it could have gone either way."

"But?" said Petra.

He pictured the lapel pin in his pocket.

"But the actual events at Downing Street are still an unknown," he turned to Ryan, "It still resonates with me what you said about the quake not being a natural event. Until we know for certain what happened during that twelve-second blind spot, the knowledge of QRI stays with us."

Each of them quietly nodded.

"So, now what?" said Theo.

Bernard looked at Diane.

"Now, you need to put everything back on main power," he said, "We need to work out how to get our magician home."

THIRD CLASS

With his eyes closed, Alec lay on his bunk and placed his right hand against the wall of his sleeping berth.

He could feel the low-level vibration of the ship's massive engines and, from time to time, he could detect the feeble swell that the Atlantic was trying to exert on the Titanic's gargantuan hull. It was hard to imagine that, in a matter of days, this incredible feat of engineering would be undone by frozen water.

Before he'd set foot aboard the ship, he'd had unshakable faith that his friends would not only find him, but also rescue him from history.

Now, surrounded by very real metallic walls and a wide ocean, doubt was continuing to consume him. He was gambling his life on the idea that eleven digits would eventually be discovered under a layer of black paint. That, he thought, and the hope that the movie he'd once watched hadn't taken too much artistic licence with the facts.

His historical knowledge of the event was so poor that he wasn't even sure *when* the sinking had happened. All he knew for certain was that it had sunk as it had crossed the Atlantic. Which could be hours or days away.

If the movie was to be believed, the disaster had happened at night, so he was trying to sleep during the day. The intention was to reduce his interactions with other people, and at the same time ensure that he was fully alert when the final night arrived. But the light from the porthole and the muted voices on the other side of the wall were making it hard to sleep.

Opening his eyes, he took stock of his situation.

His last piece of gold was gone: traded for a third-class ticket and a handful of cash. Unlike all-inclusive cruises of the future, food and drink had to be bought. Whether it was hours or days, the money in his pockets had to last him to the end.

He sat up and looked around at the empty room.

The room was low down in the ship, which suited him very well. He knew he couldn't completely eliminate interaction with others, but here he could limit his contact. In a sense it reminded him of his old Paris hotel room: a bubble that isolated him from the real world.

He got up and walked to the brass-rimmed porthole.

Looking at the dappled sunset reflecting off the honey-coloured waves, it was easy to believe that everyone aboard was sailing toward a future filled with hope and opportunity.

He felt his left hand twitch, or rather he felt the misfire of the damaged nerves in his wrist. Pressing at the spot, he checked that the gloved prosthetic was still securely strapped to his wrist and forearm.

To begin with, he'd started wearing it so that people wouldn't stare at his truncated limb. When he wore the matching *right-hand* glove, the left hand looked normal and people didn't even perceive a disability.

Over time though, he'd begun planning his exit from history, and the false hand had become less passive in its function. The adjustments he'd made to the hollow prosthesis had made him very protective of it.

He turned away from the sunset. It was time to prepare for night again.

Raising his gloved left hand, he opened the flap of cloth that covered the palm, and inspected the components in the exposed surface.

When he'd first arrived on the dark hill outside Paris, his compact flashlight had been attached to his jacket. But after several nights of painstaking work in his quiet hotel room, the anachronistic LED bulb casing and its modern power supply had been repurposed. Both now fitted snugly inside his hollow prosthetic hand. Hopefully, when the moment came, he'd be able to generate a signal that could be spotted in a QRI scan.

He knew that light itself wouldn't register, but this wasn't a problem: chemical reactions would. The merchant he'd bought iron filings from had been happy to sell him gunpowder and magnesium wire. In the future, this same request would have put him on a government watch list.

These were simpler times.

He double-checked the space where the LED bulb had once been. The magnesium wire was attached to the two exposed terminals. At the appropriate time, he'd close the switch and the power would short-circuit through the wire. According to his calculations, the build-up of heat would act as a catalyst to ignite the small gunpowder pot that was nestled next to the bulb casing. There wouldn't be enough pressure to cause an explosion, but it would certainly burn. When that happened, it would give off a distinctive energy signature that the others would easily be able to spot. When they queried the moment, they'd also be able to identify his LED flashlight components.

Recalling the old movie, he pictured himself standing on the sinking forward deck. In contrast to the movie though, he would be whirling a burning hand around on the end of its long leather straps: a glowing circle that would pinpoint his exact location to Diane and the others.

A loud bang rattled the door at the side of the room. It was immediately followed by shouts and curses.

This must be it.

Quickly closing the glove flap, he gave one last glance at the room, then turned away. As he yanked the door open, a large luggage trunk outside banged against the door frame and thumped to the floor of the corridor. At the same time, the man who had been grappling with it fell back and ended up on the floor.

"Did we hit something?" Alec's nerves were alight.

The man held up his hand in apology.

"Sorry about that, fella," his relaxed Irish tones came back, "My mistake."

"What?" Alec checked the empty corridor.

The man picked up his flat cap and pulled it back into place over his curly hair. Still sitting on the floor, he pointed at Alec's room.

"I didn't mean to go barging your door," he said, "My trunk got away from me there."

Alec looked up and down the narrow corridor. It was still quiet. The bang had just been the man's bulky luggage hitting his door. Looking back into his room, he saw that there was still light coming through the porthole. In his confusion, he'd overlooked that it wasn't yet night. The iceberg hadn't hit yet.

The man got up from the floor, dusted himself down and turned to Alec.

"You alright there?"

Alec let out a sigh of relief, "Yes, sorry."

"It was my stupid fault," he laughed, "You wouldn't mind giving me a hand, would you?"

"Hand?" Alec frowned.

The man returned the frown.

"With my luggage," he pointed at the trunk.

Alec didn't know how to reply. He was supposed to be maintaining a distance from people, but it would draw more attention if he refused. The fleeting thought *did* occur to him that, aboard a sinking ship, he may have to depend on the goodwill of others. In the days ahead, he himself may need a favour.

As Alec nodded and smiled, the man thrust out his hand.

"John Coffey."

"Alec," he shook John's hand, "Alec Dexter."

"Good to meet you, Alec," he nodded his head at the handle on the trunk, "Grab that end."

As John raised his end of the trunk, Alec reached down with both hands but lifted the handle using only his right.

"So, John," he said, "Which way?"

"Aft," he began walking backwards along the corridor, "So what's a finely dressed man like you doing in Third?"

Alec hadn't considered himself to be overdressed, certainly not in comparison to the First Class travellers he'd seen, but apparently his status looked higher than John's.

"Saving money," he replied truthfully, "Hoping for a new start."

"Ah," John nodded, "You must've boarded at Southampton, am I right?"

"Is it that obvious?" Alec deflected the question, "Did you board when we left Ireland?"

"How on Earth did you guess that?" he mocked surprise then grinned, "Been a Cobh man all my life, but when me and the missus heard about the American life, we set our hearts on it."

Alec looked down at the trunk. A life's possessions, he thought, whittled down to a few carefully chosen items that would end up on the floor of the Atlantic. He didn't know if the man would become one of the survivors, but everything suddenly felt acutely real again. The man and his wife would arrive on American soil with nothing, or they would not arrive at all.

As John steered the trunk around a corner, Alec steered their conversation away from discussions about future hopes and intentions.

"So," he said, "The biggest ship ever built."

"To be sure," John nodded, "A modern wonder. Reciprocating *and* turbine engines."

"Two engines?" Alec was genuinely interested.

"And *three* propellers," John walked backwards again, "She's a grand ship, but…"

Alec wondered if John was having misgivings.

"But what?"

"But there's days down there in the boiler room when the fires feel hotter than the blazes of damnation."

"What?" said Alec, "You work aboard?"

"For my sins," he nodded, "But to be honest, if it weren't for the White Star subsidy, me and the missus would've been saving for another year. And by then, there'd have been another mouth to feed."

The trunk hadn't changed weight, but it suddenly felt heavy in Alec's hand. In all likelihood John, his wife, and their unborn child wouldn't survive the trip. Unable to mention anything of what he knew, Alec responded the only way he could.

"Congratulations," he produced a smile.

"Ah, you're very kind," John beamed and his eyes shone brightly, "I tell you what. Help me get this thing to the lower cargo hold, and I'll buy us a drink."

Alec pictured the sunset porthole.

They were still several hours away from night. Even then, there was no guarantee that tonight was the night that it had all happened. There was still time, and it seemed wrong to reject the man's offer of gratitude.

DESTINY

Ryan found himself walking into the meeting room.

The table held several rabbit cages and hundreds of Fortean Eye magazines. At the other side of the room was the antique geography globe, except the spherical surface was shimmering like a mirage next to the whiteboard.

Long, marker-pen timelines were broken in multiple places by patches of stick men and colourful yo-yos. Diagrams stretched off the whiteboard and onto the walls where they became patches of ragged plasterboard holes, each one linked by a continuous marker-pen timeline. Moving along the line, he saw the rough holes were as tall as a door frame, and he could see into other rooms.

Dressed in black from head to toe, Petra stepped through an open hole and into a neighbouring room. Through the next ragged doorway on the timeline, he could see the same room, but it was now completely empty.

Much further along, where another doorway should have been, was the cubist portrait. In the upper left corner was a signature that flashed on and off in time with a quiet warning beep. The portrait swung open like a door, then Petra stepped through the doorway and handed him a flashing red yo-yo. As the room beyond the doorway got closer, the yo-yo flashed brighter and louder.

Composed out of cubist lines, wooden slats, and iron rods, an impaled man suddenly appeared and reached for him, screaming in agony.

Ryan snapped awake and heard his phone alarm continue to beep.

Picking up the phone, he muted the alarm and checked the time on the screen. Apparently, he'd slept for eight solid hours.

He remembered returning to his guest bedroom, but after his head had hit the pillow, exhaustion had switched off his consciousness. Almost like Bernard, he'd instantly skipped over a period of time to arrive in the present day.

Rubbing at his eyes, he swung himself out of the bed and headed to the small bathroom. Today, work would begin in earnest to query the Titanic from stem to stern, so he knew he'd need to be alert.

Standing next to the sink, he set the tap running and splashed handfuls of cold water over his face. For good measure, he ran a wet hand across the back of his neck. The jolt wasn't as good as the caffeine shot he would have had at home, but it would have to do for now.

He dried his face and put on fresh clothes.

Thinking of his home comforts, he found it difficult to imagine returning to his old house, his old life. It had been four days since Petra had met him at the cafe, and in that time the world had changed irrevocably. People were now donning black clothing and stepping through holes into the past. They were also stepping into his mind; he pictured Petra in the dream.

He walked to the door and pulled it open. Immediately, he swore in shock: she was standing just outside.

"And a bloody good morning to you too," she replied.

"Sorry," he felt flustered, "I wasn't expecting anyone to be -"

"I've been standing here all night," she said.

"What?"

"I'm just messing with you," she smiled, "Theo's found something."

"He's started the Titanic query already?"

"No," she began walking away, "but he's completed the scan of the smaller framed picture."

Ryan closed the door behind him and caught up with her.

"And?"

"With the exception of the signature," she said, "Every single brush stroke is an exact match for the upper left corner of the original painting. It's the same matter, but from different times."

It confirmed what they'd all suspected.

"Did he scan the signature itself?"

Petra nodded.

"The paint contained a high concentration of metallic particles."

"Iron filings?" he guessed.

"*Neodymium* filings," she said, "Theo thinks they might have been shaved off the metal plate. That's why we didn't see the signature when we element-queried the monastery scene."

"It blended in with the plate," Ryan found himself nodding.

There was no longer any doubt, the signature had been purposefully designed for them to find.

When they reached Diane's office, he saw that the others were already there.

Theo looked up from his tablet.

"Morning," he said, "Did Petra tell you?"

Ryan nodded, "The perfect match."

"At some point in our future," said Diane, "the sailboat picture *will* be removed from the portrait."

"Destiny," Bernard shook his head, "The unseen path that conducts all travellers."

"Let's not get ahead of ourselves," said Diane, "There's nothing to suggest a timeframe for that particular future event."

"Yeah," Petra half laughed, "Lock the damn portrait in the vault for a hundred years. Make it somebody else's problem."

"I'm sorry," Ryan now picked up on something she'd said, "The vault?"

"It's just a name," said Bernard, "At any one time, the British Museum is home to many thousands of historical pieces, but not all of them are on public display. Some are awaiting categorisation or academic study."

Ryan found himself imagining a scene from a movie he'd once seen, where a wooden crate was stored alongside thousands of others in a warehouse.

"And how many, er, 'historically rescued' items have you put down there?"

"A few dozen perhaps," Diane shrugged then tapped at her tablet, "We should really get started. Clearing buffer."

Technically, operating on main power was no different to operating on reserve, but Ryan could feel that everyone's stress levels were lower. On full power, they would be able to keep queries running continuously and view things from multiple angles without having to worry about how much energy they were burning through.

A wide area scan appeared on the screen: a four-funnelled ship on a fizzling plane of noise.

In a room that had become suddenly silent, Ryan just stared.

A live view of the past; he recalled what Diane had once said. This was now. It just wasn't his.

"Where the devil do we start?" Bernard's voice was small.

Ryan watched the ship glide on through the calm sea.

Alec hadn't relayed an exact time.

Between the Titanic hitting the iceberg and its sinking, there was a window of two hours and forty minutes. Any occlusion would only occupy one *minute* of that time, and it could appear anywhere within the confines of the ship.

"Twenty-four hours divided by two hours forty," Theo was running through a calculation, "That's nine."

"Nine what?" said Bernard.

"Nine possible locations that can be thoroughly queried per day."

"We may not be that lucky," said Petra, "The ship's enormous. It could take *ninety* queries to find him."

"Ten days?" Bernard shook his head, "Diane, I can't be here for that long. People are going to start asking questions."

Focusing on the tiny pixels that fluctuated on and off, Ryan pictured one of them being Alec: for him this was the present day, and one task would be occupying his mind. Looking at things from this perspective, an obvious thought emerged.

"Alec *wants* to be found," he said, "He knows we're looking for him, so he'll be working on the problem at his end too."

Petra was nodding.

"He'll be trying to make it easier for us."

"If he was trying to make it easy," Bernard frowned, "why did he pick the Titanic?"

"It was a chaotic event where the location itself was lost to history," Diane shrugged, "Ideal circumstances for concealing an occlusion point."

"Yes," said Bernard, "but wouldn't there have been easier places though?"

"Undoubtedly," Diane nodded, "but he doesn't have your history qualifications. We're lucky that he remembered this event at all."

Petra pointed at the screen.

"I think Ryan's right," she said, "Alec knows that we'll be standing here, and doing this. He knows that we'll be starting with this exact view."

Ryan looked over at the screen.

Jutting up from the surface of the sea, an icy-white tooth was gliding toward the ship.

TURNING POINT

It had taken at least half an hour to get the trunk down two flights of stairs and into the busy cargo hold. The room had been stacked with boxes of wildly varying proportions, and a fair amount of trunks, suitcases and items of furniture.

When he'd asked John if any of it belonged to him, he'd laughed and said that the only thing he'd be carrying for the rest of the trip was the shirt on his back, and beer in his belly.

Leading the way back up through the decks, John ably demonstrated that he knew the ship like the back of his hand. Although they hadn't retraced their steps, Alec had eventually recognised a white-painted metallic stairwell. After a swift climb, they'd returned to the more familiar territory of the third class general room at the rear of the ship, where John had made good on his intention to carry beer. True to his word, John had also presented him with a pint and thanked him for his help.

There was something simultaneously uplifting and depressing about the lively music and dancing that filled the room. The joyous celebration of new beginnings and life, superimposed with his own future knowledge, made every smile a tragic one.

He sipped at his half-empty second pint of the evening.

Here, amid the laughter, he wanted to dull the thoughts of the approaching disaster, but he'd learnt his lesson from his time in Paris: he absolutely needed a clear head at night.

John nodded at the glass in Alec's hand.

"I've never met a fella so cautious with his drink," he shook his head, "Is that why you wear the gloves?"

"What?"

"D'you think it'll stop the booze from soaking into your skin?" he laughed.

Alec laughed along with him and repeated the lie that he'd told so often.

"I get cold easily," he shrugged, "Poor circulation."

A few feet away, a cheer went up that drowned out the music.

He turned to see a man on one knee looking up at a woman with flushed red cheeks. As she gave a nod, hand drums and fiddles struck up and were then swiftly joined by enthusiastic cheers and floor stomping.

Alec drank a large mouthful from his glass.

Since setting foot aboard, he'd considered his status to be that of a visitor. Now, surrounded by the real lives of others, the notion that he might summon a portal to extract him from certain death seemed like something from a fever dream.

Although he kept his wits sharp, it wasn't long before he found himself tapping his hand along with the rhythmic pulse of the music.

During the evening, talking with John and a few others, he worked out that the Titanic wasn't scheduled to reach New York for another three days. In his mind, this equated to a halfway point. The earlier romantic marriage proposal seemed to make more sense in this context: they were celebrating a turning point. When the collection hat reached him, he was generous with his coins. They would probably never get to spend them but, in this present moment, they would be happy.

As the couple danced, John faced him with slightly glassy eyes.

"Mr. Dexter," he raised his glass, "To the one-way trip."

For a moment, Alec was unsure how to react to John's uncanny summary of the Titanic's fateful journey.

"One way?" he managed.

John frowned at him.

"It cost me everything to get here," he shrugged, "Can't exactly go back to where I came from."

Alec breathed a sigh of relief: John had meant his own personal journey from Ireland. Once more, Alec hid his knowledge and raised his glass.

"To a brave new world," he said.

John nodded and drained the remainder of his beer.

"I've been thinking," he said, "You say you've got poor circulation."

Alec discreetly protected his left hand.

"Yeah?"

"And I think it's fair to say that you're the sort of fella who likes his engineering."

Alec knew they'd talked about the ship's impressive statistics several times over the past few hours.

"What's on your mind?"

John leaned a little closer.

"What would you say to a peek at the warm engine room?"

Alec hesitated, but John continued.

"We'd only be able to stay for a minute," he said, "but if I can't use my humble stoker's privileges to bring a little joy, then what's it all about?"

The journey through the ship proved a little more indirect and, despite John's access privileges, it involved going under and around certain second class areas. Eventually they reached a corridor that, to Alec's eyes at least, looked as long as the ship.

Unlike the twists and turns they'd been taking so far, the long 'Scotland Road' corridor carried them directly to the centre of the ship. Turning off the straight route, John lead the way down a short set of steps and pushed a shiny brass key into the lock of a plain white door.

John pulled open the door and stepped inside.

Alec followed him and he felt the air get warmer. With every step along the short corridor, it got warmer, and louder. The vibrations he'd once felt in his cabin wall were present here, but magnified. Almost like a beating heart, pulses throbbed at the floor. It no longer felt like a corridor in a ship, but an artery of some immense living beast.

As John opened a small door, the room beyond exhaled a hot breath of air, and the heartbeat thundered free.

Grinning at the sheer power, Alec stepped down onto an elevated metal walkway. Through the grating under his feet, he could see a line of gargantuan pistons hammering up and down like muscular legs driving oversized bicycle pedals.

Dwarfed by the reciprocating metal shafts, the tiny people below were busily tending to steam gauges and levers, completely oblivious to the fact that they were being watched from above.

The noise was so great that he only just heard John calling to him from a few yards away.

"Over here," he beckoned.

Still smiling at the heat and sensory saturation, Alec walked over and crouched down on the walkway next to John.

"You were right," he said, "It's really warm."

John nodded, "Cos we're right next to the boiler rooms."

Alec just marvelled at the sight.

"Thank you," he said.

John smiled and pointed to the far end of the room.

"The engine crankshaft," he shuffled back to give him a better view, "It's going about seventy-five revs a minute."

Alec peered down in wonder.

The two-storey-high pistons were moving with a speed that seemed completely at odds with their massive size. From this height, it was almost like he was watching a scale model. Somewhere above them, he thought, the funnels would be breathing out steam in response to this vigorous exercise.

"Amazing," he knelt down to take it all in.

"You like your mechanical marvels, don't you?" said John.

Alec stared at the bundles of nerve-like pipes.

"Yeah."

"So I'm sorry I've got to take it off you."

Alec looked back and saw that John was pointing a revolver at him. He struggled to find words, but John had no such difficulty.

"Your precious hand," he said, "Take it off."

"John?" he raised his hands, "What the hell -"

"Hell?" John's voice cut through the warm air, "You want to talk about hell? I've seen what's inside that glove of yours. That thing'll unleash hell on us all! Take it off!"

Alec was sure that the flap on the glove had remained closed since leaving his room, but if John had glimpsed the futuristic LED flashlight components, then it could have unnerved him. Motivated by either superstition or fear, John was now acting to stop something that he believed was dangerous.

"John," he raised his hands in further submission and tried his best to speak calmly, "I can't explain it to you, but I *need* this. You're in no danger."

"Oh really?" John coughed a shallow laugh and gripped the gun more firmly.

"Look," Alec froze, "Take my money. It's in my right pocket, just -"

"I don't want your money!" John cut across him and glanced at Alec's prosthetic hand, "Man shall not reshape what the divine has cast."

To Alec, it sounded like he was quoting a theological warning about imitating the creations of a deity. The words and the aimed weapon were not a good combination.

"Please," he tried.

"Alec," John shook his head, "you're a decent fella... but that *thing* has got to go. Take it off."

Alec looked down at the engine room below.

"Someone's gonna notice that gun. They'll send people to stop -"

"Do you not *understand?"* John stood his ground, "We're completely isolated. Nobody can see or hear us. There are no damn witnesses here."

Alec raced through his limited options. If he gave up his magnesium flare, he'd lose his only beacon to the future. But if he didn't hand it over, the odds of getting rescued would drop to a deathly zero.

"Move slowly," John's eyes were alert.

Doing as he was told, Alec pulled back his left sleeve to get to the leather straps on his forearm.

"So what's your plan?" he unfastened the first buckle, "Take my wooden hand to your captain?"

"We both know it's more than that," the gun didn't waver, "but thanks for the advice."

Alec's thoughts raced.

Future technology was about to pollute the past. Although there was a high probability that the ship would sink before anyone could examine the components, there was also a chance that John's interaction with the captain could alter the balance of events on board. Suddenly, Alec could picture the Titanic hitting the iceberg differently. Or not at all.

As he started unfastening the second buckle, loud shouts and bells rang out from below. As John briefly looked away,

Alec knew there was only one thing he could do. Seizing the opportunity, he quickly pressed the button in the palm of the glove, then continued unbuckling.

John turned back to him with an anxious look on his face.

"Get it off, now!"

Alec released the last strap from his wrist and lowered the prosthetic hand to the metal grating. With any luck, he thought, the magnesium wire was already beginning to heat up.

"Back away," John insisted.

Again, Alec did as he was told. Shuffling away on his knees, he kept one eye on the hand that lay isolated on the walkway.

Abruptly, the thunderous whir of the engines stopped, sending juddering vibrations through the metal floor. Glancing down through the grating, he saw the pistons slam to a halt, and he felt the whole walkway lurch underneath him. As John staggered back, the gloved hand erupted into a white-hot ball of light.

Stumbling and shielding his eyes from the bright flare, John stepped back and hit his head on an overhead steam pipe. As he struggled to stay upright, more shouts came from below and the pistons screeched into motion again, this time in reverse.

Alec felt himself being pushed forward: the Titanic must be decelerating. In front of him, the dazed John reached out to grab a handrail. A handrail that wasn't there.

In the cold magnesium light, Alec saw the moment of shock take hold of John. There was a brief flailing of arms as he swiped at the unsupportive air, then he fell out of view.

Alec scrambled forward, hoping that John had managed to grasp onto some part of the walkway, but as he looked down he saw the stark fact. Out of view of the engine room workers, John's body lay crumpled and wedged between a mass of pipes and valves.

The roar of the engines increased and he felt the deceleration get stronger. There was only one reason why the Titanic would be trying to slam on its brakes: someone must have sighted the iceberg.

He crawled closer to the bright flare and black smoke. Logically, he knew the QRI signal was buried too deep in the ship for Diane to easily spot, but he willed her to find it anyway.

"I'm here!" he yelled out above the strain of the engines, "Find me!"

The hand burned.

He could see the plastic components inside were blackening into an unidentifiable mess. The future technology was safely melting into obscurity, as were his own chances of survival. Grabbing the handrail, he pulled himself to his feet.

"I'm right here!" he called into the hot air.

As the flames began to gutter, he moved closer and threw his arms wide so they'd be able to identify his missing hand.

"Come on!"

The flames faded into a flicker, and a grating sound reverberated through the air.

The walkway underneath him shuddered and he gripped the handrail for all he was worth. Almost as quickly as they had started, the vibrations subsided and vanished.

The pistons continued their vain attempt to slow the ship, but Alec knew the damage must already have been done.

An icy dagger had been plunged into the side of this great mechanical beast, and it would now die.

FLUX

The exposed surface of the Titanic's upper decks teemed with squirming static. At the current detail level, it wasn't possible to discern individual people, but Petra knew that's what they were looking at on the curved screen. She was almost glad that the lack of detail was sparing her from seeing their faces.

Spread across the angled decks, the crowds were amassed in two places. Dots swarmed and buzzed near the lifeboats at the centre, and an almost equal number were gathered at the aft end of the ship. Both crowds were seeking to escape the rising water that was swallowing the very front of the vessel.

As the scene continued to slowly rotate, a bright patch appeared in the air above the sinking ship.

"What the hell was that?" she looked over at Theo, "Was that an occlusion?"

"Checking," his fingers flew over his tablet.

The scene paused and then reformed. Time moved forward and the same bright patch appeared. The view zoomed in and she saw the detail level increase. The same few seconds played out again. A dot rose into view then burst into several trails of scintillating pixels.

"Distress rocket," Bernard glanced between the wall and his notes, "Twelve forty-seven a.m., about an hour after impact, an Officer Boxhall sends up the first distress rocket, apparently to get the attention of a ship on the horizon."

"Wait," said Ryan, "That's *actually* in the notes?"

Bernard nodded.

"I'm continually amazed by the details that were reconstructed from Morse transmission records and eyewitness accounts," he consulted his notes again, "People looked up to see rocket trails bathing the Titanic in light, and then the dark Atlantic waters surrounded them again."

Petra shook her head. It was both incredible and chilling that the details had outlived everyone involved in the event. She pointed at Bernard's notes.

"I don't suppose that a magician ever gave his account?"

From the look on his face, she could tell that he understood what she was really asking.

"Not that I've seen so far," he answered diplomatically, "but I'm still reading."

Diane suddenly got up from her office chair.

"Theo," she said, "Pause it."

Petra saw him quickly comply and bring the ship to a halt.

"What's wrong?"

Diane stared at Ryan.

"Something that you mentioned before," her eyes darted from side to side, "Something about a magician's flourish."

Petra now recalled it. Ryan had talked about misdirections.

"Everyone's looking up at the bright flare!" she said.

"And?" Bernard frowned.

"And," she said, "There'll be a moment nearby that went completely unobserved. An occlusion point."

"A *possible* occlusion," Diane raised a cautionary finger but nodded, "If it's going to form anywhere, it will be at a place that isn't populated."

Theo began zooming out and reframing the ship.

"Hold on," Ryan walked over to the screen, "Alec couldn't have predicted when a flare gun would have gone off."

"He wouldn't need to," Petra now realised, "He'd just need to be standing in an isolated spot when it happened."

"But..." Bernard's eyebrows were a knot.

"Listen," Diane walked to the screen, "An occlusion point forms when a quantum level *collaboration* has taken place between past and present. Alec may already have done his part by remaining in one place. We just have to add our component."

"And what's that?"

"Looking directly at it."

The view of the ship stopped turning, and Theo pointed at a detail.

"OK," he said, "I've framed up on the front end -"

"The bow," Bernard nodded, "Sorry, go on..."

"I've framed the *bow*," he pointed at the screen, "I think these sections were the forecastle deck and well deck. They're furthest from the crowds."

"Time?" said Diane.

"Frozen at three seconds before the rocket flare," he said, "At this height the scanning density is -"

"Theo," Petra interrupted, "Run it forward."

He tapped his tablet, and motion resumed on screen.

With the viewpoint locked solidly to the deck of the grey-scale ship, the fizzling Atlantic ocean seemed to pivot around it. Without fuss, a sphere of static quietly appeared in the noise.

Petra felt the laugh catch in her chest.

Diane cleared her throat.

"Theo, take us back a few seconds," she quickly pointed at the sphere's centre, "Reframe and refocus."

The image fragmented and Petra heard Theo's rapid fingertips thudding on the tablet screen. Now focused on a much smaller volume than before, the pixels blistered into clearer definition.

Frozen in time was a solitary figure. Like the cubist portrait, a man with a missing hand was folding his arms.

"Well I'll be ..." Bernard whispered above the silence.

She heard Ryan exhale a snort.

"What?" she said.

"Nothing," he shook his head, "It's just that I can picture Alec arranging things this way."

"Arranging what?" said Diane.

He pointed at the front end of the ship.

"The magician takes the bow," he smiled.

Bernard chuckled, "Jolly good."

Petra found herself smiling too. Against all odds, Alec had played his part in being found. A bow was the least that he deserved.

"OK," said Diane, "Let's run it and start to build up the metrics."

As they ran the occlusion forward, Petra began to get an uncomfortable feeling. The occlusion radius itself was larger than anything they'd encountered before. The sphere of influence covered an area that was more than ten metres wide.

"If this is supposed to be an unobserved point," she said, "then why's the occlusion volume so big?"

Theo was also frowning at the large bubble of static on the screen.

"I was just thinking the same thing."

Petra pointed to the surrounding areas.

"There was nobody on the deck nearby," she said, "There's minor perturbation to the environment but there's no influence. Diane, could we be seeing a volumetric overflow that -"

The bubble collapsed.

In its place were three figures that were running away across the deck.

"What the *hell?"*

As the figures ran, the QRI began to lose resolution and break down.

"Theo?" Diane sounded concerned.

"This isn't me," he looked shocked.

The people, and then the Titanic shifted into a blocky mass of static.

"Did we lose lock?" Diane quickly strode over to Theo.

Petra grabbed her own tablet.

"I'll check seismics. If there's been another aftershock, it could have -"

"We're still locked," Theo interrupted her, "Everything's working fine."

Diane's eyes darted between the tablet and the screen.

"Theo," she spoke quickly, "Zoom out!"

Petra could see that he was tapping the tablet, but nothing appeared to be changing on the screen.

"We should be able to see the whole ship," Theo kept working, "but I'm still getting nothing. The detail's not there."

Diane stood back from the screen.

"Maintain distance," she said, "but speed up the relative time."

"Factor?" said Theo.

"Fifty."

Petra didn't take her eyes off the screen. As the rapid tablet tapping stopped, the view shifted. She could see outlines of shapes trying to coalesce.

"Push it up to one hundred," said Diane.

Fuzzy lines and shapes jittered into outlines and volumes. The ship was visible, but every edge and surface seemed to be a ghostly approximation.

Petra felt cold.

In the early days of QRI research, they'd encountered this phenomenon at microscopic scales. What they were seeing on the screen was several orders of magnitude larger.

"Quantum flux," Diane's expression was drawn.

"At this scale?" Petra couldn't believe what she was seeing.

Diane stared and pointed at one of the more persistent edges.

"The time smoothing effect," she slowly nodded, "At a hundred times normal speed, the probability bell-curve of position data is the superposition of -"

"Excuse me," Bernard cut in, "But what on *earth* is this quantum flux?"

Diane turned away from the screen to face him.

"Heisenberg uncertainty, indeterminacy, Lorentz transform errors," she said, "We're seeing the signs that the quantum covariant field itself is in flux."

Bernard's frown deepened.

"That's not much help," he said, "Why are we seeing nothing?"

"What we're seeing isn't *nothing,*" Diane shook her head, "What we're seeing is an approximation of *everything*."

"Everything?" said Ryan.

"Every possible variation of events," Petra replied, "All overlapping each other simultaneously. We're seeing objects as a function of probability... We're seeing likelihoods that things are occupying a certain position at a certain time."

"That's why everything's blurry?" Bernard wiggled his fingers in front of his face.

Ryan was nodding.

"Like watching a busy city street on fast forward," he said, "The people smooth into a blur, but the buildings stay solid."

"Except in our case, the buildings are a ship," Theo moved his hand up and down, "and the ship itself is in motion on top of the water."

The screen suddenly changed.

The QRI returned to its normal clarity, but Petra saw the action was still unfolding at one hundred times its usual speed.

Now steeply angled, the rearmost end of the Titanic plunged downward into frothing water. In a single second, the ship had vanished from view, leaving only a few scattered lifeboats dotted on the surface.

Theo paused the scene and consulted his tablet.

"In real time," he said, "The flux lasted an hour and a half."

Petra looked at the aftermath image on the screen.

"And it clears up just as the Titanic sinks."

Diane borrowed the tablet from Theo and began making adjustments. After several seconds of quiet tapping, the view unfroze and Petra saw motions begin to reverse. Actions weren't as swift as before but, to her eye, events appeared to be moving backwards at about five times normal speed.

Lifeboats bounced up and down before gravitating toward a growing froth. As the frothing water diminished, the aft end of the Titanic rose through the surface. With arms flailing, people rocketed up out of the water and leapt aboard. The unsinkable ship continued to rise and people slid up the heavily tilted decks to grab hold of handrails.

"Those poor souls," Bernard whispered in horror.

Without seeming to affect their struggles, a wide sphere of static quietly expanded through the crowd and concealed them from view.

There had been a *second* occlusion event.

Overwhelmed by all she was seeing, Petra couldn't speak.

The ship rose higher and the occlusion rose with it. From the looks of things, it seemed that the sphere was centred on a space that was within the ship. The ball of static remained in place but then the scene quickly degraded into an impenetrable mass of noise.

Diane hit pause.

"Two occlusions," she said, "One here in the final moments -"

"And one near the beginning at the bow," Petra stared.

"Why would we retrostep twice?" said Theo, "And why is there flux between the two?"

The time continued to roll backwards on the screen, but the view remained a wall of static.

The questions kept filling Petra's mind.

"If we rescued Alec from the bow," she said, "and if we made it back *here* to the present day -"

"Then who were the three running people?" Theo completed.

Petra turned to him.

"Can you take us back to the first occlusion?" she said, "Freeze it as soon as the sphere of influence collapses."

He tapped rapidly at the tablet and the query reset.

On the curved wall screen, three figures were frozen mid-run.

One of them had a missing left hand.

The proof was irrefutable: Alec hadn't been rescued.

"Who are the other two?" Ryan frowned at the figures.

Without the benefits of light, shadow and colour, the three-dimensional silhouettes proved hard to identify.

Petra had expected to see the familiar close-fitting body suits that were worn during temporal trips, but that wasn't what she was seeing. A man wore a suit that was similar in style to Alec's, and a woman wore a dress that trailed over the deck.

"They must be other passengers," she squinted at the forms.

"But why would Alec be running with them?" said Theo.

"It's a sinking ship," she pointed out, "Why *wouldn't* they be running?"

"Good point," Theo sighed.

For a moment, they all just watched the static figures continue to fizzle on the curved screen. Only after several seconds did she realise that Ryan was staring at her. When she turned to face him, he looked extremely awkward, perhaps even slightly embarrassed.

"What?" she said.

"I had a… thought… this morning, just before you came to get me."

She recalled how surprised he'd looked when he'd found her standing outside his room.

"Go on."

"A dream actually," he said, "I was picturing holes into the past, like doorways."

"Doorways?" Diane frowned.

"Yeah."

He pulled a notepad and pen from his pocket, and found a blank page. Petra watched as he drew a small circle at one side of the page.

"I was just wondering if you could enter the past through *one* occlusion…"

He drew a wiggly line away from the circle.

"… You could then *stay* in the past…"

He finished drawing the line and drew a second circle at the end of it.

"… and then you could step back through another occlusion to come home."

Petra could immediately see what he was suggesting: there hadn't been two separate occlusions, there had been an entry point and a return. Between the two events there had been a period of time that wasn't directly observable.

"Oh," Bernard spoke quietly, "Oh my."

"Bernie?" Diane looked at him, "What's wrong?"

Petra saw him glance directly at her, and then he looked over at Ryan.

"Mr. Pryce is suggesting an entrance and an exit," he said,

"but they're not in the same place. The distance between the two is as long as the Titanic. What if the figures are you and Theo running with Alec to reach the exit?"

Petra sighed and patiently shook her head.

"We've just talked about this," she pointed at the screen, "They're not wearing our standard kit."

"And with good reason," Bernard nodded, "You'd look distinctly out of place if you wore *modern* clothing while moving through the Titanic. *Period* clothes, however, would be the perfect camouflage."

She couldn't stop herself responding sarcastically.

"So I should contact my seamstress and get her to rustle something up in my size?"

Bernard actually smiled.

"You won't need to," he said, "I think I know where we'll find it."

ICE

What surprised Alec most was how calm people were on the outer deck. Although news of the iceberg impact had spread, none of them yet knew the damage that had taken place under the water.

Children were fooling around with chunks of iceberg that had broken off and fallen onto the deck. Adults regarded the sight with a detached curiosity: a fleeting novelty that would vanish when the blocks melted. None of them knew what was about to happen.

Although his QRI beacon was gone, Alec knew his only possible rescue point was still the bow of the ship.

According to the movie, the front had sunk first, so people would be trying to get away from that area. He had to get there as fast as possible. When the time came, he wouldn't want to be battling a rising tide of water and people. At the moment though, the only thing that was remaining watertight was the class structure aboard the ship.

When he'd tried to leave the aft well deck and enter the second class section, he'd been firmly turned away by a steward. Things would have to get much worse before petty security measures broke down.

The walkway confrontation flashed through his mind.

After the beacon had burned, he'd retraced his steps out of the hot engine room and along Scotland Road, all the time haunted by the sight of John's still and twisted body. The engine room workers had been preoccupied with reversing the engines, but it was only a matter of time before the fatality was discovered.

It was possible that, as John himself had suggested, the walkway event had gone unobserved by those below, but Alec couldn't shake the feeling that his every move was now being watched. All too easily, he could imagine the ship's security officers closing in on him. Combined with the fact that he'd already lost the QRI beacon, it felt like the odds of being rescued from the Titanic were falling by the minute.

Despite the rising sense of panic that was seeping into every thought, he knew he couldn't force his way to the front of the ship. He had to be patient. He had to wait for the right moment. Picking up a discarded newspaper, he concealed his newly exposed wrist and tried not to make eye contact with anyone on the deck.

He heard a squeal of laughter and saw that children were playing a game of bowls with pieces of iceberg. A fast-moving chunk glided over the deck and clattered with the second class access steps, earning them a stern look from the steward above. Suitably warned, the children abandoned their game and went with their mother toward the relative warmth of the third class entrance.

Alec looked back at the stationary chunk of ice that the children had been aiming for. Slowly, it began to turn and slide over the deck.

NIGHT AT THE MUSEUM

Petra tapped at the frame of her glasses and looked in several different directions. For good measure, she waved her hands in front of her.

"I'm recording," she said, "Are you receiving?"

The earpiece that was synced with her glasses gave a crackle. A second later, Bernard's over-pronounced reply came through at a volume that sounded like he was trying to address a stadium.

"Receiving you loud and clear. Over."

She winced at the painfully clipped audio.

"Bernard," she said, "Talk normally and back off from the microphone."

His voice came back quieter.

"Sorry," he said, *"I can see everything clearly. It's like I'm walking up through the museum."*

That was sort of the point, she thought, but didn't say so.

Continuing to climb the stairs, she took out her phone and carried it as a prop. If anyone should overhear their conversation, it would look like she was just on a call.

"OK," she said, "Heading out now."

She pushed the door open and walked out into the Great Court.

The late afternoon sun was filtering down through the glass roof, painting everything a pale white and making her faint shadow a diffuse blur at her feet.

She'd only been walking for a few seconds when she heard Bernard sigh.

"Everything alright?" she quietly asked.

"The last time I saw this view," he said, *"I was storming off."*

"There was a lot to take in," she said, "I think I'd have needed a breath of fresh air too."

There was a slight pause.

"I owe you an apology," he said, *"I barged into you as I left. It was entirely unacceptable behaviour. I exhibited the manners and finesse of a Cro-Magnon."*

She smiled to herself. In comparison to everything she'd been through so far, the incident that had annoyed her so much earlier now seemed completely trivial.

"Don't worry about it," she reassured him, "It's all water under the bridge."

Immediately she realised that the old phrase wasn't perhaps the best thing to say to Bernard. The County Hall collapse into the Thames was, understandably, a difficult subject at the moment.

"Sorry," she said, "That was stupid."

"It's fine… I've got to face the facts of the matter. It's just taking me a while to adjust."

Petra brought their conversation back on track.

"Am I heading in the right direction?"

"Yes, take the stairs to your left."

She moved on through the upper portions of the museum. There were fewer people than on previous days, but it wasn't empty. It was easy to understand why: the British Museum was still a tourist magnet. Visitors from other countries had probably spent thousands just to get here. They weren't about to let recent events derail their already-compromised London itinerary.

She kept walking.

News of the aftershock was now almost a day old and, to avoid answering awkward press questions about a miraculous escape, Bernard was being kept out of the public eye. Although they'd all discussed a possible solution, Petra's 'virtual tour' was the only thing permitting Bernard to see above ground.

As she moved through a quieter section that was lined with colourful blown-glass vases, she asked him how he knew about the dress they'd seen in the Titanic QRI.

"It's actually more of a hunch," he said, *"When they closed the Edwardian fashion wing at the Victoria and Albert Museum, the clothing had to go somewhere, so I recommended that it should come here. After all, the rear galleries here were underused at the time."*

"Seriously?" she said, "I'm surprised that you -"

"Now," he interrupted, *"I know what you're going to say."*

"What?"

"Technically, the Edwardian period ended in nineteen-ten, which is a good two years before the ship sank. However, the fashions would have been broadly similar, so I'm hoping that... stop, go right."

She entered a dimly lit room that was filled with display cases. Behind each pane of glass, headless mannequins in neutral poses showed a wide range of Edwardian clothing. Suits, shoes, waistcoats, corsets, and dresses were all meticulously categorised and presented to a general public that was largely disinterested.

"OK," said Bernard, *"It looks like you're in the early nineteen-hundreds... Go forward."*

She'd never been the type to wear dresses but, as she walked along the avenue of past fashion, she could fully appreciate the time and effort that had gone into creating these garments. Regardless of their size, each piece had been created to last. It was incredible to think that, one hundred and twenty years after the last stitch had been sewn, these clothes were still viable.

After wandering around the displays for perhaps ten minutes, Bernard told her to stop and look directly at one of the cases.

"We're just comparing it to the QRI," he told her, *"Can you move around the dress slowly?"*

Keeping the mannequin centred, she circled it left and right.

"Anything?"

"It's close," he sighed, *"but no. The one in the QRI has a floral… something… on the upper left of the chest."*

Looking down in dismay, she caught site of a blue brooch that was laid out next to a matching pair of shoes.

"Hey!" Bernard now noticed, *"Move closer!"*

Petra saw that a woman with a pushchair was watching her. Presumably she'd seen her slightly eccentric swaying from left to right.

"They're beautiful dresses, aren't they?" she improvised around her embarrassment, "Makes one want to dance."

The woman gave a polite smile, then hurriedly wheeled her sleeping toddler away.

Theo's amused voice now came through the earpiece.

"It's a nice frock."

"Shut up," she turned and knelt down next to the flower-shaped brooch, "Is this it, or not?"

"Hold still," he said.

For several long seconds, she heard nothing from either Theo or Bernard. Eventually, she gave up and waved her hands in front of her again.

"Hello?" she said, "Are you still there?"

"Petra," Theo replied, *"It looks like we're going on a cruise."*

As night fell, the museum closed to the public.

On multiple levels, they all worked through the night to finalise the details of the rescue operation.

12.47

It had taken half an hour for the first lifeboat to be swung out. The simple movement had sent rumours rippling out through the crowd on the deck. The only reason Alec knew this was because he'd overheard someone else talking about it.

Some people were being told to return inside, dress warmly and bring their lifebelts. Others were being instructed to return to their cabins and collect their blankets. Suddenly, people were paying attention to the tilt that had been growing under their feet all along.

Now preoccupied with ship matters, officers and stewards withdrew from the well deck stairs. Taking advantage of the minor gap in security, Alec calmly walked up the steps, opened the gate to the Second Class deck, and walked inside.

He could see that the commotion here was the same, but slightly better dressed. Before anyone could approach him, he opened the nearest door and walked into the warmth.

The smell of the room reminded him of the smoke-filled bar in Paris, except the air was much clearer. All around the oak-panelled room, green leather chairs surrounded small tables; each one holding unfinished drinks and card games.

Arranged along one window, a number of moustached gentlemen strutted and smoked their cigarettes while muttering at the ongoing confusion outside.

Dumping his newspaper, Alec scooped up a neglected smoking jacket from the back of a chair and draped it over his arm. Without slowing, he walked on and pushed his way out onto another stairwell. Seeing uniformed officers descending the wooden treads, he turned aside and walked through the doorway opposite.

Spotting a line of waiters' uniforms on hooks, he discarded the smoking jacket and slipped into a white jacket. He picked up a serving tray to conceal his wrist, and walked through the restaurant. Again, he saw that people were staring out through the windows, but some were now attempting to put on their lifebelts.

"You there," a man clicked his fingers.

Alec kept walking, "Yes sir."

The man pointed at a woman near the window.

"Fetch a brandy for my wife."

Alec gave a nod and ran out of the restaurant as fast as he could.

Adopting a similar technique for each section that he passed through, he continually upgraded his apparent status and moved ever forward. All the while, minutes continued to pass and the floor continued to tilt.

By the time he'd reached the first class sections, people's radius of attention had shrunk drastically. Everyone seemed preoccupied with their own affairs, or their lifebelts, or the fact that the lifeboats that had begun to fill.

Now standing on the well deck at the bow of the ship, Alec looked out at the water. The surface was only a few feet below him.

Already, he thought, seawater had overwhelmed the lower decks at the front end. Moving in an unstoppable flow, the water would work its way aft and fill up the sections of the ship from the inside. At some point, the buoyancy equations would flip and gravity would drag it down.

Beneath him, he felt a shudder and imagined an airtight room somewhere succumbing to water pressure. He turned away from the dark sea and climbed the steps to the forecastle deck.

The deck was empty and, lacking any form of side shelter, it was freezing cold.

"I'm right here," he quietly looked up at the star-flecked sky.

The only reply he received was the distant, steam-venting roar of the funnels and the faint murmur of people. Gathering a blanket around his shoulders, he folded his arms to try to ward off the cold.

He looked around at the empty deck. There was no-one here to witness the arrival of any occlusion.

"Come on," he willed Diane and the others.

A whooshing sound caught his attention, but when he looked up, he saw it was only a flare gun. A rocket trail of sparks drew a vertical line in the darkness and then exploded into a shower of light. It must have been high up because there was a notable delay before the sound arrived. A chill ran down his spine as a strong gust of Atlantic wind blew at his back.

Behind him, two people were calling his name. It was the most welcome sound in all the world.

Whirling around, he saw Theo and Petra standing on the deck. As they both dashed toward him, he saw Theo check his wristband tether.

"Twelve forty-seven," he said, "Timer running."

Grinning from ear to ear, Alec wanted to run and hug them, but he knew time wasn't on their side. He quickly rolled up his sleeve in preparation for a tracer injection.

"We got your message!" Theo beamed.

Glancing at their outfits, he couldn't help himself.

"Fashion moves fast," he said, "How long was I gone?"

"We'll fill you in later," Petra grinned.

Alec thrust out his arm.

"Really hoping you brought my tracer with you."

Somewhat alarmingly, both of them shook their heads.

"The occlusion here is less than a minute," said Theo, "We can't bring you back in this trip."

"What?!"

"We ran the numbers," said Petra, "You might have been able to absorb the tracer, but we can't calibrate your new wristband in under a minute."

"Ergo, the occlusion retroactively agreed," said Theo, "It only stayed in place long enough to get us here."

In disbelief, Alec pointed at Theo's wristband.

"Then why the hell did you start the timer?"

Theo shook his head.

"The timer isn't for a minute," he said, "it's for an hour and a half."

While Alec's mind continued to reel, Petra placed her wristband next to Theo's: a procedure he didn't recognise.

"What are you doing?"

"Don't panic," she told him and turned to Theo, "Synced?"

Theo nodded, "Detaching tether."

Before Alec had time to yell out his objection, he felt another shiver run down his spine. As the sensation subsided, he saw Theo and Petra start running across the deck. Instinctively, he chased after them.

"Wait!" he called out, "Where the hell are you going?"

They kept running, but he heard Petra yell back.

"We've got to get to the exit!"

CLOCK

Diane turned away from the transmitter pad controls and started the clock. In an hour and a half, the tether would be pulled taut.

In theory, she knew there was no need to run the present-day clock in real time; the moment of their return *could* have been synchronised to a minute after their departure. However, keeping things in real time would give her the opportunity to run a vital data-gathering experiment.

She left the control room and walked back to her office.

Every trip made her a little nervous. The science was sound, but at the end of the day, they were always dealing with matters of probability.

In the very early days, when they were first investigating teleportation, some items *had* gone missing. The complex patterns that had represented things like rubidium-quartz cubes or ostrich eggs had simply failed to reach their destination. They'd either disintegrated into a cloud of subatomic particles, or were completely intact but somewhere else in the universe.

The recently resolved McCairn mystery only reinforced what she already knew: every time someone departed from the transmitter pad, there was always a small possibility that they'd never come back. And she'd just sent two people to retrieve the one who was already lost.

Facing the curved wall in her office, she cleared the QRI buffer and reset the temporal coordinates to coincide with the 12.47 rocket flare.

Frozen in time, the Titanic sailed out of the surrounding static; its bow notably lower than the aft. Reframing, she zoomed in on Alec and the surrounding forecastle deck. With a tap on her tablet screen, time ran forward.

Alec's noise-filled silhouette looked up at the flare, then a wide occlusion enveloped him: Theo and Petra's arrival.

As before, the occlusion remained in place for under a minute and then cleared. The three figures ran over the deck, but for every step they took, the query remained stable. Unlike last time, the quantum flux didn't obliterate the view.

She accelerated the timeframe, looking further forward into their trip.

The three of them sped to the forecastle steps, descended them with almost comedic speed, and then zoomed over the well deck. The scene dissolved into a wall of static again.

She hit pause.

She'd been able to see more than the first time they'd queried this event, but quantum flux had still rolled in to occlude the scene.

There seemed to be only one logical reason for this: it wasn't possible to see the actions that the three of them had yet to take.

As she began to mentally run through the ramifications, the screen static started to change.

Although the timeframe was still paused, structure began to emerge. Within a few seconds, Alec, Theo and Petra were visible again. She could see their sprint was paused mid-stride.

Slowly she began to understand what had happened.

While the QRI had been paused *here*, events aboard the ship had continued to move forwards. Events there were moving out of fuzzy probability and becoming resolved outcomes. In reaction, the quantum flux was clearing in its wake. In effect, the past had caught up with her stationary QRI feed.

She looked at the three of them frozen on the screen.

Her data-gathering experiment had worked.

As long as she kept the query delayed by a few seconds, she'd be able to view events as they unfolded.

Using Theo's false-colour overlay system, she targeted the rubidium-quartz combination in their wristbands.

A dull red dot overlaid itself on Petra, and two appeared on Theo: clearly he hadn't given Alec a replacement wristband yet.

She resumed playback.

Their grainy silhouettes joined the chaotic swarm of people within the ship. At times it was difficult to discern their three individual profiles, but the red dots moved in the same direction. After moving down and through the third class open space, they descended again.

"What are you doing?" she murmured at them.

On the almost sectional view of the ship, she could see that the seawater had breached several rooms below them. The forward cargo hold was flooded, turning old motorcars into submarines. The letters in the mail room swirled like the flakes of a snow globe.

She zoomed out slightly.

Before Theo and Petra had departed, they'd all spent many hours poring over the plans of the Titanic. They'd even run a QRI on the ship *before* its maiden voyage. Using a frozen moment in time, they'd explored the empty deck layouts in detail and discussed the possible routes that the rescue might take. Despite all of this, Diane could see that they'd already started to improvise.

They were moving through a third class corridor, and far lower in the ship than they'd discussed. From Diane's point of view, they were caught between the water that was rising unseen behind them, and the quantum flux that obscured the unknowns that lay ahead.

The red dots moved on.

TILT

Petra led the way along the busy corridor and did her best to mentally filter out the shouts. Filtering out the expressions on people's faces was impossible though; their anxiety was clear, and it was on the rise.

Seeing the signage for the Swimming Bath, she navigated past two men who were carrying bags, then ducked into a short side corridor.

"In here!" she called to Theo and Alec.

Opening the watertight door, she quickly moved inside and they followed her in. After Theo had closed the door behind them, she turned to look at the first class swimming pool facility.

Against one wall of the long room were spacious changing cubicles, each one fitted with dark wooden doors. On the other side of a handrail, and occupying half the width of the room, was the pool itself. Within the walls of the pool, the water appeared wedge shaped: its level higher at one end than at the other. It took her a moment to realise that the surface was, of course, still horizontal. It was the rest of the ship that was tilted.

With every step they took, their environment was shifting and changing around them.

"Hello?" she called out.

Her voice echoed off the hard walls, but nobody answered.

"This will have to do," she turned to the others, "I can't imagine too many people wanting to swim at the minute, can you?"

"Fair enough," Theo began walking along the line of cubicles, "I'll double-check we're alone."

Alec glanced back at the door, "What are we doing here?"

She kept her voice low.

"We need to recalibrate your replacement wristband. I was hoping to find an unoccupied cabin, but I don't think we can wait any longer."

Theo reached the far end of the room, gave them a thumbs-up and started walking back again.

Alec shook his head.

"Still can't believe that the whole entrance-exit concept was Ryan's idea."

"I can hardly believe it myself," she agreed, "I think we got so used to operating within the limits, that we got…"

"Limited?" he said, "I guess he's got the advantage of looking at things as a novice."

Theo walked past them and stood guard by the door.

"OK," he said, "Let's get this done."

Petra lifted up the outer part of her dress and accessed the pocket that she'd roughly sewn into the petticoat. She pulled out Alec's customised injector and the palm-sized rubidium scanner.

Alec shook his head in amazement.

"I've been wondering how you were going to compensate for the tracer degradation," he nodded, "But I had no idea that you'd be bringing so much kit back here with you."

She straightened her dress.

"This glorified rucksack has its uses," she said, "Nobody of this era expects a woman to be carrying scientific equipment, least of all *future* equipment."

She saw him point at the label on the injector.

"Top Hat," he read, "Is that one mine by any chance?"

"It seemed apt for a magician," she nodded, "Hold out your hand."

"Wait," he said, "If you inject it now, the isotope will have degraded by the time we get to the exit point."

"We're not using rubidium eighty-two," said Theo, "Even inside an injector, the isotope would have degraded within a few minutes of us getting here."

"So what are you using then?"

"Rubidium *chloride*," Petra told him, "As a biomarker, it'll be absorbed just as easily."

"It will," Alec frowned, "but it won't be an exact match for my bio-pattern."

Theo held up the replacement wristband.

"This band is entangled with your bio-pattern back home," he then pointed at the scanner, "Once we measure the *dispersion* level of the rubidium chloride -"

"You can *mimic* the isotope distribution," Alec now nodded, "and create a tether overlay. Nice."

"You're welcome," Petra smiled but then noticed he was shaking his head, "What?"

"I'm seriously hoping these sorts of trips don't become a habit," he said, "but if they ever did, then we have *got* to work on streamlining the tether process."

"Necessity's the mother of invention," said Theo, "Before now, we've never had to consider retrosteps that were longer than a minute. Free from that limit, we'll be able to explore options."

"But for the time being," said Petra, "we know that the *limited* version works. So, for safety, that's what we're going with."

Alec glanced at the injector and wristband.

"Belt and braces," he nodded.

She administered the tracer, then placed the scanner's measuring clip on his index finger so that the analyser could begin its work.

"So, what happens when we get to the exit?" he said.

She pictured the rear of the ship.

"We each use our own pre-flight booster injector," she said, "When the tether goes taut, it'll pull back the exact same patterns that left the transmitter pad."

She saw him look down at his left forearm.

"Well," he said, "Not *exactly* the same pattern."

Theo gave him a tight-lipped smile, "Sorry."

Alec sighed and shook his head.

"It wasn't your fault," he now seemed to force a smile, "You should've seen my replacement hand. It was a work of art. I hollowed out the -"

"Hold on," Petra couldn't help interrupting, "You *made* a replacement?"

"Modified," he gave a shrug, "I was surprised at how advanced prosthetics were in this time. It was mostly wood but, with a glove on, you really couldn't tell."

"What happened to it?" said Theo.

While the analyser continued to work, Alec described the covert magnesium flare that he'd built into the palm. Alec explained how he'd met John Coffey, and then told them about the events in the engine room. It was horrifying to think that it had happened against the backdrop of the iceberg impacting the ship. All things considered, Alec was lucky to have escaped with his life.

The scanner gave a quiet beep.

She unclipped it from Alec's finger and gave it to Theo.

He took it from her and retreated to one of the changing cubicles. Kneeling down at the side of the slatted seat, he connected the wristband and scanner.

"It'll take me a few minutes," he called over his shoulder.

Alec pointed at the water and smirked.

"You realise that this gives a whole new meaning to the idea of *pooling* our resources."

Theo gave a groan, "Maybe we should leave him here."

Alec smiled and raised an apologetic hand, "Sorry."

While Theo worked, Petra kept one eye on the water level within the pool. Although the orientation of the room looked identical to when they'd walked in, the surface of the water now seemed more steeply angled. The tilt of the ship must be increasing, she thought, and they still had two-thirds of its length to cover.

"The costumes were a nice idea," Alec looked between both of them.

"We had a little help," Petra admitted, "In the query, we saw the three of us leaving the forecastle deck."

"Whoa," Alec's eyes widened and he looked round at the swimming pool, "Does that mean that all of this, right now, is queryable?"

"Nope," she shook his head, "Straight after we saw ourselves, the QRI got swamped with quantum flux."

"What?" he said, "At the *macroscopic* scale?"

She told him about the temporal averaging effects that had enveloped the whole ship, and her theories that might account for the phenomenon.

"So," Alec pointed upwards, "Diane can't see anything that's going on here?"

"You know how it goes," she gave a shrug, "In terms of quantum observability…"

"There are no damn witnesses," Alec seemed distracted for a moment.

She smiled and pointed to the flower brooch on her dress.

"Well, maybe *one* witness."

Alec looked at it and smiled.

"A camera?" he said, "Like your spectaculars?"

"*From* my spectaculars, actually," she said, "Ugliest piece of DIY hacking I ever did, but I couldn't exactly go wearing your high-tech frames around here could I? It was Bernie's idea, but he owes me a new pair of specs."

"Wait, what?" he said, "Holroyd came *back?*"

"Long story," she simplified, "but he thinks that if we can bring back a continuous video of the trip, it will act as physical proof that retrostepping exists."

"Why would we need proof?"

Theo stood up and walked out of the cubicle.

"Things started to get a little out of control after you left," he said, "There was a second quake."

Alec froze, "Is everyone alright?"

"Physically, yes," said Theo, "but the Government's in the middle of the biggest shake-up in centuries. We don't know who's going to end up in control. The video will give us proof of Query's capabilities. Hopefully it'll persuade anyone in charge to keep the museum lights on."

Petra saw him glance at her brooch and then look around at the swimming pool.

"I guess it would be pretty hard for anyone to fake all of this," he said, "All the people..."

She knew exactly what was on Alec's mind. It was something that she herself was grappling with. On previous missions, she'd never encountered anyone else. Now, operating outside of occlusions and embedded in history, she was exposed to the full humanity of it all. Alec had been doing this for months.

"I can't imagine what you've been through," she said.

"For a while, I gave up," he stared at his feet, "Resigned myself to living back here... *So* glad you found the message."

Petra exchanged an awkward glance with Theo.

"We would've found it eventually," she said, "but actually it was Ryan who joined the dots first."

"Seriously?" Alec looked up, "Who is he? Mr. Abstract?"

Petra thought of the boxes of Fortean Eye magazines.

"If you stare at something long enough," she shrugged, "I guess you see all sorts of weird connections. We owe him."

Theo held up the wristband.

"Then let's go and thank him."

Alec took the band, but then seemed to realise that he couldn't put it on by himself.

"Could you give me a hand?"

Theo smiled and shook his head, "Been planning *that* one for long?"

"About three months," Alec smiled back.

Theo took it back from him and secured it to Alec's right wrist.

"Mr. Magician," he said, "Try not to make this one disappear."

She saw Alec's eyes suddenly well up and he pulled them both into a hug.

"Missed you so much," his hug tightened, "So much."

HISTORY

Ryan watched the three red dots on the screen. They separated themselves from the background squirm of people-static and he saw three figures move into a room at the side of the ship.

"Where are they?" he turned away.

Bernard glanced back and forth between the screen and the tablet in his hands.

"I believe they're in the Swimming Baths," he said, "Why would they go there?"

"It's quiet," Diane pointed at the screen, "Nobody else is in there, so it's a good place to run the wristband calibration. You wouldn't want to be trying that in a busy corridor."

He could tell that Theo was moving along a line of cubicles because two red dots were accompanying a single figure. When they'd finished the calibration, each of them would have their own dot.

He saw the three of them gather together and begin a conversation but, as ever, there was no sound.

"I wish we could hear what was going on."

"You and me both," Diane stared.

"With Petra's recorder," Bernard smiled, "you'll be able to play back the whole thing when they return."

Ryan looked at the scene that slowly rotated on the curved screen. Given the immediacy of the QRI interface, it was easy to think of these events as happening in the present moment. He had to remind himself that he was viewing history, not a movie with a missing audio track.

Bernard squinted at the static.

"I dare say that one could run the video alongside the query," he said, "The audio correlation *alone* would make quite a compelling proof."

Diane turned away from the screen.

"This obsession with proof," she said, "How worried are you that we might lose control of retrostepping?"

He walked away from the screen and sat on the sofa.

"I'm just preparing for possibilities," he shrugged, "History is replete with examples of what happens when hierarchies collapse. In the turmoil, power is seized and new orders arise. With all that's going on around Westminster, there may *already* be someone waiting for the right moment to take control of this facility."

Ryan realised what he was saying.

"You think that having video proof could give us protection."

"Possibly," said Bernard, "You're the only ones who know how it all works."

Ryan looked back at the screen.

Time had clearly moved on. The silhouettes of Theo, Petra and Alec now carried their own independent red dots.

Diane stood and handed him the control tablet.

"Zoom out, Mr. Pryce," she said, "Let's see where they went next."

RISE

Petra checked the timer on her wristband. In a little over an hour, the Titanic would be bound for the floor of the Atlantic.

The wristband recalibration had been necessary, as had the route briefing that they'd given to Alec, but it had all cost far too much time. The water at the far end of the pool had continued to rise. The tilt was increasing.

Theo handed her the rubidium scanner.

"Here," he said, "You'd better put this away. We can't be leaving out-of-place artifacts back here."

She took the device and, after stowing it in her concealed pocket, she pulled open the door.

Immediately, freezing cold water washed in and flowed over her feet. It wasn't enough to knock her over, but she could feel the weight of it dragging at the hem of her dress.

"Grand Staircase!" she shouted, "Go!"

The situation had degraded significantly outside the swimming pool. The corridor was flooded and there was a definite direction to the flow. Although the water was shallow, she could see it was rising and heading toward the rear of the ship. People were shouting and dashing through the water, sending icy waves lapping against the walls.

A mother and child waded past her at speed, both wearing lifebelts and smiles. A glance at the mother's face told her that the smile was purely for the child's benefit. As the pair splashed on, the mother turned and looked directly at Petra.

For one second, their eyes connected. The woman said nothing, but Petra felt the entirety of the woman's fraught desperation burning itself into her mind.

She felt Theo push her around a corner and she saw the base of the Grand Staircase. Water was coming down the steps from above.

She remembered Bernard mentioning the eyewitness accounts, but she was now seeing it for herself. Their intended exit route, up through the centre of the ship, was itself beginning to flood.

"The E deck inundation," Theo spoke Bernard's words aloud, "Everything's tipping over to port. No choice, we've got to climb."

Fighting the weight of the water in her dress, she grabbed the handrail and mounted the stairs. The people to her right were overtaking her, despite carrying small pieces of luggage. The icy cascade continued to drag at her feet and her legs began to ache with the effort.

As she set foot on the next floor up, she stopped to take a breath, but the people behind her didn't. They pushed her aside and continued moving up the staircase. The thought of climbing another five flights to get to the first class deck filled her with dread.

She grabbed hold of Theo and Alec, and pulled them to the side of the wide corridor.

"Need another route," she shook her head.

"One more flight," said Theo, "Once we're up there, we'll

have a straight run through first class reception and dining saloon."

"Wait," Alec pointed along the corridor, "I know this level. We're in Scotland Road. If we need a straight run, go this way. It'll take us to -"

Shouts interrupted him.

The stairs up to the next deck were a dense mix of people and downward flowing water. As Petra watched, someone tripped over backwards and landed, neck first, on the lower steps. It was the woman she'd seen mere moments before. She could see the child was pushing his way back down the crowded staircase, calling out for his mother.

Petra didn't recall moving, but she found herself crouching at the woman's side, fighting against the cascading water, and desperately trying to turn the woman face up. When she succeeded in rolling her over, it was quite clear that the fall had killed her. The same eyes were staring up at her, but they were now empty.

She could feel Theo pulling at her and telling her that they had to go, but she fought him off. All she could see was the stricken face of the child.

The logic of their situation disappeared in a heartbeat. Instinctively, she stood and scooped up the child; she'd climb every last step to get him to the lifeboats.

"Petra!" Alec was shouting at her, "We can't!"

The child in her arms fought with all his weak might.

Withstanding his kicks and blows, she faced the stairs and started climbing the cascade. All the while, Alec and Theo were begging her to stop.

She'd got no further than three steps when the cascade became a sudden waterfall. Her feet were knocked out from beneath her, and she felt the crystal-sharp bite of the cold water flooding over her head.

Fighting to get her head above water, she saw the ceiling above her. Pipes, beams, and lightbulbs were sliding past her at speed. She was being swept along the corridor. She felt the flow twisting her onto her side, then her head went under again. As her own yells emerged as bubbles, her clothes scuffed along the floor, and she came to a sudden halt.

Struggling onto her elbows, she pulled her head from the water and drew deep stuttering breaths from the air.

All around her, people were trying to get to their feet. In the deeper water behind her, Theo was on his hands and knees. Ahead of her, checking his wristband, Alec was trying to sit upright. Only now did it hit her that the child she'd been holding was gone.

Hauling herself onto her hands and knees, she cast around trying to spot him, but all she could see were adults. Most were trying to get up, but a few were face down and motionless; crimson trails leaching from them into the rising water. The ship was already claiming its first victims.

Theo arrived at her side, clutching his ear and clearly in pain.

Before she could speak, he gritted his teeth and thrust out his hand.

"Time to move," he pulled her up, "Help me with Alec."

They quickly waded through the water and helped Alec to stand. Immediately, she could see that the cold water had affected him severely.

She and Theo were wearing neoprene drysuits under their clothing, a precautionary measure against the cold that they knew they'd encounter, but Alec had no such protection. He was shivering badly. If they didn't get him dry, she feared that only *two* people would be making the return trip.

"He's gonna freeze," said Theo.

Petra saw the water was still rising. The wedge shape that she'd seen in the swimming pool was duplicated here on a larger scale. The water around them was shin deep, but the doors at the far end of Scotland Road were submerged. In the distance, the water wedge began swallowing one of the ceiling lights. It fizzled into a shower of sparks, and then the lighting overhead dimmed for a second.

"We've got to get to higher ground," she said.

"N-n," Alec stammered and shook his head, "D-Down."

"Down?" Petra checked.

His head shuddered as he nodded. He raised an arm in the direction of the shallow end of the corridor, then began walking. Grabbing an arm each, they both helped him. Clearly he had an idea, but he couldn't tell them in words.

SILHOUETTES

Ryan watched in horror as three red dots were swept along Scotland Road by an angular slice of water. Once more, three static-filled silhouettes became more noticeable against a background of human anguish. The three of them had survived but he could see they were moving more slowly, and were huddled together more tightly.

He was still getting used to operating the QRI viewer interface, so he was having to think about each action carefully, but he didn't wait for Diane's next instruction. He moved the side view of the corridor to the left, and zoomed in on the three figures. The one in the middle only had one hand.

"Alec must be injured," he realised.

Theo and Petra were on either side of him and helping him to walk.

"Bernard," Diane didn't take her eyes off the screen, "Find the E deck floor plan. Work out their likeliest route to get up to the -"

"Aft D deck," Bernard nodded and immediately focused his efforts on his tablet screen.

Ryan watched the three of them moving along the

corridor, ankle deep in water. Behind them, other silhouettes struggled through a fizzing mass of static that was creeping higher and moving along the corridor.

"Ryan," Diane absentmindedly pinched her thumb and index finger together, "Zoom out. Show me the side view."

It took him a few seconds to carry out the instruction, but after he'd finished, the screen refocused.

The bow of the ship was notably lower in the water than the mid sections and, to his eye at least, the aft portions looked slightly raised from the surface of the sea.

"OK," Bernard was still staring at his tablet, "They'll head for the central stairwell, go up a deck, and then probably move through the second class dining saloon. That should put them ahead of the flood."

Over the next few minutes, they discovered that Bernard couldn't have been more wrong. Not only had they headed *down* the stairs, they'd headed back toward the bow.

"What's in that area?" Diane circled her hand over the screen.

"The engine room," Bernard frowned, "Why on earth would they be going there?"

Ryan saw the three figures enter a short corridor, but then the view seemed to become less clear. Ripples of static seemed to wash over them.

"Diane," he held out the tablet, "Am I doing something wrong?"

She took the tablet and began tapping at its surface.

The red dots cleared from the display, but the figures remained in place. A few moments later, he saw patches of light blue flitting across the screen.

Diane's frown cleared.

"It's water vapour," she said, "Steam."

The three figures stopped walking across an elevated walkway and, much to everyone's surprise, began to quickly undress Alec.

"Oh my," Bernard averted his eyes.

Petra's silhouette took off Alec's coat and began folding it and then twisting it. Light blue pixels gathered on the material and then cascaded off it. He saw Theo do the same thing with Alec's shirt and trousers. Ryan realised what they were doing. In one of the warmest places on the ship, they were trying to wring out Alec's wet clothes.

It had been Theo's idea to wear their drysuits under their clothing. At the time, Ryan had been surprised that they'd had such specific items on standby, but as Petra had pointed out, occlusion event disasters didn't always end in fire: one of their previous trips had required the use of scuba gear.

Alec, of course, hadn't been wearing a drysuit when the box truck accident had thrown him into the past. He must have been freezing when the water had flooded the corridor.

Theo and Petra laid Alec's clothes flat on the walkway and then did the same with Alec himself.

"What are they doing?" said Bernard.

"If I had to guess," said Diane, "They're trying to prevent hypothermia."

A moment later, Theo and Petra began rubbing at Alec's limbs, perhaps trying to encourage circulation. They kept this up for a few minutes before Theo checked his wristband. There seemed to be an exchange of words, then he got to his feet and dashed off along the walkway.

"Where's he going?" Bernard pointed.

Theo left the upper engine room and exited by the same narrow corridor that they'd used to get in. A moment later, his silhouette had climbed a short set of steps and moved into a group of people.

Ryan felt a rising sense of panic.

"I can't see him."

Diane froze the display.

"It's OK," she tapped at the tablet, "Element overlay is

still showing us the effects of the steam… but if we retarget rubidium…"

A red dot pinpointed Theo's location and Ryan breathed a sigh of relief. Almost immediately though, he saw an odd effect.

In the part of the screen that was displaying Alec and Petra, he saw their red wristband dots, but there were also fainter patches of red within Petra's dress. He walked to the screen and pointed at them.

"What are these?"

"Ah," Diane nodded, "They're the rubidium chloride injectors."

"Why didn't we see these other dots before?" Bernard frowned.

"Before," she said, "I was filtering specifically for the rubidium-*quartz* in the wristbands. But at the moment it's highlighting anything that contains concentrations of rubidium. It's easy enough to correct though."

As she raised her tablet, Ryan realised what was bothering him.

"Wait!" he stopped her.

He looked at the red patches in Petra's hidden pocket.

"What's wrong?" Diane studied the screen.

Ryan pointed at the two faint dots.

"If Petra's supposed to be carrying all three return injectors," he said, "Where's the third one gone?"

LABYRINTH

With the pain in his water-filled ear singing loudly, Theo dashed on through the corridor. This section was above the rising water, but the floor was bright with the sheen of damp footprints. The people who'd made them were now long gone.

The lights flickered.

He had to find dry clothing for Alec: the wet items they'd taken off him weren't going to dry out fast enough. He knew he only had a matter of minutes before the flood would catch up with him. If he stayed here too long, the water would cut off his route back to the others.

Finding the first available open door, he pushed inside. The cabin was compact and sparsely fitted with bunks and a single washbasin. The tap was still running, but the flowing water was angled off to one side: a measure of how much the ship was continuing to tip.

A quick check of the bunks revealed that no clothing had been left behind. It was the same in the next room, and the next. On his fourth attempt, now significantly further along the corridor than he would have liked, he found a cabin with an abandoned suitcase; its contents strewn over the bunk and floor.

Dashing over fallen papers and photographs, he quickly rifled through the clothes and discovered an oversized pair of trousers, complete with braces. Rummaging on, he found a woman's woollen cardigan, and a shirt that could have been used as a small parachute. They would have to do.

Quickly bundling them up into the shirt, he dashed out of the cabin and ran back along the corridor toward the engine room. Even as he ran, he could see ceiling lights in the distance sparking and flickering off.

Skidding round a corner, he bolted down a short flight of steps and ran through the access way. The engine room was exactly as he'd left it. The great pistons below him were motionless, but the incredible warmth was still present, presumably because the boiler rooms were still generating heat that couldn't be used.

As he ran across the raised walkway, he saw that Alec was now sitting up and his shivering was less severe.

"You were gone ages," said Petra, "Everything OK?"

"The flood's on its way," he unravelled the clothes, "Help me with these. Alec, we can't stay here."

"Understood," Alec gave a nod, then did his best to assist them with the process of getting dressed.

The woman's cardigan went on first, being the smallest item. The wristband snagged a few times on the wool, but they quickly confirmed it was still secure. The voluminous shirt came next, followed by the baggy trousers. Not having the time to adjust the braces, Theo unclipped the front buckles, wrapped them tightly around Alec's waist and tied them in a double knot.

"Belt *and* braces," Alec smiled, "Very thorough."

Checking their wristbands one last time, they set off along the walkway and a moment later they were back in the cold air of the ship.

The short steps that Theo had raced down a few minutes ago had become a miniature water feature. He could see a shiny film of seawater sliding down the vertical drops of the steps. As he began to climb, the film thickened into a chaotic flow.

"Move!" he yelled.

With every step he climbed, the splashes deepened. When they reached the corridor level, the tilt that was causing the flood was painfully apparent. The angled water was no longer an exaggerated optical illusion. He could now *feel* the tilt in his legs.

Barely outpacing the cold sea that pursued them, they ran on through a labyrinth of corridors. Theo's damaged ear and the echoing walls made it difficult for him to tell which direction sounds were coming from, but he could hear Alec and Petra's voices somewhere behind him.

Pushing his way through a door, the narrow confines of the corridors became a wide open space. Red-and-white linoleum floor tiles, wood-panelled walls, and wicker chairs all surrounded a wooden staircase that rose up and out of view.

"Did we get turned around?" Petra looked back, "Is this the Grand Staircase?"

Alec shook his head, "We're in Second Class."

"You're sure?" she said.

"Trust me," he pointed at the stairs, "You don't forget lugging a heavy trunk around."

Behind them, a gush of water flooded under the door, and then proceeded to push it open. The wicker chairs that were closest to the door got caught in the swell and, as though they were four-legged creatures, began to meander away from the danger.

"Go!" Theo pushed Alec and Petra ahead of him, "Don't stop before D deck."

The staircase zigzagged between floors.

Owing to the ship's tilt, the first flight of stairs was angled down slightly, so Theo found the ascent was made easier. The next flight was in the opposite direction though, so the angle was steeper and it felt more like he was trying to stride up a ladder.

With the sound of rushing water coming from below, he led the way and continued the climb; the ship's fickle assistance alternating with every change in direction, and his compromised inner ear doing its best to upset his already conflicted sense of balance.

He knew they had to reach the rear section as fast as possible. Their remaining thirty minutes would have been perfectly adequate if the ship had been horizontal, but the flat floors were now becoming inclines. If they didn't speed up, the decks themselves would soon become too steep to walk over.

LOST

Diane concentrated on the curved screen and excluded all other thoughts. Reviewing the earlier moments of the QRI, she quickly discovered where Petra had lost one of the injectors.

As the cascade of water had knocked her off her feet and washed her down Scotland Road, the injector had been jostled from her pocket. When she'd lost her grip on the child, the injector had got caught in an eddy and had been whisked away to a lower deck.

For all intents and purposes, it was irretrievable.

The wristbands were intact but, with one of the injectors missing, the tethers would leave one of them behind. Worse still was the fact that she could see all this, but was powerless to warn them.

There was a light tap on her shoulder, and she became aware that Ryan had been trying to get her attention.

"Is the occlusion still there?" he said, "The one at the exit?"

It was a valid question, she thought. Eventually, the three of them would become aware of the injector problem. At that point, they may choose to stay together, rather than abandon the one who would be stranded. If their priorities then shifted to getting off the sinking ship, then the exit occlusion may never have happened.

She quickly tapped the end index point into her tablet and ran the query in reverse. As before, the aft of the Titanic un-sank and rose through the surface of the ocean. Once more, a wide occlusion un-collapsed into a static-filled sphere and then the query entered the quantum flux period where nothing was visible.

For some reason, the exit occlusion had still been part of the final events.

"Does that mean they all make it back somehow?" said Bernard.

"Not necessarily," she said, "One of the tethers won't be able to get a lock. At best, two of them may come back."

The monochrome noise continued to fizz.

"Forgive me," Bernard frowned, "but couldn't we just look for wristbands in the moments after the, er, occlusion disappears?"

Ryan was nodding, "We know the occlusion is centred on the upper aft store. We could check that same space one second after the exit closes."

"Wouldn't that tell us who got left behind?" said Bernard.

Diane quickly reset the query and focused on the aft store.

Running time forward, the second occlusion collapsed. The ship began its final plunge, and she could see the torn interior. It was clear that some people hadn't made it out in time. Some silhouettes were still struggling, others simply floated motionless in the middle of water-filled rooms.

Steeling herself for what she may find next, Diane added rubidium to the element overlay, and refreshed the screen. Not a single red dot was present.

She ran time forwards, backwards, and even checked the neighbouring rooms, but the result was the same: the injectors weren't there.

"Could they have escaped?" said Bernard, "If they *did* go through the second class dining saloon, they *could* have decided to head up to the boat deck."

"And do what?" said Ryan.

"And get to the lifeboats that... damn," he suddenly paused, "Women and children first. Petra may be alright but..."

Diane tried to keep her thoughts rational.

While they'd been spending time investigating the loss of an injector, time had been progressing for those aboard the Titanic. For every action that became a resolved part of history, the quantum flux would be clearing in its wake. New portions of their journey through the ship should now be available to view.

She reset the query again, and focused in on the last time she'd seen the three of them together: Theo had left Petra and Alec behind in the engine room.

Increasing the speed factor, she watched the events unfold at five times their normal speed. Like a hummingbird, Theo zipped in and out of rooms and flew back to the engine room, where a bundle of clothes exploded onto Alec. Pursued by a fast wash of water, the three of them zigzagged through a maze of corridors and rocketed up a set of stairs.

"Yes!" Bernard beamed, "They went to the surface!"

Almost as soon as he'd spoken, the red-dotted figures suddenly halted their ascent, left the staircase, and began speeding along an internal corridor.

They hadn't gone for the lifeboats.

As far as she could tell, they were broadly trying to stick to the original plan.

The view degraded into a squall of quantum flux: the time-accelerated query had apparently caught up with the events aboard the ship.

She rewound the view until the flux cleared, and returned

the query to normal speed. Now only a few seconds behind their actions, she could again witness their progress.

She heard Bernard take a deep breath.

"How long do they have left?" he said.

"Less than thirty minutes," she watched the three of them moving through a narrow busy space, "The closer they get to the aft store, the more we'll know."

She watched the screen in silence, an uncomfortable feeling of inevitability eroding her thoughts.

Ryan, who hadn't spoken for a while, now cleared his throat.

"Their exit room," he said, "How big is it?"

Overhead, the lights flickered.

EXIT ROOM

Making his way aft with Theo and Petra, Alec passed several of the people he'd seen earlier in the third class general room. Their good cheer and levity had vanished; colourful smiles and brightest hopes now replaced by grey lifebelts and darkest fears.

Alec thought of the couple who'd got engaged. He thought of the young boy who had, in all likelihood, died when the staircase had catastrophically flooded. Looking to his left, he could see that Petra was similarly blank-faced and was lost in her own thoughts; fate had snatched the child away while she'd been trying to save him.

He thought of John Coffey again, and the look that had been on his face as he'd wielded the revolver. Despite being the one holding the gun, despite repeatedly telling Alec that nobody would be able to see what he was doing, John's look had been one of desperation and fear. The entire encounter had apparently been driven by a belief that the prosthetic hand was violating some sort of holy principle.

He passed a man who was clutching a fiddle.

Perhaps fear just made people behave in unpredictable ways, he thought.

Alec could feel the deck was getting much steeper now. While his mind dealt with the peculiar sensation of navigating the tilted stairs and walls, his muscles burned with the effort of running uphill. One way or another, he thought, the journey must be very close to the end.

He felt his footing slip and he fell; his hand hitting the deck hard. He was only on the floor for a matter of seconds before getting up again, but the cold metal seized the opportunity to steal a little more heat from him. In its dying moments, the ship seemed to be lashing out at the infestation within its hull and was taking what it could in order to survive.

As they pushed on, they encountered fewer people. Any passengers they did meet were all speeding by in the opposite direction. No-one tried to stop them, or tried to tell them that they were going the wrong way, or tried to tell them to get to the lifeboats. Alec, Petra and Theo were now simply obstacles to be avoided in the scramble for the surface decks.

Through an open door, he saw a coat lying on a bunk. Warmth, the thought flashed through his mind.

"Hold up!" he called out.

He dashed inside, snatched the coat, and returned to the corridor. A few doors away, Theo was at a corner, anxiously glancing between him and the way ahead.

"Come on!" his beckoning hands were a blur, "It's right here!"

Fighting the incline, Alec chased after Petra and Theo. When he rounded the corner, he saw them both standing next to a closed door.

"How long?" he quickly put on the coat.

Theo checked his wristband.

"Fourteen minutes," he began unbuttoning his shirt.

"What are you doing?" Alec frowned, "Weather too warm for you?"

"The storeroom door's locked," he said, "I'm getting us inside."

Theo reached inside his shirt and pulled out a large key on a string.

"How the hell did -"

"We queried the lock," Petra cut short his question, "before the ship left Belfast."

"And three-D printed the key," Theo held up the chunky plastic duplicate and approached the door.

"Stop!" Alec stepped closer, "Plastic key, metal lock? What if it snaps? What if the mechanism's rusty or -"

"Right now," Theo inserted the key, "the mechanism's brand new and well oiled."

Alec knew that holding his breath wouldn't affect the resilience of the plastic, but he found himself doing it anyway. He watched Theo slowly turn the key. He heard a brief scrape of metal, and winced. Theo adjusted his grip and continued turning. There was a sudden click, and he saw the key turn freely in the lock. Without waiting, Theo grabbed the door handle and pulled.

The door opened and Alec let out his breath.

At the same time, the storeroom let out a few boxes.

The small pieces of luggage exited through the open doorway, slid across the sloping floor, and crashed into the opposite wall.

It took them another minute to clear the boxes that had fallen and gathered around the storeroom door. All the while, the ship continued its relentless drive to redefine the concept of horizontal.

When they got inside the room, they realised that the problem was only going to get worse. The boxes that were stacked vertically against the end wall would topple as the ship prepared itself for the final plunge: an event that would happen at the same time as the rapidly approaching exit occlusion.

With ten minutes to go, they began hauling the boxes away from the far wall. They worked as quickly as they could, but it was a continually shifting landscape. As the room kept tipping, some of the taller stacks fell and redefined the surface that they were able to stand on. As fast as they could clear a space, new debris would fall into it. Eventually, in their desperate attempt to clear the end wall, they were just throwing luggage and boxes to the far corners of the room, and hoping to keep themselves upright.

Alec was just about to reach for another box when he felt a deep shudder travel through the room. He froze and saw that Theo and Petra had done the same.

"Decompressions," said Theo, "It's started."

Petra flung a crate of bottles crashing against the side wall and she began hauling at the material of her dress.

"We should get ready," she said.

As a rumble vibrated the floor, Alec saw her actions halt.

"Petra?" he climbed over a crate to get to her.

She didn't reply, but her movements were becoming more frantic.

Something was wrong.

Overhead, the lights flickered.

THE BACKUP

The lights above Diane's head flickered.

For a moment she suspected that there had been another aftershock, but when she checked the seismic sensors, she discovered that everything was still in perfect registration. The link to the past was intact.

There *had* however been another power failure.

Looking at the map on her screen, she could see that a large power outage was affecting several blocks to the north of the Thames.

Exactly as designed, the museum's backup supply had instantly taken over. In decreasing order of priority, it had first protected any active retrostep equipment, then QRI functions, and then finally the more mundane electrical systems like lighting.

Again, they were operating on backup power.

Unlike last time though, their reserves weren't starting at one hundred percent; since the box truck incident, there hadn't been sufficient time to accumulate a full charge.

Ryan's exit room idea complicated matters.

Computationally, it was brute force and unrefined. Physically, it was borderline reckless. In power terms, it would burn through their backup power very quickly. In short, it was a plan that she herself would never have considered. But given their time constraints, she knew it was probably the best chance they had to get everyone home.

She looked at Ryan.

The signature had come into their lives and turned everything upside down. She wasn't a superstitious person, but it was now hard to tune out the feeling that someone had painted his name either as a warning, or as an endorsement.

She didn't believe in the vagaries of fate or destiny, but solid science had shown her that the exit occlusion still existed. Future possibilities had resolved because of actions they were about to take. The exact *way* that the events unfolded was still up to her though.

"Ryan," she said, "You *do* realise the ramifications?"

For a moment, he seemed to study her face.

"Tell me you can do it," he didn't flinch, "Tell me Theo's mathematical boost will hold."

Theo's tenfold topology increase *had* worked for London County Hall, but she knew that the geometry would be radically different for Ryan's solution.

"Technically, yes," she said, "It's just that -"

"Twenty-three minutes," he pointed at the screen, "Is it enough time?"

"Yes," she said, "But -"

"Who else *is* there?" he glanced behind him, "No offence, Bernard."

"Genuinely, none taken," said Bernard, "But can the recall tag things be *used* that way?"

Diane nodded.

Normally, the tags were configured to define the minimum amount of space necessary to surround an object for transport, but she knew that was adjustable.

"I can increase their radius of inclusion," she said, "Each

tag would then overlap the other and define a larger recall volume."

She could see Bernard arranging his fingertips to visualise the tetrahedral space.

"A triangle-base pyramid," he said, "Four vertexes?"

Ryan nodded.

"One tag each," he said, "Alec, Theo, Petra and me."

FOUR MINUTES

Alec could see Petra was panicking.

He saw her give two injectors to Theo, but then she kept rapidly searching between the folds of her petticoat.

Another deep rumble pushed at the floor.

Face pale, eyes wide open, Petra stopped her search. He saw Theo read the injectors and become as still as her.

He didn't need to ask her what was wrong.

Three people. Two injectors.

One of them wasn't going home.

A muffled decompression filled the quiet air.

Alec heard faint, distant yells echoing in through the door. Presumably, the three of them now had no time to get to the lifeboats.

"How long do we have?" Alec quietly broke the silence.

Theo handed the injectors back to Petra, then turned to face him.

"In about four minutes," he said, "You and Petra go home."

The room began to tilt faster.

Somewhere, a box fell down and he heard glass smashing.

Expressionless, Theo pressed at his wristband.

"Tether pre-sync running," his voice was flat as he turned to Petra, "When you hit the minute mark, inject your booster."

"Theo…" he said, "There's gotta be *something* we can do."

"There is," he said.

"What?" Petra stood ready.

Theo took off his wristband.

"Make sure you don't leave this here in the past," he held it out for him.

Aware that this moment would haunt him for the rest of his life, Alec saw his own hand reach out and take hold of the device.

Theo let go.

"According to eyewitness accounts," Theo was saying words, "the ship broke in two before sinking, so this whole room…"

The words were continuing, but Alec couldn't focus. His own actions had led them both here. His hidden message had set in motion a chain of events that had condemned Theo to death. The room that was supposed to be their exit would become an icy tomb.

He grabbed hold of Theo.

"Get to a lifeboat!" his voice broke, "You can send us a message. A telegram. *You* can tell *us* where to find you!"

Theo just looked at him.

Again no words were necessary.

Alec heard the wristband emit a quiet tone. In thirty seconds, they'd use the injectors. A minute after that, he'd never see him again.

A grating screech shuddered through the silence, then the whole room dropped.

For one instant Alec pictured the Titanic shearing in two, and its rear half crashing back into the sea. Then reality arrived.

In a catastrophic release of force, the storeroom became

upright again, sending him sprawling across the floor and sending crates toppling into each other.

He heard Petra yell, then the lights flickered again.

As the immediate clattering stopped, Theo shouted out.

"Everyone OK?"

Alec looked over to see that Petra was clutching her arm.

"... knocked them straight out of my hand," she was saying.

"What?"

"I lost the injectors!"

Alec dashed to her side and started hauling at the freshly thrown luggage. At the same time, Theo scrambled over boxes.

"How long?" he yelled.

Alec quickly checked his wristband, "One minute twenty!"

If they didn't inject their tracers in the next few seconds, their bodies wouldn't have time to absorb the chemicals. The tether would have nothing to latch onto.

Between a suitcase and a large trunk, he suddenly saw a gleam of metal.

"Here!" he shouted, "Help me!"

As Petra and Theo pulled the gap wider, he saw the metal was a squat cylinder. An injector. Reaching into the gap, he grabbed hold of it and pulled it out. It was marked 'Top Hat'.

Petra must have read the label too because she stopped moving and looked at him.

"We're out of time," she pointed to the injector, "Alec, you need to take it."

"We need to keep *looking!*" he stood up, "Yours has got to be around -"

"Alec!" she shouted over him and raised her wristband.

It was emitting another quiet tone.

The final minute had begun.

The whole room began tilting again, but Alec could see

that it was all happening much faster than before. Baggage and boxes crawled across the floor, then quickly started scrambling and leaping over each other to get to the opposite wall.

The lights above him flickered and faded.

As darkness swiftly swallowed the space, he felt the air buckle.

RETROSTEP

With four recall tags safely secured in a waist pouch, Ryan sprinted back along the corridor.

He knew where Lab One was, but he'd never been inside. He'd been in the lab next door to it, and he'd seen its massive net, but the room that held the transmitter pad had remained off-limits to him. Until now.

Heart hammering, he sped to the number pad at the side of the door and punched in the four digits. As soon as the lights above the door switched from red to green, he pulled the door handle and dashed into the room.

And stopped.

Ahead of him, he saw a floor pad that was similar to the one he'd seen in Lab Two, but this one was surrounded by densely packed machinery.

Directly above the pad, a large torus shape was slowly rotating. Its circumference was made up of long metallic tubes that followed each other end-to-end around the wide ring; each one rotating, or counter-rotating, on its own axis.

A deep hum permeated the whole space, reverberating off walls and bouncing off all manner of pipes and glassy-looking panels. All around him the air itself felt alive, as though static electricity was about to crackle through it at any moment.

"Three minutes, Ryan," Diane's voice echoed through the room, *"We don't have time for the wonder tour. Get to the pad."*

Glancing up, he spotted a balcony and observation window in the upper reaches of the room. On the other side of the glass, Diane was looking down and pointing to the transmitter pad.

Giving her a thumbs up, he ducked under an archway of thick cables, and moved quickly to the centre of the room. Feeling very much that he was about to leave behind everything he knew, he tentatively stepped onto the pad.

"Stand in the middle," she said, *"Keep as still as you can."*

All around him he saw coils of densely wound copper that were interlaced with iridescent threads of quartz. As he kept still, a high-pitched whistle evaporated into the ultrasonic range and he felt a ripple passing through him. Staring at the surrounding tubes and metalwork, his mind chose this moment to remind him of the McCairn photo.

When the convict had woken up on this pad, he'd have been surrounded by all of this, he thought. It was hardly surprising that the man had been freaked out by what was around him.

"So don't freak out," he quietly told himself.

"No need to freak," Diane's matter-of-fact tones came through a nearby speaker, *"The scan's complete."*

He hadn't realised that she'd be able to hear him.

"Great," he recovered, "What's next?"

"We prep your tether," she said, *"To your right."*

He looked to the right side of the space and saw that a wristband was clipped into a shallow recess. It was a metal-link band that could have passed for a modern-day watch, except the display area was matte black.

"It doesn't hold your bio-pattern," she reminded him, *"but it will link you to it via the tracer. To your left."*

He saw the pneumatic injector nozzle at the left side of the rig.

He took a deep breath, something that Diane apparently noticed.

"You're doing well, Ryan," she told him, *"OK, the tether's ready."*

He heard a click and turned to see the wristband's display briefly flash on and off. Following her instructions, he unmounted the band from the recess and put it on.

"Are we ready?" he asked.

"Almost," she said, *"Now I need you to listen carefully."*

Ryan looked up, but he couldn't see the observation window. All he could see was the spinning torus above him.

"Go ahead."

"You know that we can't get an accurate scan of your arrival coordinates, don't you?"

"Yep," he said, "It's still occluded."

"Correct, so I back-extrapolated the position of the exit room by querying the trajectory of the Titanic after it went under the -"

"Diane," he closed his eyes, "I'm nervous enough already. I get that this is your best guess."

There was a pause.

"I'm sending a large volume of air with you," she said, *"but the landing... well... it's going to be rough."*

He pictured the storeroom at the aft of the ship.

According to Bernard, the ship's generators had failed just before it sank. Without electrical power, the Titanic's final moments would have been in complete darkness.

Thinking of the actions that Alec must once have taken, Ryan reached up and turned on his jacket-mounted LED light.

He knew the timings that were involved. Once the rubidium-82 tracer was in his bloodstream, there would be approximately 16 seconds to confirm absorption and begin the trip: the trip that had caused the exit occlusion that they'd already seen.

For one moment, he felt like a passenger: events were driving *him*.

The speaker crackled and Diane's voice came through.

"It's time."

As he presented his wrist to the injector nozzle, she spoke again.

"Thank you, Ryan," she said, *"We'll see you soon."*

"I hope so."

"QRI timer in sync… Injector in three, two, one."

He felt a sharp pinch at his left wrist as the tracer entered his system. Walking to the centre of the transmitter pad, he began mentally counting down from sixteen. Picturing an uncertain floor level, he bent his knees slightly.

The machinery above him began to rotate faster. The individual segments of the torus lit up; their combined twisting and rotating motion tracing out overlapping sine waves of light.

"Tracer absorption confirmed…"

His mind raced. He was really doing this. His next step would take place over a century into the past.

"Direct query still in occlusion," Diane reported over the increasing noise, *"Retrostep coordinates confirmed."*

The torus now accelerated. Its undulating waves of light warped and strobed into an encompassing ring that seemed to be rotating both forward and backward at the same time.

"Auto-commit locked in," Diane was saying, *"Good luck."*

Around the base of the transmitter pad, lights came on and strobed in sync with the torus segments above. All around him, a hum pulsed at the suddenly viscous air.

As he closed his eyes, the present day ceased to exist.

Standing at one side of Lab Two, Bernard pressed the button and watched the tension increase in the steel cables. As the motorised winches wound in the cables, the corners of the wide net peeled themselves off the floor and rose into the air. The outer edges of the net lifted from the floor, and within a minute, the low central section separated itself from the ground.

Then it stopped.

He pushed at the button again, but the net rose no further.

He felt a cold sweat break out on his brow, but then remembered Diane's instructions: the catcher mitt was supposed to do that.

Quietly cursing himself, he mopped the sweat from his forehead and quickly moved to the control panel for the pneumatic support rods.

As instructed, he adjusted the recoil pressure to account for the fact that *four* people would now be returning instead of three. He didn't understand the digits he was entering, but in matters of calculation, he trusted Diane implicitly.

"Bernard," her voice echoed through the room's loudspeaker, *"The clock's running. One minute!"*

He entered the last of the digits into the keypad, closed up the panel, and hit 'enter'.

At the corners of the net, the support rods hissed then slowly telescoped upward, raising the whole hammock-like assembly higher into the air. After a few seconds, the rods locked into place with a mechanical jolt and sent a light ripple through the elastic mesh.

Satisfied with his work, Bernard turned to look at the rest of the room and saw that the cubist portrait was still lying on the floor. Next to it, on what the others had called the bunny pad, was the signed sailboat scene that Theo had been analysing earlier.

In less than a minute, this room would become much busier. Considering the importance of the two artistic works, he thought it was probably best if they weren't just left on the floor.

Moving as quickly as he could, he crossed the open space and lifted the large portrait by its shortest edge. Levering it upright, he could feel that it wasn't exactly heavy, but it was a little unwieldy.

Shifting his weight from side to side, and pivoting the canvas on alternating corners, he started walking the portrait back across the floor.

Petra felt the room tilting.

The cold realisation hit her: the ship was starting its terminal dive.

Their rescue plan had failed, and there was no backup.

She was going to die here.

Like everyone clinging to the exterior deck, she was going to drown in the icy depths of the Atlantic.

It felt like her final moments were almost unfolding in slow motion: one last high-definition experience for her adrenaline-flooded senses.

Luggage was tumbling, as were Theo and Alec. She could hear the quiet, tortured screams that were echoing in from somewhere above. The young boy's terrified face flashed through her mind. The lights above her flickered; a dying, pale-yellow strobe that fell into a darkness so dense that it felt as if her eyes were closed.

She felt the air pull at her lungs, then a dim light returned.

It wasn't coming from the ceiling.

Accompanied by a thick punch of expanding air, a ball of light erupted in the middle of the storeroom, blasting aside fallen and falling boxes in its wake.

The light snapped back to a singular spot, then a figure fell out of the air and landed in a pile of toppled suitcases.

Almost immediately, the figure scrambled to get to his feet, sending pained curses and bright-white LED beams scattering around the dark room.

"Ryan?!" she now recognised him.

He stood upright, reached for a pouch at his waist, then doubled over again and vomited.

She tried to get to her feet, but the room kept tilting. The storeroom doorway would soon lie beneath her. Already she could hear the rush of water and feel an icy wind. The rising water was pushing the remaining air out of the ship.

Theo and Alec were clambering over to Ryan, who was still trying to speak.

"Four tags..." he retched and then pointed between the four of them, "Like Bernard rescue... but pyramid..."

She saw Theo rapidly drawing triangles in the air with his finger, then he spoke with equal speed.

"Ryan, are we supposed to make a pyramid return volume?"

Still doubled over, Ryan gave a muted thumbs up and patted at his waist pouch.

"One tag each," he coughed.

Bracing herself against a large case, she pushed herself upright and crawled over the floor that was fast becoming a rising wall. The rushing sound suddenly got louder, and she turned to see water bursting in through the doorway.

With a fresh kick of adrenaline, she sped over the shifting luggage landscape. To her right, Alec thrust out his hand and pulled her over to where the other two were taking the tags from the pouch.

She saw Ryan look at one of the tags, turn it on, and then hand it to Alec.

"This one's... assigned to your wristband."

As Ryan did the same thing for Theo, she looked around at the rapidly flooding room. Cases were floating on the severely angled water. Already she could feel the air pressure changing as the rising water squeezed the space that they were in. Stretching her jaw, she felt her ears pop, and the rushing sound got louder again.

Ryan handed her a tag.

"Keep tight hold," he managed.

"OK, a pyramid," said Alec, "Three of us need to stay low, and form a base."

"And one of us stands up in the middle," Theo lifted his tag above his head.

Petra heard the thirty second warning coming from all of their wristbands.

Ryan checked his wrist and then activated his own tag. As he glanced between them all, he seemed to remember something.

"Listen," he raised his voice over the sound of the rushing water, "Diane says not to get too close to each other."

It made sense, she thought.

"To keep our bio-patterns separate?" she asked.

"I'm afraid I didn't have time to -"

With a sudden jolt, their small island of cases and boxes collapsed and she was tipped into the icy water. The drysuit took the brunt of the thermal shock but the tilted walls still disoriented her.

Shaking the water out of her eyes, she ignored everything except the angle of the water which would always try to stay horizontal.

A second later, her revised perspective snapped into place: the storeroom walls and floor were rapidly dropping through the surface of the water. Amid the floating cases, the others were fighting their water-logged clothes and doing their best to stay above water.

As she thrust out her arms to begin swimming toward them, she heard the wristband emit the fifteen-second warning. Only now did she realise how far apart they'd all drifted after the fall.

They wouldn't reach each other in time.

Again she felt fate slowing the hands of her personal clock.

She looked at Theo, Alec and Ryan frantically trying to push cases out of the way on the surface of the rising water.

A terrifying new thought flashed through her mind: everyone was floating in the same *plane*. When the tags defined the shape that would return, that shape would be blade-sharp flat surface. The tether would simply bring back an atom-thick slice of the four of them.

She could think of only one way to restore the three-dimensional volume.

"Listen!" she yelled, "Lift your tags! Face away from each other!"

"What?!" Ryan shouted.

"Just *do* it!" she took a deep breath.

Without waiting for their reply, she ducked under the surface of the water and began swimming straight down. They may not be able to form a pyramid *above* water, she thought, but an inverted one would define the returning volume just as effectively.

With every stroke and kick, deep rumbles pulsed through the water. The lower deck rooms had already started decompressing.

The ice-cold water welcomed her deeper, pulling at her heavy dress and numbing her skin. As the faint light from above receded, she felt the water was resisting her less. She slowed her swimming, but the water continued to get colder and she felt herself twisting to one side. Too late, she realised what was happening. Within an already sinking ship, water was being sucked *down* to fill the decompressed decks that were somewhere below.

She was being dragged deeper.

Clutching the tag tightly, she tried to turn around and kick for the surface, but she felt her leg scrape over a straight edge.

In the last glint of visible light, she saw the storeroom doorway receding from her. In total darkness, she felt herself getting pulled head first around a corner and deeper into the ship.

Her lungs screamed for oxygen and urged her to take a fresh breath from the seawater, but she clamped her hand over her mouth and fought it. Immediately in front of her eyes, she saw her wristband display was strobing rapidly. A single second remained.

Thrusting her tag out in front of her, she closed her eyes.

Bernard leaned the large portrait against the side wall and stepped back to look at the fragmented man: the solution to, and source of, so many of their problems.

Suddenly, Diane's voice echoed around the room.

"Precursor spike!"

As he whirled around to look up at the net, the loudspeaker clicked and her voice returned, filled with panic.

"Bernard get out of there!" she yelled, *"The returning mass is -"*

He didn't hear the rest.

Arriving like the crack of thunder, a pinpoint of light tore itself into a wide, glassy bubble that expanded at lightning speed, pushing the air out of its way and knocking him off his feet.

Looking up, he saw the sphere was so large that it had ripped a hole through the net and was touching the floor beneath it. Light swirled around and through its shimmering surface then, as if a desert mirage was evaporating, he saw outlines coalescing into a vast physical form.

Seemingly balanced on a single lower point, a heavily skewed wedge shape filled the width and height of the room.

As its indistinct volume rapidly condensed into intricate detail, he understood what he was seeing.

Hanging motionless in the air was a three-dimensional, Escher-like slice of stairs, corridors and rooms.

As though held in place by invisible walls, translucent water occupied every single space; the debris within it frozen in time, like bubbles in blown glass.

Before he could blink, it seemed that time was suddenly granted permission to move forward.

The lower pointed end skewered the floor, sending water gushing sideways and ejecting a woman in a dress. Now pivoting about its narrow end, the gigantic wedge began a terrifyingly slow fall.

In a cacophony of screeching metal and room-wide vibrations, the topmost section impacted the side wall, slowed, and began gouging claw marks down through the feeble concrete. The water within the structure didn't slow. Still accelerating under the same gravity, the water fell freely to the floor as one solid mass, sending a tidal wave crashing against the walls and washing in his direction.

Scrambling backwards, he saw the upper end of the wedge shape rip free of the wall. At the very top, luggage was toppling off a sloping floor, and two men were desperately trying to stop a third man from sliding over the edge.

The whole structure rolled onto its side.

A gargantuan mass of water and iron beams slammed into the bunny pad, instantly obliterating the small oil painting that had been resting on its surface.

Bernard kept frantically crawling backwards, but the tidal wave caught up with him. It was now only a few feet high, but it effortlessly lifted him up and threw him against the side wall.

Ice-cold water wrapped itself around him and tried to drag him under, but he fought it for all he was worth.

Struggling up onto his knees, he caught sight of the woman in the dress.

Now that she was upright and clear of the fast-moving water, he could see it was Petra. She was taking great, splashing strides through the water toward the wider end of the structure.

As he hauled himself to his feet, he realised the metallic screeching had stopped. The bizarre, wedge-shaped cross-section of ship had come to rest.

"We're OK!" a voice came from above.

He looked up to see Alec, Theo, and Ryan perching on a pile of boxes that had gathered in the corner of a sliced-through room.

Above the continuous noise of water cascading through metalwork, he heard Petra laughing and couldn't help smiling.

Everyone was home.

Figuratively and literally, they'd also brought home a slice of history.

"Hey Bernie!" Alec called down to him, "You're gonna need a bigger vault!"

He knew Alec was probably right, but standing shin deep in freezing cold water, his first thought wasn't about storage. The room was in the lowest part of the museum; the water had nowhere to go. This was going to be one messy clean-up.

Looking around at the debris in the water, he saw something that almost made his heart stop.

Against the side wall, jutting out of the shallow water like a shark fin, was a corner of the large cubist portrait that he'd moved earlier.

As he got closer, it became clear that the canvas had snapped across a diagonal. The cubist man beneath the cold seawater was now an irretrievable wreck of torn cloth, but the sailing boat scene in the upper left rectangle of the canvas had survived intact above the gently lapping waves.

He heard Petra wade through the water and stop at his side.

"So *this* was how it happened," she said.

Unable to find words, he simply nodded.

Whether they liked it or not, they appeared to be travelling along a path that destiny was prescribing for them.

He now saw Petra glancing around.

"Where's the smaller one?" she said.

With a heavy sigh, he pointed at the mass of ironwork that was intersecting the ruined bunny pad.

"Gone," he said.

The rain-like sound of draining seawater filled the air and sent echoes washing back and forth around the closed room.

"Come on," Petra began wading back through the water, "We need to get everyone dry."

COFFEE

Cocooned in warm blankets, Alec sat in his meeting room chair and drank from his coffee cup. He'd been away for so long that he'd almost forgotten the taste. There had of course been places to buy coffee in Paris, but consuming it had required a trip to a cafe, and careful pre-planning of how he'd minimise his interaction. Here, drinking it required no mental dexterity. Everything here was instant and available.

He knew that the novelty of being around modern trappings and perspectives would soon fade, but for now he savoured the heat of the ceramic mug, the warmth of the air around him, and the brightness of the lights above his head.

With the exception of Diane, everyone else at the table was similarly wrapped in blankets, holding hot mugs in their hands, and nursing their aching muscles.

Bernard was alternately frowning and nodding as the others talked him through what they believed had happened in the final moments aboard the Titanic.

Very much like the incident in the box truck, the sync tags had done exactly what they were designed for: they'd worked to define a volume of space that would return to the present.

But when they'd drifted apart, the three tags in the storeroom had defined a room-wide triangle. The fourth tag, which *should* have been immediately below them, had been dragged out of the room and pulled to a lower deck. The resulting volume hadn't been a neat inverted pyramid, it had been a distorted wedge. Thanks to Theo's tenfold increase in addressable mass, the wedge had returned containing an angular cross-section of flooded rooms and corridors.

The returning physical matter had been so massive that it had taken every last watt of power to define and teleport. The impact of the thirty-metre-long structure had also created a tremor so large that it had knocked the seismic sensors offline.

Alec finished his coffee, tucked his hand back into the warmth of the blanket, and looked at the large, wrecked portrait on the table.

Metzinger's 'Man with a Pipe' now contained neither the man nor the pipe.

As if fulfilling its own bizarre temporal prophesy, the sailboat and lake section had remained intact. Everything else was a torn and ripped mess. Even the black tie area that had contained his iron filing message had been destroyed during the catastrophic Lab Two flood.

He quietly worked through the logic. At some point, the ruined portrait would be trimmed to size, inherit a signature, and be put in a neodymium-backed wooden frame. As for the version that had already gone through these events, its somewhat circular lifespan had come to a tragic end under the crushing weight of the Titanic shard.

As he glanced over at the intact sailboat segment of the torn canvas, an alternative perspective occurred to him: perhaps this was where the framed painting had actually *begun* its circular lifespan.

"Interesting…" Bernard was reading from his tablet.

"What is?" Alec leaned forward.

"It says here that the cubist portrait also came to be known by other names."

"Which were?"

"American Man..." Bernard frowned, "American Smoker... I wonder why that was?"

Alec told them how Metzinger had misidentified his accent because of a phrase he'd used in a Paris bar. Alec thought that the alternate names were perhaps evidence that he'd had some sort of effect on history, but Diane wasn't so sure.

"When it comes to QRI and retrostepping," she said, "their time-resolved nature means that the past remains unchanged. Any interactions we make, or *will* make, to the past are *already* part of our history. Nothing changes."

"But..." said Alec, "didn't we just rip up the operating manual?"

"How do you mean?" she frowned.

"Occlusions are points where any interaction is completely contained," he glanced at Theo and Petra, "But we just weaved our way from one end of the Titanic to the other. That's hardly what I'd call contained."

"We might *think* we've changed things," she pointed at the broken portrait, "but ultimately, I'd say that events are still unfolding as before."

Having spent a significant amount of time in the past, he thought Diane's view was coldly deterministic. If what she was saying was true, then the choices he'd made in the past weren't actually choices at all; a perspective that made him feel deeply uneasy.

He saw Theo shrug.

"Even if you *did* influence Metzinger," he said, "the fact is that we're all embedded within this timeline. There's no way for us to step outside the system to compare before and after."

Ryan snorted a quiet laugh.

"It *felt* like I was stepping outside the system," he held his stomach, "Talk about motion sickness."

Theo patted Ryan on the back.

"I don't know if you were always 'supposed' to come and get us but... well..."

"Thank you," Alec completed for him, "Thank you everyone."

When he looked over at Petra, he could see that her thoughts were a world away.

"Petra?"

Her focus returned and she quickly adopted a smile.

"All I can say is that it's the last time I'm wearing a dress for any of you."

Alec raised a finger, "Never say never."

She laughed along with everyone else, but then shook her head.

"Still can't believe that we changed nothing."

Bernard sighed and picked up his tablet.

"Eyewitness accounts mention nothing of your activity aboard the Titanic," he said, "In some ways, I think that's a testament to how well you all blended in."

"OK," her voice was quiet, "but you know that's not what I meant."

Bernard looked away and nodded. After tapping and swiping the tablet screen, he sighed again and reported that only 710 people had survived.

For a moment, the room went quiet, then Ryan looked up.

"You mean seven hundred and *eleven* survivors."

Bernard looked at the tablet and shook his head.

"I'm afraid not."

Theo now sat up straight and glanced at the others.

"But it *has* to be seven hundred and eleven."

Alec saw Diane nod in agreement.

When he asked why, she told him that she remembered

highlighting the number 711 on the curved screen during their Titanic research.

Alec exchanged glances with Bernard who shrugged. Neither of them had been here when the others were doing their research.

Suddenly, Alec felt a chill.

"Maybe the survivor report counted one less person, because I ended up back here."

He saw Petra slowly sit upright.

"There shouldn't be *any* discrepancy between our recall and recorded history," she looked around at everyone, "We *did* change the past."

Alec expected Diane to offer some sort of counterargument, but she simply nodded to herself.

"I hate to admit it," she said, "but I think my original hypothesis may be in need of some revision."

Bernard put down his tablet.

"But what about the portrait," he said, "Didn't you say that everything's unfolding in the same way?"

"We may be bound for the same destination," Diane was frowning, "but perhaps our *route* has now changed."

Alec considered the long route that the ruined canvas had already taken to get here. Even now, he could picture it standing on the easel with the paint still wet. Jean had talked about cubism being an artistic view of dimensional truth: a concept for holding time, motion, and the observer himself in an indeterminate state. In a more modern era, he thought, the Mysterious Metzinger could have been describing quantum probability.

Under his warm blanket, he felt the faint misfire of the nerves in his left wrist. As had become habit, he instinctively reached to press at the spot, and again he felt the uncomfortable absence of the prosthetic.

The engine room confrontation flashed through his mind.

Things could have gone so differently if he'd had the chance to use the magnesium beacon properly.

"Bernard," he glanced at the tablet, "could you check something for me?"

"Of course," he said.

"Could you see what you can find on John Coffey?"

"Ah," Bernard nodded, "The man obsessed with your..."

Alec took a deep breath. He'd have to get used to the idea of people not quite finishing sentences when it came to matters that involved his hand.

Bernard worked at the tablet for a while, and then frowned.

"Hmm," he said, "According to the White Star records, Mr. Coffey was crew, but he was never aboard."

For a moment Alec thought that Bernard may be trying to spook him, so he found himself smiling. But when the smile wasn't returned, he realised that it wasn't a joke.

"I met him," Alec insisted, "I spent *hours* with him. He knew the ship like the back of his hand. He was a boiler room worker."

"Indeed he was," said Bernard, "but he didn't go on the journey."

"What?"

"It seems that John Coffey sneaked off the ship," Bernard read out the details, "He hid under some mailbags and got himself transported to shore before the ship left Queenstown."

"But... that's *impossible."*

"Yeah, that one got me too," Theo nodded, "We're not talking about Queenstown in New Zealand. Apparently, Queenstown is the old name for Cobh."

"Indeed," Bernard put his tablet down, "The name only changed in nineteen-twenty."

Alec now found himself doubting his own memory.

He was pretty sure that John had said he'd lived in *Cobh*

all his life, but that place name hadn't existed until eight years *after* the Titanic disaster. Either something was amiss, or he was just exhausted. Given what he'd been through, he suspected it was probably the latter.

The meeting room lights flickered.

"Ah," Diane consulted her tablet, "I think the main power is back on."

He saw Bernard take a very deep breath.

"Is it time?" he looked nervous.

"Not quite," she shook her head, "I want to build up a little reserve power first."

Again, Alec felt that the others knew something that he didn't.

"What did I miss?"

They told him about the London County Hall collapse and the ingenious way they'd extracted Bernard from the rooftop, despite him having no tether. As Alec listened though, he began to understand the scale of the potential consequences.

Minutes before the collapse, dozens of politicians had witnessed Bernard leaving the main hall, but he hadn't yet been counted as a survivor. As far as the world was concerned, Bernard was still missing. If he made a miraculous and unscathed return now, a day after the aftershock, it could focus unwanted attention on them.

"OK," Alec nodded, "But what has *that* problem got to do with building up reserve power?"

Diane glanced over at Bernard.

"We've talked it through," she said, "and we all think there's one solution. One that will keep retrostepping concealed."

Bernard was quietly nodding in apparent contemplation..

"The hourglass sands are but borrowed moments," he sounded like he was quoting a poem, "They return whence they came."

Alec frowned at him, "What?"

"My rescue was temporary," he said, "I have to go back."

Alec pictured Bernard retrostepping onto a collapsing rooftop and being plunged into the Thames along with tonnes of concrete: sacrificing himself in order to protect the secrecy of their operation. He found himself shaking his head at the thought that everyone had decided this cold-hearted plan was actually a viable solution.

"After *everything* we've been through, we're *not* sending him back there to die in some -"

"Die?" Bernard looked both alarmed and amused, "Good heavens no! At least I very much hope not."

Diane quickly clarified what their intentions were.

"Assuming we can get the timings right," she said, "We're going to send Bernard back thirty-three hours."

The timing sounded very specific.

"Why thirty-three?"

"It's just after the news channels started speculating about which ministers had died in the County Hall collapse."

"In the chaos," said Theo, "Bernard can show up and get himself accounted for."

"If there's no mystery," Ryan shrugged, "There's no attention."

When Alec pointed out that Bernard's sudden arrival would generate quite a *lot* of attention, Diane reminded him that occlusions didn't work that way. As ever, the arrival location would be in an unobserved spot. In Bernard's case, it would be downstream from the media frenzy that was focused on London County Hall and Westminster Bridge.

Clearly, they'd given this a lot of thought.

"When did you work all this out?"

Petra glanced over at Bernard.

"One night in the museum," she said, "Bernard's idea."

"Please," he shook his head, "We all brought it together."

Alec looked at Bernard and considered the physical strain that he was volunteering for.

"And you're willing to go through all this?"

Bernard reached into his pocket and pulled out a gold lapel pin.

"Miranda gave me this in twenty ten," he stared at the roman numerals, "I wore it every day. She wanted me to work closely with you."

Alec felt a stab of regret that they'd so actively deceived him.

"I'd say you already *have* been working with us," he said.

Bernard paused and then frowned.

"What?" asked Theo.

Bernard ran his fingers over the shiny MMX lettering.

"Miranda May," he smiled and looked around at them all, "Minute Men."

Alec could see the others were now smiling too.

"What about the X?" said Petra.

Bernard raised his finger and drew a cross over his heart.

"My promise to keep it a secret."

RETURNS

Standing in the guest bedroom, Ryan pulled on the last of his clean clothes. At some point soon, he'd have to go home and pick up new supplies. On the bedside table, his phone was flashing a discreet light.

As he bent to pick it up, muscles that he didn't know he possessed cheerfully announced their presence. He suspected it would be like this for quite a while. Every so often, his minute-long luxury cruise would provide him with another painful souvenir.

Pausing to permit himself a small wince, he moved a little slower and collected his phone. He tapped the screen and listened to a voice message.

"Hey Ryan, it's Omar. I've been out of cell range for days, so I've only just seen the news about London. The Fortean front webpage is down, so I just wanted to check you were OK. Drop me a text or call me, I'll be on this number for the next day. Yeah, so, I hope you're alright, er, talk soon."

Ryan saw that the message was already a day old, so he'd missed any chance to call him back. By now, Omar would have moved on to the next leg of his Egypt trip.

As an image of the pyramids flitted through his mind, he

wondered whether they'd somehow been the source of his inspiration for the recall tag formation. He supposed he'd never know for sure. As he was beginning to understand, the causality of things wasn't always apparent.

A knock came from the door.

Apparently, it was already time for Bernard's retrostep.

He looked at the phone and decided that the outside world could wait a little longer for its Fortean tales. Tossing the phone onto his bed, he headed to the door and opened it.

"I knocked this time," said Petra.

"Thanks," he couldn't help smiling.

"Well," she smiled back, "I didn't want you to vomit in surprise."

"I'm never going to live that down, am I?" he said, "Considering it was my *first* retrostep -"

"You did well," she patted him on the shoulder, "Better than well actually."

He closed the door, and they both started to walk along the corridor. Immediately, he noticed that she was moving as carefully as he was.

"You too?" he said.

"Yep," she nodded, "I think I must've hit every corner as I got dragged down."

Ryan didn't know what to say. She'd had the worst experience of all of them, but had said the least about it. He'd injured himself during his mid-air arrival, but she'd suffered the terror of half-drowning in complete darkness.

Attempting to steer her away from the memory, he pointed ahead of him and adopted a sarcastic tone.

"Oh good. Stairs."

"Try doing it in a dress," she shook her head, "So glad to be rid of that damn thing."

"You weren't tempted to wear it for Bernard's big send off?"

"No," she smirked, "I didn't much care for the colour."

After a minute of climbing stairs and moving along connecting corridors, they arrived at the waiting room.

Unlike the first time he'd been brought here, Petra now led the way and walked straight through to Diane's empty office. Somehow, without the fizzing static on the curved wall, the room seemed even emptier.

"I thought I was watching the departure from here," he said, "Where are the others?"

Petra didn't answer. She just kept walking until she reached the plain door behind Diane's desk. He'd always assumed that the door was a store cupboard, but as Petra opened it, he realised there was a whole room on the other side.

The arrangement of spaces here beneath the British Museum had always made it hard for him to visualise where things were in relation to each other. The room in front of him tied together the various viewpoints he'd seen over the past few days.

On opposite sides of the room, wide windows overlooked two vast spaces.

Through the broken and missing glazing to his right, he could see the time-displaced wreckage that had been transported from 1912. Looking like a real-life cross-section diagram, the partial floors and walls slanted down to the seawater that still covered the floor of Lab Two.

Through the other window, below a balcony walkway, was the mass of machinery and cables that surrounded the transmitter pad. He could see that the large torus was already spinning.

Between the two windows, behind a wide control console that was bristling with screens, Diane looked up.

"I thought you might appreciate a live view instead."

Still taking in the sights, he just nodded and walked further in.

Like the satisfying last few pieces of a jigsaw, the various things he'd learnt over the past few days began to slot into geographical place.

He pointed at the broken window.

"Didn't you say Lab Two was a sealed space? No observers?"

Diane nodded.

"Roller shutters normally shield the view," she nodded, "but they run off main power."

"I'll add it to the repair list," Petra joined her at the console, "How's everything looking?"

He saw Diane glanced to her right.

"They're in final prep."

Ryan walked over to the window and looked down at Lab One.

The wide, spinning torus was clearly visible. Below it, at the side of the transmitter pad, he could see that Alec and Theo were talking to Bernard while tying a large block of polystyrene to each arm.

Alec turned to look up at the window. As he gave a thumbs up, his voice came from a speaker on Diane's console.

"OK," he said, *"We're all set."*

With no need for a tracer, preparations for Bernard's one-way trip had apparently been fairly swift.

Using a microphone in the console, Diane addressed the room below.

"To reiterate, Bernard," she said, "While you're in the past, you must *not* make contact with us. Back then, we were busy trying to rescue you, so you *cannot* interfere with those events."

Ryan saw him look up toward the window.

"Understood," he nodded, *"I'll only make contact with you again after this present time."*

"Not a moment sooner," Diane replied.

As Theo guided Bernard onto the transmitter pad, Ryan

lost sight of them below the spinning ring of counter-rotating elements. A few seconds later, Theo backed away.

"OK, he's on the pad," he said, *"We're exiting now."*

The elements within the ring lit up, and again Ryan saw the flickering of intertwined sine waves.

Above a growing hum, he could hear Alec reporting that they were clear of Lab One. He was distantly aware of Diane's continuing verbal checklist, but his attention was focused on the transmitter rig's mesmerising ballet of motion and light. Helix formations rippled in both directions around the circumference of the ring. Again he got the impossible impression that it was spinning in opposing directions at the same time.

Accompanied by a deepening hum, rapidly pulsating lights came on around the base of the transmitter pad.

Caught in the strobing light, the spinning ring seemed to be held completely motionless, as if rotating neither backward nor forward.

For a fraction of a second, all light under the ring seemed to shift toward redder tones, and then it dipped into a perfectly black void. Light itself wasn't leaving the pad.

In no time at all, the patch of darkness pinched itself into a point.

Thirty-three hours earlier, above the dark waters of the Thames, a man quietly appeared in the night air.

Seen and heard by no-one, and with large polystyrene blocks attached to his arms, he dropped into the water. After kicking his way to the nearest bank, he untied his disposable flotation aids and allowed them to drift away with the other pieces of river debris. The man then straightened his soaking wet tie and moved off into the shadows.

Ryan saw the dark point vanish as if it had never existed.

The strobing lights fell out of sync with the ring and for a moment he saw the bidirectional spinning effect again. Then the ring quickly began to lose speed and the illusion dissolved away.

"Transmit complete," Diane spoke over the fading hum, "Theo, Alec, volume integrity check."

"Moving in," said Alec.

Looking down on Lab One, he saw Alec and Theo dash to the transmitter pad and walk under the slowing ring.

"E.M. stable," said Theo.

"Transmit buffer clear," Alec added.

Ryan turned to face Diane and Petra.

"Does that mean that he's back in the past?"

Diane glanced around the room.

"We didn't cease to exist," she said, "Which means one of two things. Either everything went well, and he did nothing to affect the last two days."

"Or?"

"Or, he didn't arrive at all. His bio-pattern -"

The desk phone rang.

The three of them exchanged looks, then Diane reached out and tentatively pushed the phone's speaker button.

"Hello?"

There was a slight rustling sound, then a voice came through the speaker.

"I believe the reports of my death have been grossly exaggerated."

Ryan laughed out loud.

"Where are you, Bernard?" Petra was smiling.

"In the Great Court Reading Room," he said, *"I actually got here a few minutes ago, but I knew I had to wait."*

"Stay there," Petra now laughed, "we'll be right up."

MMX

Diane looked up at the glazed roof of the Great Court. The dark night, and her tiny reflection, were gone. In their place was a clear, pale-blue morning sky. The new day almost felt like a fresh new start.

Accompanied by the others, she started climbing the limestone staircase that spiralled around the central Reading Room tower. To her right, Petra and Theo were still talking about the Downing Street damage.

"But," Petra was saying, "the twelve-second occlusion we saw was *way* too short to be a retrostep."

"At this point, I don't think we can rule it out," said Theo, "We've only just discovered a radical new way to interpret occlusions. The Westminster quake *could* be a result of factors that we haven't even considered yet."

Although Diane nodded at the idea, she found herself distracted.

Over the past few hours, certain details from their various conversations had begun to bother her.

Alec had mentioned that the man calling himself John Coffey had used a town name that was either wrong, or extraordinarily prescient. It was possible that Alec had misheard John, but she doubted it.

When she thought about their 3D-printed storeroom key, and the QRI method they'd used to acquire its shape, it gave her an uneasy feeling: despite not being a crew member, John had similarly possessed the perfect key to enter the secure engine room.

Then there was the matter of the gunpoint confrontation itself.

John had lured Alec to an isolated location where their actions would go unobserved. Even after doing this, he hadn't just pulled the trigger and killed Alec. His entire focus had been on separating Alec from a hand that looked out of place.

Out of place things, she thought.

She found herself glancing over at Ryan. In the days to come, he would no doubt have his own unique take on this developing puzzle.

As she reached the top of the steps, she saw who was ahead. Dressed in a suit that looked like a duplicate of the damp one he'd been wearing five minutes ago, was Bernard Holroyd.

On seeing them all, he straightened his MMX lapel pin and smiled broadly.

"Good to see you," he adjusted his tie.

The simple action told her that something must be wrong.

"Bernard?"

"Please," the smile remained in place, "Let's talk."

Before she could reply, he turned and walked toward the door of the Reading Room.

When the main power had returned, the automatic scanner rig must have resumed its previous task, because she could hear the whir of its mechanisms. As she walked toward the open doorway, she could see that the machine had almost finished scanning the stack of Fortean Eye magazines.

Inside the room, she saw two men that she didn't recognise.

Both of them were wearing earpieces.

She stopped and looked behind her. A similarly dressed pair of men had reached the top of the spiral stairs and were turning to guard the way they'd just come.

"It's alright," said Bernard, "They're with me. Everyone come in."

Making her way hesitantly into the room, she kept one eye on the men next to Bernard. In turn, they assessed her and the others in the same way.

Feeling as though the situation was slipping out of her control, she rounded on Bernard.

"What's going on?"

Bernard glanced at the men, "Wait outside."

She watched as the two of them left the room and stood on either side of the doorway. A second later, the door was closed and the room became quiet. The only sound now was the background whir of the scanning rig.

"For the past thirty-three hours," Bernard walked over to the central worktop, "I've been dreading this."

"What did you *do,* Holroyd?"

He reached into his pocket and brought out a blue brooch. Diane immediately recognised it as the concealed camera that Petra had been wearing.

"I took it back with me," he said.

Diane glanced over at Petra, thinking that she'd been involved somehow, but she looked just as stunned by the news.

He set the camera brooch down on the worktop.

"The MOD has seen the video."

The scanner continued to whir, but she felt her own mental mechanisms jar to a grinding halt.

Mere minutes had passed for her and the others, but he'd had well over a day to orchestrate this manoeuvre.

The security detail outside the door must be MOD, she now realised. In all likelihood, there would now be more men on the ground floor, securing the entrance.

A further realisation now clicked into place. To have had the foresight to take the brooch with him, his planning must actually have begun before he'd even departed for the past.

She'd underestimated him.

At the same time, he'd betrayed her.

She looked him up and down, and hoped that her contempt would be apparent. She and her team had saved his life, yet *this* was how he was repaying them.

At a time when London had been suffering tragic devastation, she'd foolishly made an ally of him.

"I should have heeded your words," she said.

"What words?"

She locked eyes with him.

"Beware allegiances that are forged in tragedy," she recalled, "Isn't that what you said? How *right* you were."

He returned her stare.

"And as you once said to me, when you shook my hand," he said, "Better the devil you know. You could have ended up with a complete stranger."

Although this was true, she didn't want to concede an inch. She just shook her head.

"Perhaps I've ended up with a stranger anyway."

Her retort seemed to have the desired effect. She saw him become more still. In that moment, she felt an illogical sense of victory. The same petulant child that had disobeyed him days ago had stamped its foot again.

"Diane," he quietly shrugged, "I'm not the enemy here."

She jabbed a finger at his lapel pin.

"What about the promise?" she said, "You said you'd keep retrostepping secret."

He lowered his head and looked down at the pin.

"Before you sent me back," he said, "I knew I wouldn't be

able to keep it secret. Not because I wouldn't try, but because you would keep running things the same reckless way."

Diane let out an exasperated breath, but realised that she had no counterargument. Theo was still deaf in one ear, Petra had almost drowned, Alec had lost a hand, and a large slice of Titanic had ruined Lab Two.

Except for the background whirring of the rig, the room remained quiet.

Bernard looked around at them all.

"A handful of people on the planet know how to build and operate the retro-topology equipment. And yet, each time the situation degraded, the favoured solution was to send *more* of those people into the problem. The decisions put lives at risk, and threatened the future of the Mort program."

"Maybe we should've left you on the roof then," Theo spoke out.

Bernard cast his arms out wide.

"This is *precisely* my point," he said, "Emotional reactions are driving decisions."

"Without those 'emotional' reactions," Petra stared, "You wouldn't *be* here."

Bernard sighed.

"True, but someone else would have come here instead. Maybe not at this instant, or in a month, but eventually someone else would be standing right here," he looked around at them, "And unlike me, they wouldn't owe you their life. They wouldn't owe you a single thing."

Diane saw Alec glance over at Theo and Petra, who in turn looked at Ryan: an unspoken chain of gratitude. On multiple fronts, Ryan's involvement had saved each of them. Bernard included.

"Diane," he shrugged his rounded shoulders, "Speaking as someone who's just had their life saved, I can tell you that it makes you think about the fragility of it all. QRI espionage and valuable elements may have been the initial goal, but *retrostepping* is a tool of unspeakable power. *Mort* will literally have the power of life and death."

In the cold light of day, she knew he was right.

What had started off as minute-long occlusions that retrieved lost artifacts, had rapidly become something else. They'd already seen the evidence. Occlusions were now doorways, and the long corridors between them were opportunities to fundamentally change the past.

At the side of the room, the last magazine fed itself out of the scanning rig and the machinery whirred to a stop.

In the quiet lull that followed, Bernard looked around at them all.

"You succeeded in saving yourselves," he said, "but Mort could save many others."

"What?" Petra folded her arms.

"You know that your QRI reports have been used to foil terrorist plots, but imagine being able to *undo* the ones that we didn't see coming. Picture the simple accidents of fate that could be reversed. Think of the lives that Mort could save."

Diane understood what he was driving at.

She was used to thinking of the past as something that took place decades ago, but she hadn't really considered the sort of history that was only a few days, or few hours, old.

Before she could respond, Alec raised his truncated wrist.

"History isn't something that can be controlled or tamed. It bites back."

Bernard exhaled a tired-sounding laugh.

"History," he said, "and the perspectives of the people who inhabit it, are concepts I am well versed in."

"Not like me," said Alec, "I can assure you."

Diane saw Bernard pause for a moment, then he cleared his throat and faced Alec.

"Indulge me," he said, "You've experienced the perspective of living *within* history."

"You know I have," Alec glared back at him.

"And when you were back there," Bernard raised a finger, "did it feel like the past? Or did it feel as real as the present moment?"

"As real as I'm talking to you now."

"So, in other words, the people in history lived their lives in their own present, just as we are living ours?"

"Yes," Alec was frowning.

Diane felt her patience wearing thin.

"Where the hell are you going with this?"

He slowly turned and looked directly at her.

"This is where I'm going," he said, "What if our present day, this *exact* minute, with all its innate tangibility and realness… is in fact the past."

As he continued to stare at her, she felt the cold chill of a genuinely new perspective: the idea that none of them were at the forefront of time's leading edge.

Judging by the silence and drawn faces around the room, she guessed that the others were having similar thoughts.

She saw Bernard's posture relax slightly. As he spoke to the quiet room, all signs of confrontation were absent from his voice.

"People in the near future could be querying everything that lies beneath the British Museum at this *very* second, and we would know nothing of it. So the question is, do we want those people to be a future version of *us?* Or do we want those people to be *strangers* who discovered a very poorly guarded facility?"

There was no choice here, she realised. To safeguard QRI and the fledgling retrostep program, the operation had to be protected. If they wanted answers to the many questions that had just been unleashed, then the British Museum's best kept secret would have to be placed into much securer hands.

Whether they were ready or not, the Ministry Of Retro Topology had to become a reality.

The silence in the air was broken by a discreet beep from

the scanning rig screen. A moment later, Diane felt her phone vibrate.

Another AI correlation must have been detected.

She looked over at Ryan, who was standing closest to the rig. She couldn't see the display, or the details of the connection that had been found, but she could see the expression on his face.

"Ryan?"

Turning away from the screen, he glanced around the room.

"I should've packed a bigger suitcase."

THE SECOND PLACE

RETROSTEP BOOK 2

Excerpt

Standing on the rear footplate of the bus, Bernard Holroyd watched the gated entrance of Downing Street sweep by.

Perched like eagles atop tall metal security gates, the large video cameras scrutinised the people below. Presumably the very bus he was riding on had also just been captured and preserved for posterity on an inch of videotape.

At some point in the past, he thought, the street that ruled the world hadn't even *had* security gates. If people were so inclined, they could walk off the neighbouring streets and stroll up to the lacquered black door of number ten.

Things were simpler back then, he thought. Or perhaps things were just more complicated now. The technology certainly was.

Mobile telephones could now be carried in the palm of your hand, fax machines were being replaced by lightning-fast email, and satellite dishes were sprouting like metallic mushrooms from every other house in the land. 1996 was undoubtedly a time of modern marvels, he thought, but there was no telling what the new millennium would usher in.

Thankfully, some technologies were slower to change. He handed over his coins and the bus conductor ratcheted out a receipt. Absentmindedly folding the paper into a miniature plane, he watched the world go by.

Being a lifelong student of history, the evidence was clear to see: London was a tapestry of bygone eras. Although several parts of this road had been destroyed or rebuilt, other areas had persisted since the Georgian period. Like some great omnipotent traveller, he thought, he was gliding through disconnected patches of history and seeing them all at once. Not a bad perspective for someone in their late twenties.

With the ding of a bell, the bus approached Parliament Square and drew to a halt. Posting his tiny aircraft into the rubbish bin, he stepped off the footplate and into the weak afternoon sun. A moment later, and with a cough of diesel fumes, the bus rounded the corner and headed toward Westminster Bridge.

In the distance, he could see the ongoing construction works for the Jubilee Line extension. An entire city block had been painstakingly demolished to make way for the new addition to the underground tube network. He knew the massive engineering project had suffered several setbacks in the past few months, but today the site was a hive of noise and activity.

Although the construction cranes swung and loomed over the site, they themselves were dwarfed by the imposing edifice that was Westminster Clock Tower: a worldwide symbol of historical permanence and order. Even when the tower couldn't be seen, the sound of Big Ben's deep tolls brought the same iconic image to mind.

Ringing out suddenly, the siren of a police car wailed past him at speed and accelerated toward the Houses of Parliament. More sirens rang out and he turned to see that two police escort bikes had stopped in the middle of the busy junction and were blocking all traffic.

Like a dizzy spell that lasted only a fraction of a second, he felt the ground move ever so slightly, then the view ahead of him slowly began to change...

THE FORTEAN EYE COVER STORIES...

FROM THE AUTHOR

Thank you so much for reading *The Minute Men*.

If you liked it, it would help me enormously if you could give me some stars or (if you're adventurous) a short review.

Your voice really does make a difference.

Having good ratings means that I can keep writing new books and giving you things like...

AN ARCHIVE OF FREE BOOKS

If you'd like The Fortean Eye Cover Stories, or other free ebooks for your digital shelf, then head over to:

www.Futurewords.uk

Thanks again, hope to see you there...

Also by Simon Winstanley

FIELD ONE

BLACKBOX: BARCODE

FIELD TWO

BOUNDARY

EVA

THE BRIDGE

INSIDE THE FIELD (illustrated guide)

REZ POINT

THE OLYMPUS KEY

THE REALITY FORGE

Printed in Great Britain
by Amazon

62012593R00201